ABOUT THE AUTHOR

Diemme Black is an author of sexy romance fiction. She has been married to her husband for over a decade and is still madly in love. She is a very busy mom and couldn't be prouder of her kids. Diemme likes to travel to all different beach destinations, and loves the sun and the sand. She thoroughly enjoys reading other romance and erotica novels.

Other books by Diemme Black include:

Inked My Life (Book 1 of The Tattooed Heart Series), which was published in 2014
Rocking Me (Book 1 of the Rokk Me Hard Series), which was published in 2015

If you want more information on Diemme Black, including her published and upcoming books, please visit and follow her at:

https://twitter.com/diemmeblack
https://www.facebook.com/diemme.black
https://www.facebook.com/diemmeblackauthor
https://www.instagram.com/diemmeblack
http://amzn.to/2bxJyoz
http://bit.ly/goodreadsDB
http://www.diemmeblack.com

BY DIEMME BLACK

ISBN 978-1-941432-04-4

STRUMMING ME

BOOK 2 OF THE *ROKK ME HARD*™ SERIES

© Copyright 2016 Diemme Black Publishing LLC

Cover designed by Shanoff Formats. Visit Shanoff Formats at http://www.shanoffformats.com.

First Printing, 2016

Printed in the United States of America

To all of you who support me, understand me, and unconditionally accept me for who I am. I dedicate this book to you.

TABLE
OF CONTENTS

CHAPTER
ONE

Sarah

When Ali and Jace dropped me off after we returned from Los Angeles, everything appeared to be fine. The front lights were on because of the timer. The lawn was neat and tidy, and the door was a welcome site. It felt good to be home. Then I opened the fucking door.

The front door opened to the living room, which was the first room I saw. Sofa cushions ripped. Papers everywhere. Broken glass from my picture frames all over the furniture and carpets.

Then I walked into the next room in my house, the kitchen. Glasses and dishes were shattered. Even my little potted plant was turned upside down and there was dirt all over the floor.

Who the hell did this? Michael – that was the first name that came into my mind. I knew he was angry at how we left things – he had posted so much demeaning and insulting shit about me on Facebook after he stormed off in rage during our last time together. Did he expect me to come running back, begging for forgiveness as though I had done something wrong? That's why he did this? To me? To my house? It was a complete disaster.

Holy shit, what if Michael was still here? I ran to the door and was about to run outside, but instantly stopped. I wasn't leaving my home. This was my house. I paid for it and I worked damn hard to buy everything in it, everything that was now ripped to shreds. I went back into the kitchen and grabbed a knife from the knife block. Yeah, like I had the balls to stab someone. On second thought, I put it back and went to the hall closet. My golf club bag was there. I took out the nine iron and slowly went down the long hallway that led to my bedroom. The door was open, not the way I left it. Whenever I leave the house, I close the bedroom door behind me. I slowly pushed it completely open and saw the mess that was my bedroom. My makeup was all on the floor. The vase of flowers I had on the nightstand was shattered and flowers were all over my bedspread. The bedspread was ripped and there was down from the comforter everywhere. My clothes were in a heap in the middle of the room, some off the hangers. I could tell some of the clothes were ripped or cut and that my perfume and shampoo and stuff were poured all over the pile of my clothes. But thankfully no one was there. I looked into the adjoining bathroom – another mess. My shower curtain was pulled from the rod, the rod was on the floor and the mirror over the sink was shattered.

One more room to check, the office. Again I raised the golf club high over my shoulder and headed to the spare bedroom I used as an office. The door was open a little bit, and I opened it the rest of the way. Again, a disaster. Papers were everywhere. The computer was thrown on the floor and plugs were strewn about. Crap, my car. I hadn't come in through the garage as I usually do. Ali had dropped me at the front door. I didn't want to see my car. I went to see if the door was locked from the garage into the house; it was. I would deal with that later. I just wanted to turn around and leave. I did not have the head for this shit right now. But this was my home and it was violated. This was a personal attack on me.

I picked up the phone and, would you believe, I was about to dial Matt. Boy did I have it bad for him already. No, I couldn't call him, much less let him know what was going on. Would he really want to be with me, with my obviously psycho ex around and dealing with our break up like this? No, I had to keep him far away from this mess. If I called Ali, she would have to tell Jace; there was no way she wouldn't tell her fiancé. And no doubt he in turn would tell Matt, his band mate and virtual brother since childhood.

There was only one person I could trust to keep his mouth shut, my brother. I dialed him and was so happy to hear his voice when he picked up.

"Hey, Sarah, you get home okay? Good thing you sent me that text about what Michael posted. I was able to unfriend him from mom and dad's account so they didn't see it."

"Thanks, Joseph, you're the best. I wish I could say that this is a happy how-the-hell-are-you-call, but it's not. I just got home and my place is trashed. I mean, seriously trashed. Can you come over and help? And please don't call mom and dad. I don't want them all upset and worrying."

"I'm already in the car, on my way. Call the police, Sarah. You have to have them dust for prints and get Michael for this. You know it was him. Call them now on conference with me so I can hear that you're okay until I get there. Now, Sarah!"

"Ok, calm down. I'll call them now." I dialed and clicked the phone so Joseph could hear the call. I told the 911 operator that I just arrived home from the airport and my place had be ransacked. The operator asked me if I was alone. I told them my brother was on the other line and on his way to me, but I had searched the house and there was no one else here. She said that she was sending the police and that I should go back outside of the house until they arrived. I did what she said and waited only a few more minutes until Joseph showed up, shortly followed by a police car.

The police had me wait outside while they searched to make sure the house was empty. Then they walked with me through the house so I could see if anything was missing. I didn't see anything obviously gone, but with such a mess, I couldn't be sure. Then I told them about not going into the garage. They went first and as luck would have it, the car was there and untouched. Well, that's one blessing.

"Miss March, do you have any idea who would do this?" Detective Edwards asked me.

"Yeah, I know someone who would do this, her ex. She just gave him his walking papers. He's the only one who would want to hurt her like this," Joseph answered to the police officer.

"You have a bad breakup with… what is his name, Miss March?" he asked me.

"Michael, Michael Mailtlin. You see we were both in Los Angeles for a concert a friend was putting on for New Year's Eve. We were having a bad time while we were there, fighting a lot. Finally he accused me of cheating on him and started yelling and acting crazy at everyone there. I told him I hadn't cheated on him and to stop being an ass. He didn't, so I told him to go home. I stayed a few extra days and then I flew back today."

"That's not all. He put up some nasty things about Sarah on his Facebook page, saying he caught her cheating. But he put it in a very vulgar way if you know what I mean," Joseph added.

"Miss March, has Mr. Mailtlin ever done anything like this before?" the officer asked.

"Never. My sister isn't an idiot. She would never have stayed with a psycho much less have agreed to marry him," Joseph jumped in to answer.

"I was asking Miss March," the officer countered back.

"No, nothing like this. But the truth is we've been drifting apart for a while now. I just didn't want to face it. But he has been changing. He's been more easily aggravated and upset lately. See, he's an artist and he has a very big show coming up and just seems overly stressed about it. I have been letting a lot slide, but this? I would never think he would do this."

"Has he ever shown you a violent side before, Miss March?"

"Look, I know you have to ask these questions. I get it's your job, and you don't know my sister, but she is a strong, tough woman. She is the last woman I would ever know who would stay in that kind of relationship. If he even tried to lay a hand on her, she would have shot him to the curb long ago," Joseph said looking fiercely at Detective Edwards.

The officer turned to look at me and I just put on my best face. "He's right, I wouldn't have taken it. He's never been abusive toward me, other than verbally, and that's just lately."

"Well, Miss March, it's going to be a few hours until we can let you have full access to the house. We have to photograph and dust and go through everything. But, even if we find Mr. Mailtlin's prints, he was still your fiancé so it would make sense that his prints would be here. Unless we can find evidence at his place that he did this, we won't automatically be able to press any charges against him. Now has he threatened you in any way, over your voicemail or in a text, which would help us get you a restraining order against him?"

"No, nothing like that," I answered.

"Here, this is what he posted on Facebook about my sister," Joseph said and showed the officer his phone with Michael's Facebook page open.

"Not very nice of him, but not really a threat either. This guy just seems like a real jerk, one you should consider yourself lucky to be getting rid of. Is there somewhere you can go until we're done here? I could call you before we leave and then you can come back in and sort through things."

"I'll take her to my place," Joseph said.

The officer handed me his card and told me to call if I realized anything was missing, or if I found anything that would point to Michael. Then he told me he'd call me before they all left so I could come back. He wrote phone numbers on the back of his card, to a cleaning service and a locksmith. I thanked Detective Edwards and walked over to Joseph's car. He was on the phone, but I knew he wouldn't call my parents because I made him promise. Maybe just one of his friends to keep a lookout for Michael. I hoped Joseph didn't think he was going to start a war with Michael. I had enough testosterone right now without his getting into shit with Michael. Whatever, I was beat. I got into Joseph's car as he got off the phone, and without another word we were headed to his place.

When he let us in, I was almost scared that I would walk in and find his place a mess too. But it was just my wild imagination. The place was in perfect order; that is, for a single guy's place. I moved a bunch of clothes off the couch and fell onto it. Joseph slumped down next to me, and I could see he was eyeing me.

"I'm sorry to drag you into this," I said.

"Are you kidding? I'm your brother, that's what I'm here for. But I want to know everything, now. Did something happen with this guy Matt? Is he the reason Michael really freaked out? I mean, I could care less what you did, but I want to know the truth."

"The night Michael started with me, nothing happened with Matt. I was at Jace's house and Michael got all over me about my hair. He said I had only cut and colored it to look like I was a Blacking Out whore. I couldn't take his shit anymore. Lately I don't seem to do a thing right. So I walked out of our room and headed for the backyard. Matt's house is directly next door to Jace's. Matt heard me crying and came over to talk to me. We only talked. That was it. He did hold my hand and walk me back to the door in the morning. That was what Michael saw. That was it, Joseph, I swear. Now after Michael left, I did kiss Matt and fall asleep next to him. But that's it and Michael has no idea about that. And you and Ali are the only ones who know about that, and she's not saying anything, so neither are you."

"And when you say Matt, you mean Matt Lewis of Blacking Out? The guy you've had a secret crush on for years?" Joseph smiled at me.

"Yes, that would be the same Matt. And about that, keep it quiet. I don't want him to think I kissed him because of a silly crush I had on a rock star. Just keep it to yourself," I sternly said.

"Tell me the truth. Did you end things with Michael all because of Matt? 'Cause I mean, I know how amazing you are little sis, but one kiss with this guy doesn't mean he's going to stop being a rock star whore and settle down."

"I did not end things with Michael because of Matt. The end of Michael and me has been coming for a while. Everyone seemed to love him so much that I just let a lot of crap slide. You all seemed ready to welcome him into the family, so I felt stupid to just pull out of everything."

"Sis, we welcomed him for you. None of us ever really liked him. We liked him because we thought he made you happy."

"Do me a favor, forget about what you think my feelings are. If you hate someone I'm dating, please tell me. That doesn't mean I'm always going to listen to you, or care, but don't lie to make me feel better, okay?"

Just then the bell rang and Joseph got up to answer

the door. Running through the door were Ali and Jace. Oh crap!

"Are you okay? Why didn't you call us? We would have turned right around. I should have let Raymond or Jace walk you in the door. I'm so sorry." Ali was close to tears and running off at the mouth about how this was all her fault.

"Ali, I'm fine. I didn't want to call you because I didn't want to bother you guys."

"How could you even think for one second that you're a bother. Do you have no idea that you're my sister? You idiot," Ali said.

"I didn't realize that Joseph called you guys. You didn't have to rush over here. I'm fine. Can't say the same for my house, but I'm fine."

"How bad is it?" Jace asked.

"I seriously don't think there's anything at all to save," I said.

"I cannot believe that fucking prick did this to you, all because you didn't fly straight home to deal with him," Ali said. Now she was in pissed mode.

"Joseph, I think you should be properly introduced. This is Jace Wicks, Ali's fiancé. Jace, my brother Joseph March."

"Man, it's a pleasure to meet you. Ali and Sarah both speak about you all the time and how lucky they are to have you as a brother," Jace said as he shook hands with Joseph.

"Good to meet you too, and congrats on your engagement, man. But I'm still her big brother; hurt her and I'll kill you. There are tons of places to dump a body here in Vegas," Joseph said, not one hundred percent joking. Ali was basically my sister since grade school, and Joseph always treated and protected her the same way.

"Ease up, big brother, he's one of the good guys," Ali said and got up to put her arms around Jace's waist. "Now let's get down to business. What's our first move here? What do we do with the house?" Ali looked at me waiting for my answer.

"To be honest, I never loved the house. It was affordable and close to you two, and mom and dad. But I truthfully don't know if I can ever get the image out of my head of it all torn to bits."

"I was never crazy about that house either, Sarah," Joseph said, and Ali shook her head to agree.

"Okay, step one, we clean it up and box up whatever isn't broken. So we'll probably need about one box for that. I guess we'll need to call for a dumpster to get rid of the furniture and broken stuff. Then I'll have to call a realtor to put it on the market. Then I'm going to have to start looking for a new place. God it's going to take forever to make enough money to replace everything."

"What about insurance? They have to help with the cost of everything damaged, right?" Ali asked.

"Seriously, Sarah, I don't know what you're worried about. You have to know that Matt is going to see this as all his fault. He'll probably just go out and buy you a whole new fucking house," Jace said.

"No! I don't want Matt to know about this. It's my problem, not his, and he is not going to storm in here like a testosterone-filled caveman and just fix everything," I said as I stood up over them all for emphasis.

"Too late for that, honey. Jace called him after Joseph called us. He's already on a flight," Ali said with a smile.

"Oh God, Jace, please tell me you didn't," I said.

"Sorry, Sarah. If it were Ali, I'd want to know. Not

to be throwing my brother under the bus, but you have to know he's got the hots for you," Jace said.

"Yeah, he couldn't get on a commercial flight, so he hired a charter plane to get him here. Raymond's waiting for him at the airport now, ready to bring him over," Ali said.

"What are you upset about? You like this guy, so what's the big deal if he wants to come here and help out?" Joseph asked.

"Because this is my mess, not yours or yours or yours or his. I can take care of this myself." I stormed from the room and went to Joseph's bedroom and shut myself in.

CHAPTER
TWO

Matt

Was this flight ever going to fucking land? I had to get to Sarah. I couldn't believe that cocksucker would wreck her house. Fuck it – I'm a rock star. I'll just buy her a new one. I was going to have to talk to Raymond about getting her a security system and her own security team until we put this asshole away. Let's see, what else needed to get done? I had to call a realtor to find her a new place. I had to call my decorator from L.A. and get him out here to decorate with Sarah. I knew she would want to pick stuff out. Then again, maybe I would just buy a place for myself and have her move in with me, that way I could keep an eye on her.

I knew I was probably getting ahead of myself, but I already knew how I felt about her. Forget about the fact that she had the body and face of an angel. Angel made for sin, that is. She was smart and funny and successful and not overwhelmed with who I was and what I did. She was already loved by the guys. But when I heard what happened, my blood started to boil that I wasn't there for her. I knew I should have flown to Vegas with Sarah, Ali and Jace today. I knew it was stupid of me to wait. After all, we were all making our way to Vegas this week anyway to get ready to record the new album. Why didn't I just go with her? Why, because I didn't want her to know how I felt about her.

Me and my stupid pride could have gotten Sarah killed. What if she walked in the house while Michael was trashing her house? What if I was the one who caused all this? No matter how long it took, I was going to make it up to her. I'm a goddamn lead guitarist in a rock band, and no one was going to get in my way.

Thank God we were landing. I had to get to her. Good thing Raymond was waiting; he could get me to her fast. I got my bags and guitar and rushed off the small plane. Raymond quickly took my things and loaded them in the car and we were off. I was shaking my legs through the whole ride, just so anxious to see Sarah and see for myself that she was okay.

I practically ran from the car and kicked in the front door of Sarah's brother's house to get to her. Luckily Jace knew I was on my way so he was there to let me in.

"Where is she? Is she all right?" I asked in a rush, looking around the room and finding everyone but her.

"She's fine, Matt, just very pissed at all of us. She locked herself in Joseph's room. Matt, this is Joseph, Sarah's brother."

"Pleased to meet you, Joseph. I know this is your place and your sister, but do you mind if I try to talk to her?"

"Be my guest. First door down the hall on the right," Joseph said smugly, folding his arms over his chest, as if to say no way Sarah would let me in and talk to me. Maybe she wouldn't but I had to try.

I knocked on the door. "Sarah, it's Matt. Can I come in?"

The door opened and Sarah flung herself into my arms. Oh, yeah, this felt right, Sarah in my arms. I felt her shaking more than I heard her crying. I pushed her gently in the room and kicked the door closed. She just held on to me and had her head buried in my neck. I sat down on the bed, and took her into my lap. She finally pulled back and looked at me.

"What the hell are you doing here?" she asked.

"Jace called and said that someone tore your place up. Where else would I be?"

"So you came here to rescue me?" Sarah asked in disbelief.

"I came here to be with you and do whatever you let me do for you. I already told you the other night how I feel about you, and that I want to be with you. Did you honestly think I wouldn't come running here?"

"I don't want you running in to save the day. I can handle this."

"I know you can. I just had to make sure you were okay for myself. When I heard what happened, I needed to get here. I'm sorry if you don't want me around, but I'm here and I'm not going. If you're not ready for a relationship, I get that. I'll wait. But then see me here as a friend."

"I don't want you here as my friend. But I don't want you to save me either. I have to fix this alone. I don't want you to leave, but you have to let me get this straightened out by myself."

"Look, I already know what a strong, independent woman you are. Everyone out there knows that too. Independent doesn't mean you can't have help. If for nothing else, Ali looks like she's going to cry at any minute. Your brother looks like he's going to kill someone. Even if it's not for you, let them in and let them help."

"Does the same apply to you? Do I have to let you help so you can feel better?" she asked me with a smile.

"It would be nice. You'd make me feel better if I could do something. But I don't want to push. I'll take my cues from you. Sound good?" I asked.

She kissed me lightly on the lips. And, hell yeah, I returned the favor. It was just starting to get interesting when there was a knock on the door. Sarah jumped from my lap and sat next to me. I told whoever it was to come in.

"Sarah, the police just called on your phone. They're ready to leave. Do you want to go back and take care of things?" Joseph asked.

"Let's rally the troops and get going," she said and got off the bed.

I got in the back seat of Joseph's car while Sarah was in the front. Ali, Jace and Raymond followed behind us. When we got there, there were police and tech crews loading up bags of stuff. On the outside the house looked well taken care of and right as rain. But then we all walked inside. All of our jaws dropped. The place was a mess. How Sarah could still be standing tall, I had no idea. If I walked into my place and all my stuff was ruined, I'd be total bullshit. This was one tough chick I had. None of us could speak. Thankfully, Raymond was ex-military and had seen hell, so this wasn't too bad for him.

"Sarah, I spoke to a Detective Edwards. Here's a list of evidence that the tech crews took. You'll get everything back after the investigation is over. He also said to call him if you realize anything else is missing. I think we should all spread out and take an area. We should use bags and boxes. I'll make a run to the store and get boxes and tape. Garbage bags for things obviously ruined and boxes for stuff that can be fixed or should be saved for Sarah. Ali, you and Jace take the kitchen. Joseph the living room. Sarah, you and Matt take the bedroom. Are there any other rooms, Sarah?" Raymond asked.

"There's a spare bedroom I use as an office, but it's trashed too."

"I'll take that room when I return. Jace, take this until I'm back." Raymond took a gun from the back of his jacket and handed it to Jace, who quickly put it in the waistband of his jeans.

"You guys don't have to do this. I can get through everything myself," Sarah said.

"Okay, um, Sarah, we're just going to ignore your hard head and get to work," Ali said and went toward the kitchen asking Jace if he even knew how to use the gun if the unfortunate moment should arise.

No one listened to Sarah. They all followed Raymond's orders and spread out to work. I took her hand and told her to lead me to her bedroom. She gave my hand a little squeeze and led the way. This room seemed to be the worst. What was left hanging in the closet was cut to ribbons. Her comforter was torn up. There was down stuffing all over the floor. I didn't know where to begin. I asked Sarah to go get the bags. While she was out of the room, I took out my phone and started to take pictures of Sarah's stuff. I would replace what I could for her. I had a feeling she was going to try and resist my buying her anything so I had to figure out a way to do it, and have her accept it. When I want to do something, I don't take no for an answer.

CHAPTER
THREE

Sarah

It took us until around one a.m. to get the house reasonably cleaned up. Everyone looked totally beat. I was so ready for a bed, with Matt wrapped around me. Oh crap, I would have to tell my brother that I wasn't staying with him so I could stay with Matt at Ali's house. I didn't see this going too well. But I just needed Matt right now, and a soft bed.

"Okay. Thanks, guys, but we're done here. I'll call the dumpster company tomorrow and have all the crap taken away. But for now, let's all get some sleep. Sound good?"

"Sounds good to me. Let me guess, you're going to stay at Ali's?" Joseph asked and thank the Lord I wasn't the one saying it.

"If you don't mind, Joseph. I will feel better at Ali's with Raymond and his gun there. Thank you for everything, big brother. I'll call you tomorrow." I hugged Joseph and he was hugging me and not letting me go. I could understand, he was scared. I hugged him super strong back and then he felt comfortable to release me. We looked at each other for a second, and I hoped he knew my smile was real. I was going to get through this.

"I'll talk to you tomorrow, sweetie. Have a good sleep. Love you," Joseph said and then turned to his car and left.

Matt took my hand and walked me to the car. We all

piled in the car and headed to Ali's house. Everyone was too tired to talk. We just drove in silence. When we got to Ali's we all filed out and just headed in to sleep. Matt and I went straight to the guest bedroom. He walked in behind me and locked the door. I turned to him. He walked toward me and hugged me. I snuggled into his neck and breathed in his scent. He smelled so good, like the trees in the forest. I loved his scent.

"Matt, I think we need to talk," I said and pulled back from Matt to look at him.

"I was going to say the same thing, but I thought maybe the morning would be a better time to talk," Matt said.

"I think I need to get this out now." I sat on the bed and Matt sat next to me. "I'm happy that you flew out here to be with me. But I'm not used to being the damsel in distress. I know you came here with these grand ideas of taking care of everything and fixing everything. And as much as that is appealing right now, I can't let you just come in and take over everything. I have to end this thing with Michael the right way and for all the right reasons. I like you, Matt. I like you very much. But you are not the reason that I'm ending it with Michael. I've been thinking about it for a long time. I need to know what you want from me, what you're after with me. If it's just a good time, that's fine, but tell me now."

"Is that how you see me? Do you think I jumped on a plane, which I had to charter to get here, because I just wanted to screw you? Seriously?"

"I'm sorry. I just want you to tell me, why me?"

"What do you mean, why you?"

"I mean, you haven't been in any relationship for very long. You've been hopping around from girl to girl. Then the other night, you tell me you want me, that you want just me and you want me to end things with Michael. I don't know why you'd meet me and within two days, act like you're done, like you just want me. Why? I mean you have to understand how insane this all sounds."

"Sarah, what the fuck did this guy do to you?"

"What do you mean, what did he do to me?" I asked, appalled.

"What did he do to you that you can't see how amazing you are?"

"How can you possibly know how amazing I may or may not be after knowing me such a short time?"

"Sarah, we've talked until the sun came up. Day after day while you were in L.A. we shared a lot with each other. You showed me who you were, and I did the same thing. I've never been like that with another person, except for maybe Jace. It meant something to me, something real. I know this has been fast and scary and confusing for you, but I'm not going to just sit here and pretend this isn't happening between us. I'm not going anywhere, and I'll wait as long as you need to get where I am. I think it would be better if I slept on the couch and gave you some space tonight." Matt went to leave, but I blocked his way.

"Matt, wait, please don't leave. This is all just a lot for me to take in right now. And I think I do know you, you're right. I bet the whole time on the plane, all you could think of was first killing Michael, and then how you would buy me everything to make it all whole again."

"No, I thought of buying you everything first, then killing Michael."

I laughed and put my hands to his face. "You are an incredible man and I do not deserve you, but if you're telling me you're here for more than a few nights, that you want something real, I'm in too. But you have to just try and not jump in head first right now. I have a lot to get through and I just need to do some of it on my own. Got it?"

"I got it. And I am here for the real deal, Sarah." He leaned down to me and kissed me. I kissed back with everything I had. I was so into Matt. I only hoped he'd still be into me if he found out about me. This whole tough girl thing was such a big lie. I just wanted him to be my knight in shining armor. I knew he could be, if I could just keep everything secret from him.

I went into the bathroom and got dressed in a pair of sweats and a long sleeve top that Ali lent me. Matt had some stuff with him, and when I got out of the bathroom there he was, no shirt on, and baggy workout pants hanging off his cut waist. Oh crap, I'm done for. There is no way I can just sleep next to this guy. He was doing this on purpose. The other times we slept next to each other, he was fully clothed.

"Hope you don't mind," Matt said, with a hopeful smile. "I only took so much stuff when I packed. I'll get some more clothes tomorrow. In fact, what do you say we go shopping together?

"Neither my taste nor my budget fits into your life-style, Matt. I'll just head to the mall with Ali," I said and got into bed.

"I shop at regular shops, Sarah. I'm not into the whole hundred-dollar-jeans thing. I mean, they're still just jeans and a t-shirt. You pick the store, and we'll go. But please, just let me do something. Let me pay for some things. You know, if you don't let me buy you some stuff, Ali is going to go with you and just use Jace's credit cards. So wouldn't it be better to have me pay than Jace?"

Shit, he had a point. Jace had given Ali his credit cards while we were in L.A. and now that they were getting married, what was his was hers. She would make sure to buy everything. She was already doing so much. "Okay, what about this. I'll let you buy me some stuff, but you let me work it off."

Matt's eyes bugged out of his head.

"Not with sex, idiot. I'm in PR. I can help you guys while you're recording here. I can set up a meet-and-greet, or a few magazine interviews, stuff like that to work off the money. What do you think?"

"I think it's a great idea. You know, play your cards right and show the guys what you're made of, and maybe we can make it a permanent job," Matt said.

"What do you mean?" I asked, very surprised.

"Well, we fired Allen. So we need a manager."

"Matt, you can't be serious. You're just going to offer me a job not knowing what kind of worker I am, what kind of connections I have? I have no experience managing a band."

"Okay, don't get all crazy on me. It was just a suggestion. Let's go back a few steps. Let's start where you said you'd let me buy you some stuff to replace what got lost and you can work it off, getting local gigs. Sound good?" Matt asked and looked appeased.

"For now, let's just think about sleep." I hugged him and kissed his cheek. We both climbed into bed and Matt held me to his side. It felt so right. He was holding me so tightly, it was almost a bit uncomfortable. My back was still killing me, but if I asked Matt to ease up on his hold, he might get suspicious. So a little discomfort for keeping things hidden wasn't too bad. But I just needed sleep. Like right now. And it came quickly.

Matt

I noticed that Sarah flinched when I held her. Why, was I holding her too closely? Was I going to fast? But that's how I am. I want something, I get it. I wanted her, and I wasn't going to hide it. My parents said that I've always been like this, like when I came home with Jace when I was a kid in school. I told them that he was my best friend and that we had to keep him because his parents were mean to him. From that moment on, I always had Jace with me. I had asked him to be my best friend and he said yes; that was that. That meant he was my best friend and brother. He was always at my house and always with me.

My parents knew that there was no getting Jace to leave once I brought him home. Thankfully for me, my parents have always embraced my all-or-nothing attitude. I only hoped that Sarah could learn to love it. I know I wasn't easy to get along with. I have always been very impulsive. When I got my first big check from our debut record, the first thing I did was buy myself a car and my parents a house in the same day. Then after the second check, I bought my mansion and convinced Jace how cool it would be if we lived right next door to each other. Jace, who liked to think everything out, knew I would keep on him, so he gave in and bought the house.

It was the same thing with Sarah. When I first saw her, with her short rocker girl hair and slamming body, walk into the room in Jace's house, I knew I had to have her. She was gorgeous, and I just wanted to get her in my bed. Later that very same night, I had to take a cold swim in my backyard to try and cool off from thinking of her, especially after I found out she had a fiancé. But then I found myself sitting in the backyard. I was trying not to think of Sarah in that low cut tight dress with my peeling it off her. That's when I heard someone crying. I was scared it was Ali. So I walked into Jace's backyard and found Sarah sitting at the edge of the pool. I practically sprinted to her and was ready to tear her fiancé apart. I put my arm around her and held her until she was able to talk. Then she told me how she was having second thoughts about her and Michael. Yea for me! I gave her my true opinion. Seriously, I didn't tell her to lose him just so I could have her. I thought that there was no way this fabulous girl should be crying, ever. Much less over a fiancé who would make her feel like shit. I held her until she was able to go back into Jace's house. But I already knew, I already knew she was mine. Now I just had to make her realize it.

I watched her sleep. She was so beautiful. Her little pert nose, her full pouty lips, her beautifully arched eyebrows. As she slept, there were no worry lines etched on her forehead. She looked like an angel to me. My angel. Now I just had to figure out a way for her to accept all that I wanted to give her. Maybe I should talk to her brother, or Ali. I didn't want her back to that freaking house ever again. She shared too many memories with Michael there. I wanted to get her somewhere safe. I knew that Jace and Ali would probably move out to L.A., but there was a good chance they would keep the Vegas house. We were going to record here, so I needed a place. How could I get her to accept a whole house from me, and let me live with her? Or I could just buy the house for myself, convince her to move in with me while her house was up for sale, and hope eventually she'd just want to stay.

But Sarah was so independent. How the hell was I going to pull this off? Okay, Matt, one day at a time. For now be happy that Sarah is fine, and at least has agreed to let me take her shopping and replace her stuff. That was a step. With Sarah, I was going to have to try baby steps instead of the leaps I was used to taking.

I tried to stay up the whole time, to make sure asswipe didn't show up and start with Sarah. But eventually

I fell asleep holding her. It was like a dream when I woke up and smelled coffee. But then the reality hit me, and this was better than a dream. Yes, there was coffee, but there was also Sarah in my arms. We started the evening with her nestled against my front. Now she was lying across the bed and her head was resting over my chest. I smiled and knew that this was what I wanted. I wanted to wake up to this woman constantly. Yeah, that's where I was. But I also knew Sarah was nowhere ready for all that. How could I reign myself in? Sarah started to stir, so I didn't have to worry about it at that moment.

She looked up to me with her beautiful brown eyes. They were shining at me and she smiled when she realized that I was holding her.

"I thought I was dreaming of you. I'm happy that it's real, that you're really here with me," she said.

"You better get used to me quickly, babe," I said and kissed her forehead.

"Sounds good to me. Hey, I smell coffee." Sarah tried to roll out of bed, but I grabbed her arm and tugged her back into bed with me. I tried to kiss her, but she slammed her mouth shut and tugged away.

"I have morning breath. There is no way I'm kissing you before I brush my teeth, now let go." I did and she swayed her hips as she walked into the bathroom. I could watch her ass every minute of the day. I rolled over right onto my morning wood and groaned. I just wanted her lips, her face, her everything. I had to stop thinking about her for a few seconds and get my wood under control. I was pretty sure Jace wouldn't want me walking into Ali's kitchen with my dick poking out of my gym pants.

The aroma of the coffee pulled me to the kitchen, and there wrapped around each other in the kitchen were Ali and Jace. I was so happy for my brother. I was psyched he found Ali and that she loved him back as strongly as he loved her.

"Cut that shit out, you two," I said in a joking voice.

Jace and Ali pulled apart and gave me a big smile while they went back to cooking at the stove.

"Where is Sarah, is she okay?" Ali asked me.

I walked to the coffeemaker and poured myself a cup of the god's juice and then shook my head. "I think she'll be fine soon. I offered to take her shopping today to get her some new clothes. At first she wasn't having it, but I struck a deal with her. Ali, I'm gonna need some help here. You know how Sarah is, all having to do everything by herself. I want to help. But I don't know how much I can do without turning her completely away."

Ali walked over to the table where I was sitting and took my hand. "Matt, I can see how you feel about her. And I have to say, she is one lucky woman. Jace has already explained to me that you're an all-or-nothing kind of guy. But you're going to have to reign it in a bit. She just completely lost everything she worked her ass off for. You have to go as slowly as possible. She's into you too. But she's going to be fighting herself to do this all on her terms, not yours. Just give her a bit of room to breathe."

"I know you're right. I only hope that I can tone it down and keep her happy at the same time."

"What are we talking about?" Sarah walked slowly into the kitchen all fresh faced and smiling. I knew it was all an act. But in a way, I loved that about her. She didn't want anyone to be worried about her. She wanted to be strong, which just made me fall harder for her.

"We were talking about all of us going shopping today," I said with a smile directed toward Ali and Jace.

I knew Ali would have my back, but I would have to

make this up to Jace. He hated shopping.

"All of us?" Sarah asked happily.

"All of us," Ali answered happily too.

At that point Ali and Sarah started to do a little happy dance in the middle of the kitchen. What the fuck is it with women and shopping? Jace and I were laughing at their ridiculous display. But we both loved that we were in the financial situation where we could spoil these two.

"Lovely happy dance, ladies. Now can someone please get breakfast finished so we can go crazy shopping?" I laughed to the women.

Ali and Sarah finished making breakfast while Jace and I stood watch over the ladies. I was jealous of Jace. I wanted Sarah to look at me the way Ali looked at him. Or maybe envious is a better word, because I was happy for him, but I wanted it for myself.

We all ate breakfast together and enjoyed the light conversation. Things didn't go deep about what Sarah was going through, or what her next move would be. I had to get Jace aside and talk to him about Sarah helping with promotional shit while we were here. I also had to talk to the other guys and make sure they were okay with everything. While I had raced to get here for Sarah, I called them all to tell them what had happened to her place. They all had fallen in love with Sarah and knew how I felt about her. So I knew it wouldn't be a problem, but I felt like they still had to have a say in the decision I made.

I told Ali and Sarah that Jace and I would clean up since they cooked and told them to get ready. That's when I hit the subject with Jace. He was one hundred percent good with it and said he knew the guys would be too. That was one hurdle cleared. Now I had to find a house, and get Sarah to move in with me. No biggie.

CHAPTER
FOUR

Sarah

We all piled into Jace's truck and Raymond drove us to shop. I didn't know where we were going, but I knew we had to try and be as discrete as possible. The first time Ali and Jace went shopping at the mall together was a disaster.

"So, I know we can't do a mall. Where are we going to shop?" I asked.

Matt answered, "Well Ali told us your favorite place to shop. So I had Jeff call ahead to the store and they're waiting for us, and only us. So go shop yourselves, silly ladies," he said and smiled that megawatt smile that had my heart flip in my chest. That's when the old ugly doubt came creeping in. I knew he cared about me. He proved that by flying all the way here just to be with me. Not to mention he offered me the world.

But I was nothing. I didn't feel like a woman who deserved this; I just felt like a stupid woman who deserved all the shit that was flying her way. The only thing I could do, if I really cared about Matt, was to get him out of this mess. The only way to do that was to make him and the rest of the band go back to L.A. and record there. In time, he'd give up pursuing me. After all, other than my family, all men gave up on me eventually.

I was deep in my sad depressed thoughts when we pulled up to the store which was situated in the corner of a strip mall. There were two women waiting by the doors. When Raymond pulled up to the curb, we opened the doors ourselves and walked toward them. They greeted all of us by name and when we were safely inside, they locked the door and pulled down the rolling curtain so the glass doors were covered from view. One woman walked over to Ali and started to speak to her, and the other one, Laurie on her name tag, came toward me.

"Hello, Miss. I'm Laurie and I am here to assist you with your shopping today. As I understand it, you're in need of a whole new wardrobe. Where would you like to start?" She was roughly the same age as me. But she was striking. She was tall and lean and had long blonde hair that was pin straight, yet had a beautiful body to it, and golden green colored eyes. She seemed to give me a bright smile, but I knew women too well. I knew it was all an act. I bet the minute I was in the dressing room, she'd walk over to help herself to Matt. I could already see the cogs turning in her head. Bitch.

But why was I upset? I just told myself that I needed to be fair to Matt and send him away, so why should I care if a skinny tall dish wanted Matt? Because I did. Damn, I was fucked up. I had to speak to Ali soon and have her help me. She always trusted me, now I had to trust her.

I just offered a smile as fake as the one Laurie had on her bitch face. I looped my arm through Matt's arm. "That's so sweet of you, Laurie, but Matt promised me he would take me shopping, and I want him to help me. But thank you anyway." With that, I pulled him toward the dresses.

"Want to tell me what all that was about?" Matt asked through his low laugh.

"She was practically eye fucking you. The minute she shoved me into the dressing room she was going to move in on you."

"So you had to mark your territory?"

"What if I was? Just be happy I didn't piss all over you," I smiled devilishly.

"I think she might need a little more convincing. Right now she's checking me out while your back is turned away from her. Why don't you stick your tongue in my mouth and show her that I'm marked?" He winked at me.

I was calling his bluff. I didn't think he thought I had the guts to do it. I put my fingers through his hair and brought his lips to mine. I started the kiss with power. I didn't start out slow and sweet; I pushed my way into his mouth, and he moaned upon my tongue mixing with his. He had his hands wrapped around my waist and was pulling me harder to his body. I felt his erection straining against my stomach. That made me moan and deepen the kiss even more. The sound of someone clearing her throat made us pull apart.

Ali was standing there with a huge smile and tons of clothes hanging on a moveable rack next to her. "Can I steal your woman away for a few minutes so we can shop? I promise to give her back," Ali said as she came closer and took me by the arm. Matt laughed and told me that he would be in the men's section if I needed him. Wow did I need him. That kiss. A fucking kiss and I was wet. Seriously wet in the panties. What would it be like if he really touched me? Ali snapped me out of my sexual fog by pulling clothes off the rack for me. I had to admit, I wasn't tall and leggy, but I was medium height and thin. I didn't have to try a thing on. I have always been a size six. I added things to the rack that I wanted. But for every one thing I added, Ali added three more. I gave her a face, but she told me that this was supposed to be fun and the boys had the money to spare, so why not.

I looked around for Matt and when my eyes found him, he was already looking at me and smiling that sexy I-want-to-fuck-you smile. I smiled back and he mouthed for me to get more stuff. Okay, whatever made this man happy. I loaded up on shirts and sweaters, pants, jeans and skirts. There were only a few dresses that would work for my job. But I was even loving their shoe selection. I was trying to pick out two handbags when Matt came over to me and shook his head.

"No, put those back. We're going somewhere special for a purse. Trust me," Matt said in my ear and then kissed the back of my neck, instantly sending goose bumps down my whole body. I shook the chill away and went to find Ali. She told me that we were going upscale next and, as here, someone was waiting for us and the store would be closed for us. I didn't know how Ali adjusted to all this so quickly. When I started to protest to her that this was all too much, she hugged me and told me to deal.

"Sarah, Matt wants to do all this for you. Please just make him happy and accept it. I don't want to break Jace's confidence, but he told me that Matt has never acted this way over a woman. Ever. For once, enjoy someone trying to take care of you."

Ali was right. I was used to being self-sufficient. Even with Michael, I usually paid for everything. He was an artist and when he did sell a piece, he usually spent the money on buying more art supplies. Not that I wanted to have a pity party or a shit-on-Michael moment, but it hit me right there. Michael never opened the car door for me. I never walked in first anywhere we went. He never even seemed bothered when I paid for things for him. I always thought he acted that way because he didn't want to insult me by thinking I was less than him or beneath him. But the more I thought about it, he was just as ass. Matt was beside me again and walking my purchases to the front. He had quite a bit for himself as well. After all the clothes were added up, I turned away so I didn't have to feel badly about the amount of money Matt had spent on me. We were all heading to the car and loading our stuff in when none other than Laurie ran out to the car and asked Matt to come back inside, saying he had signed the wrong receipt. Matt walked back in and I got into the car. We talked about what we should all do for dinner while Matt was in the store.

"I know, let's go to that fondue place," I said.

Ali clapped her hands together and was in the mood for fondue too.

"There's no food in fondue. It's bread and cheese. How the hell is that dinner?" Jace asked.

"Honey, they have steak and lobster and shrimp and chicken too. You cook it all yourself in a pot and there are different courses of the meal. Trust me. You'll love it. Plus the place has very private tables. If you guys keep your heads down on the way in, we can sit in the back and not be bothered," Ali said.

Matt came into the car, looking really pissed off. "Man, what's the matter with you?" Jace asked.

"That chick tried pulling me back inside."

Matt fumed, running his hand roughly through his hair. I was a bit confused as to why he was so angry.

"Dude, what am I missing? Girls try to get their hands on you all the time. Why so pissed about it?" Jace asked. I was glad I wasn't the only one who was lost.

"Yeah, but she knew I was there with someone else. I mean, what the fuck?"

Seeing that he meant every word he said, I knew what I had to do. Fuck my not being good enough. Whatever forces that brought this man into my fucked up life, I thanked them in my head and crawled onto Matt's lap, facing him with my legs on the sides of his hips, and started to devour his mouth.

I heard Ali trying to stifle her laugh, but all I cared about was kissing the shit out of Matt.

I heard Jace turn around in his seat and laugh too. I didn't care if the whole world wanted to laugh at me right now. The feel of Matt's lips on mine, the way he sucked on my tongue and stroked my mouth was making me wetter and wetter. I wanted more. I moved my hips, slowly grinding into his hard dick. He started to moan and then realized that we weren't alone and broke the kiss first.

"What the hell was that about?" he asked all out of breath.

"I didn't know that men like you really existed," I said through raged breaths.

"Hey, I have a guy like that right here in the car too you know," Ali snorted.

"Yeah, but I'm not allowed to kiss the fuck out of Jace, Ali."

I climbed off Matt's lap and he took my hand in his. I loved the way his calloused fingers rubbed the back of my hand. I was truly happy in that moment. How could this day get any better?

We pulled up to the back service entrance of one of those upscale shops I never go to. There were two security guards waiting for us. Raymond got out first and went to speak to them. He came back shaking his head and looking pissed.

"Man, they just told me that they can't close down the whole store for us. But they'll keep people away and have a full team of security around you guys." Raymond looked straight to Ali. "I'll stay with you, Ali. You too, Sarah. Let security stay around the guys. We'll go in separately. Might be better that way."

"Just take care of the girls. Ali, promise me that no

matter what, you will listen to Raymond," Jace implored.

Ali just shook her head and proceeded out the door with Raymond, and as I was about to join her, Matt tugged on my hand, bringing me back to him.

"Listen to Ali and Raymond, please. No matter what may happen." Matt kissed my hand and then let go.

Ali and I walked together first, with Raymond on our heels. A security guard was waiting for us and asked where we wanted to go first. Ali said lingerie without so much as batting an eyelash. The security guard nodded and started to lead the way. No one bothered us or even seemed to notice that we had security with us. We went up the escalator and were led to the lingerie department. Ali grabbed my arm to try and make me more comfortable.

"Is it that obvious that I am not loving this?" I asked.

"You have to get used to this part of it. You're around celebrities all the time. This is just the reality of it. Come on, let's spend some money. And I think I know exactly what you should get for Matt."

Ali ran over to a rack that had beautiful panties and matching bras. There was a black lace number that I knew would rock Matt's world. But I couldn't do it. I couldn't get into bed with Matt yet.

I pulled the outfit as I walked to another rack of bras. I needed a whole new wardrobe of panties and bras. The ones I was wearing were all I had left. I started to find my size and colors that I liked, and before I knew it, I was walking to join Ali in the dressing room. I had grabbed a ton of stuff, but I loved each and every piece I had. We were still waiting for the boys when Ali and I were getting bored. She took out Jace's card and paid for the whole lot. She said it was more a present for Matt than me anyway. Then we told the security guard to take us to the handbag section.

We walked straight to Louis Vuitton and that's where we stopped.

"Ali, I cannot spend Matt's money on a bag like this. It's so unnecessary. Any bag will do. This is too much."

"He asked me to get you here. This is what he wants. Enjoy." I grudgingly started to check out bags when we started to hear gasps and yelling and even screams. We turned to look at each other. The boys were here and everyone knew it. Security led Matt and Jace to the counter where Ali and I were standing, looking at purses and wallets. They made a human shield so the boys could stand with us. Matt put his hand to my back and asked me what I had decided on. At least that's what I think he asked me. The massive crowd behind us was yelling for Jace and Matt to take pictures, sign some-thing, and just look at them. This was not too much fun now. I wanted Matt there with me, but while he was with me there was chaos. I quickly picked a purse and wallet and let Matt pay and then practically begged him to let us get back to the car. He nodded and Raymond helped. Ali and I moved past the crowd.

As Raymond held Ali and me by our arms and tried to maneuver us away, some bitch purposely stuck her foot out and tripped Ali. Ali didn't go down though, Raymond held her up. Ali turned to her and the bitch actually spit in Ali's face and started to scream that Ali was a bitch who took Jace away from her. Raymond just kept dragging us along. I started to cry. This was crazy.

Raymond got us to the car in record time and asked Ali if she was okay. She wiped her face with a tissue and said she was fine. That's when she saw me crying and grabbed my hand.

"Sarah, did they hurt you? What's the matter?"

"That was crazy, Ali. That bitch actually tried to trip you and spit in your face."

"Honey, don't worry about me. I'm fine. Did you get

hurt?"

"No, but I don't know if I'm cut out for this heavy shit." I started to shake a bit. Ali held me close to her side and just kept rubbing my arm. It wasn't long before the boys were back. Matt went to the front seat and Jace hopped in the back with us as soon as Raymond told him what had happened to Ali.

"Baby, are you okay?" Jace asked as he pulled Ali to his arms.

"I'm fine, just another crazy-ass fan. But I think Matt might need to calm Sarah down," Ali said.

Jace and Matt both turned to look at me and saw my tears. Jace jumped out of the back seat and Matt was there in an instant. He even jumped over Ali to be next to me.

Matt took my face in his hands and looked into my eyes. "Baby, what happened? Are you hurt?" he asked.

"No I wasn't hurt, they only hurt Ali. But that was crazy."

Matt held me to his side and rubbed my hair, saying over and over that he was sorry.

"Well, I don't know about everyone else, but I'm freaking starved and just want to go home. How about In-N-Out and then we just stay in and watch some movies?" Ali asked.

We all agreed and headed to get food and hide in Ali's house.

After we ate, we all settled on the couch and started to argue over which movie we should all watch. I was the most silent, still trying to understand what happened today. I didn't even hear them when they asked me what my vote was. Then I felt Ali nudge me.

"I'm sorry, what?" I asked and saw three very worried faces.

"Sarah, would you mind if I speak to Ali and Jace alone for a minute?" Matt asked.

I shook my head, still feeling as if I were in a daze, and went to the guestroom. I closed the door and started the shower. I just wanted to run the hot water over myself and clean myself of the huge mess that today was.

Matt

"What's up, man?" Jace asked.

I started to pace back and forth in front of Ali and Jace. "I looked at a bunch of houses online last night while Sarah was asleep. There's a great place, fully furnished, and it's in a gated community with a lot of security. I can start to rent the place ASAP and I want to take Sarah with me. Being with you guys is great, but you just got engaged. You need privacy and I don't want to leave her here, or have her find another place. I want her where I can keep her safe. We still don't know what that prick could do to her if he found her alone."

"Matt, we don't mind having you guys here," responded Ali. "Actually it's been kind of fun. I don't know if it's such a good idea to have Sarah away from us. Here there are always people to watch out for her."

"I know you're only thinking about Sarah, but I think it has to be her decision. Ali's right, we don't mind having you guys here. Besides, Ali likes to be gagged. Right, honey," Jace teased Ali.

"Seriously, Matt, I think Jace is right. I think we have to see what Sarah feels comfortable doing. Matt, she's my sister like Jace is your brother. I love her the way you love Jace. I would tell you if I didn't want you guys here. In fact, it actually makes me feel better that you're both here. If you want to talk to her about getting a house, feel free. But don't push it or do it thinking that we don't want you here." Ali walked over to me and gave me a huge hug. "Go talk to her. But explain everything to her. That was one of the problems she always had with Michael. Michael only chose what he wanted to tell Sarah and left her in the dark most of the time. I know you want to rescue her, but again, go slowly."

I shook my head and went to the guestroom to talk to Sarah, leaving Jace and Ali in the living room. I softly knocked on the door waiting to see if Sarah answered. There was no answer so I opened the door. I heard the shower and looked toward the bathroom door. It was slightly ajar. The glass shower had bubbled glass, so I could see the outline of her body, but I couldn't see her clearly. I was getting hard just looking at a blurred outline of Sarah. I knew she was naked, and wet, and I could feel the pre-cum wetting my boxer briefs. I took a few deep breaths to try and calm my hard dick.

The shower turned off. I turned my back on the door and heard Sarah gasp as she saw me through the crack in the door. She didn't close the door, but wrapped herself in a big, white terrycloth robe and then walked out to the bedroom.

"I'm decent. You can turn around now, Matt," Sarah said in a soft sleepy voice.

I turned around and felt like the breath was knocked out of me by looking at her natural beauty. Her hair was pushed back off her face and still wet. Her makeup was gone and there was a fresh pink glow to her face. She looked like an angel, and I was concerned that once I talked to her about the idea of getting us a house she would vanish. I knew I was moving fast, but it all just felt right.

"Sit down, Sarah. I want to tell you what we were talking about out there." I sat at the edge of the bed and Sarah sat right next to me, with her body turned to face me, tucking her feet underneath her. "You know that we decided to record here because Jace wants to be closer to

Ali and she still has the rest of the school year to get through. Ali and Jace had offered that I could stay here with them and that was what I originally was going to do. But this whole thing with your place being broken into, I had another idea. I thought since it's not safe for you to stay at your place, and I feel like I'm in the way here with Jace and Ali, maybe you would want to stay with me. I was thinking of renting a house in Misty Brook. It's a very safe, gated community with tons of security. The place is fully furnished. The house that I was looking at that I liked the most has five bedrooms and separate bathrooms. So you could have your own room and privacy when you want it. But I'd be there with you as well, so you wouldn't have to be alone. I know it sounds kind of crazy. But I want you safe and I want to be with you. This would be a good fit for both of us. You won't have to go back to your place, you can have more space, and we would have each other." She was looking at me with a completely blank look on her face. I couldn't read her at all. It was killing me.

"That was what you were talking to Jace and Ali about? Do they want me to leave?" she whispered out like a small child who was just reprimanded.

"No, they don't want you to go at all. In fact, they both said they thought it was a better idea if you and I just stayed here. But I wanted to see what they thought about the idea before I came to you with it. But I don't want to push you, I just wanted to give you the choice."

"I don't know what I want. I don't know what I want to do. Believe it or not, the whole house thing with you sounds pretty good. But I just feel so safe here with Ali and Jace and you. How about we just stay here a little longer, and when I know that nothing else is going to happen, then we could look at a place to rent. How does that sound?" she said teary-eyed.

"Why are you getting upset? You look like you're going to cry." I grabbed her hand and started to kiss the inside of her palm.

"It's just that I can't believe you like me this much. I really don't understand it. What have I done to make you do so much for me? I just feel like I don't deserve all this. I feel like all I can give you is my shitty situation right now. What if Michael's not done with his crazy shit? I don't want to drag you into it. You already feel like you have to protect me. That shouldn't be your job, Matt."

"This is what I want to do. I know it all seems too fast – Ali told me to go slowly with you – but that's just not who I am. When I want something, I go for it. When I feel something, I feel it fast. I have been trying to act all normal and slow around you, but I can't do it. I want to tell you how I feel. I want to shower you with stuff. I want to be with you. I know I'm throwing a lot at you so soon. But if whatever this is between us is even going to have a shot, you have to know the real me and I have to know the real you. This is who I am, Sarah. I love my friends and family. To me they are one and the same. I would give them anything, even my life. You fit in the category, but in a different way. I've never felt like this with anyone. I want to be with you all the time, and when I'm not with you I'm thinking about you."

"Stop for a second. Pease, Matt. This is a lot to take in. I do want to know the real you. I like that you move fast. I like that you want to protect me. I like who you are. I'm just not used to depending on someone. Michael was always dependent on me. I always had to be the strong one, the one holding him up and helping him out. I'm just not used to someone wanting to take care of me. But I do like it. It makes me feel special and safe. I just feel like this is all happening so quickly and I just feel like a slut."

"What the fuck are you talking about?" I screamed at her, angry that she would refer to herself that way.

"Matt, when I met you, I was wearing another man's

ring. Then a few days later, I'm in your arms, kissing you, with his ring still on my finger. Now I'm sleeping with you every night, making a fool out of myself by attacking you in the store today because I didn't want that bitch to come on to you. None of this is how normal people get together."

"If you ever talk about yourself like that again, so help me I'll throw you over my knee and spank you. Second, not to sound like a dick when I say this, but I'm a fucking rock star. Nothing about my life is normal at all. I think you saw that today. Besides, is how Jace and Ali got together normal? She didn't even know who the fuck he was when she fell in love with him. So how is this insane? At least you know me. I'm showing you who I am. And I could care less about whether or not you had a ring. Ring or no ring, from the moment I laid eyes on you, you were mine."

Sarah made a move toward the door. I had my heart in my throat that she was going to walk out the door. But when she got there, she locked it then slowly turned to look at me. Sarah took two steps toward me and then launched herself into my arms. I caught her and she attacked me, kissing my neck, licking and biting. I carried her over to the bed and sat on the edge with her straddling me. I lost my fingers in her short soft hair, guiding her to my mouth.

"This is what I want. I want to be yours. Only yours." She continued to work my mouth. "Matt, touch me please, touch me," she panted.

I pulled my mouth back from hers. "No, Sarah. Not yet. I want that fuck to have his ring back before I touch you more. I know I sound like a caveman. But I have to know that you can really be mine."

"How do I give him back the ring when I can't even stand to look at him?"

"I'll give it back to him."

"Oh, yeah, that's so not happening. I could ask Joseph to do it, but even that is dangerous. I don't want anyone I know to have to be near him. If I know him, he'll just start bad mouthing me and someone will hit him and then it will blow up even worse than it already has."

"I know, we can call the detective that's in charge of your case and ask him if we could arrange to give the ring back to Michael."

"That's a really good idea. I'll call him in the morning. Good thinking. So you're not just hot as all hell, but you're smart too."

"You think I'm hot as hell?" I smirked.

"You know you're hot, asshole."

"But I like it when you say it. I also like the way you're sitting on my lap. But I can't guarantee to be a gentleman much longer if you insist on staying on top of me." I looked down at the bulge in my jeans, which was very, very visible.

Sarah looked to where my eyes were and moaned and then started to rock against my hard jeans. "Sarah, no, I can't do this. It's too much."

Sarah ignored me, moved her robe and directed her naked pussy over my throbbing constricted cock. Then she continued to rock against me, kissing me hard and moaning as she rocked. "Didn't you ever do this when you were younger? Did you always just go straight to sex? Let's play a little. What do you say?" she asked as she continued to rock over my constrained dick. "Oh God, Matt, I think that I'm getting close, baby. Just a little longer and I'm going to… I'm going to cum."

I put my hands under Sarah's thighs and pulled her closer to my cock as she rocked against me. Her telling me that she was going to cum set me on fire and had me ready to blow. But just as I was trying to control myself and my horny dick, she added fuel to the fire.

"Matt, whatever you do, don't stop. I'm so fucking close." She started to buck harder and faster against my straining jeans. The more she moved, the closer I came to embarrassing myself. But right now, I could care less. I wanted to get her off and if I wet myself in the process, who cared? Sarah started to make little gasping noises. Then she was gasping louder and louder. She gripped my shoulders as she threw her head back and screamed out my name at the top of her lungs. That rocked me. I lost it and shot a load in my pants. She was still trying to catch her breath when I took her hair and brought my mouth to hers. I could not believe I just wet myself by Sarah simply rocking against me. That shit hadn't happened to me since high school. She was wrapped around me, giving to me as much as I was giving to her. I don't know how long we kissed. But when we broke apart, it still wasn't enough. It would never be enough.

"I haven't done that since high school. But shit that was hot. Did you cum?" Sarah asked as she eased back off me.

I looked down at my pants, and they were soaked. I couldn't tell if it was all from me, or from the both of us. Sarah looked at my pants and turned away from me. "Is this all me, or both of us?" I asked her.

"Yeah, I um, cum a lot when I cum. So that's probably me," she said and didn't turn back to look at me. I got up and walked over to her, turning her around to look at me.

"That's the fucking hottest thing I've ever seen. You're fucking amazing." I held her to me and she gripped me back. Then I excused myself and headed to the shower. By the time I got out, Sarah was in bed, asleep. I threw on a pair of boxer briefs and crawled in next to her. I tried to do it as slowly as possible so I wouldn't wake her. But when I finally lay all the way down, she snuggled close to me and threw her legs over mine and rested her head on my chest.

"You're my knight in shining armor, Matt. I feel like I'm in a dream," she said in such a sleepy voice.

I kissed the top of her head. "I'm real, baby. And I'm not going anywhere. Sleep well, Sarah."

CHAPTER
FIVE

Sarah

I had never fallen asleep that easily with Michael. I never snuggled with him. He always needed his space. But Matt was different. I wanted to be wrapped around him and he enjoyed it. I thought over everything he had said to me yesterday. I wasn't the spontaneous kind of girl. I didn't live life by the seat of my pants. I thought everything out. At least I thought I did. But staying with Michael for so long when things were so bad, maybe I needed to make a change. Maybe I should throw caution to the wind and just jump right in. Matt had no problem doing it with me. Why should I? I knew he was one of the good ones.

The first night he found me by Jace's pool crying myself silly, he was warm, caring and just listened to me. The only people I ever felt that at ease with were Ali and my family. From the very moment he met me, he stuck up for me and was on my side. Michael had beat me down in so many ways. I walked away from him, and now it was my chance to walk away from the fear I had. The fear of living life and loving it.

I watched the easy rise and fall of Matt's chest. He looked so peaceful and calm. He was one of those people who you could instantly tell was good on the inside in addition to being hot as sin. And it didn't hurt that he could make me cum all over him. Now there was only one more thing to be done until we could really start moving forward. I had to give Michael back his ring. I watched Matt for a few more minutes, then as silently as I could, I climbed out of bed and grabbed my phone. I padded into the bathroom and gently closed the door behind me.

I looked up Detective Edwards' number on my phone and pushed talk. He answered right away.

"This is Edwards speaking," he gruffly answered.

"Detective Edwards, this is Sarah March, we met the other night when my home was ransacked."

"Yes, Miss March, I remember. What can I do for you?"

"I know this sounds like a lot to ask, but I have to give my ex-fiancé back his ring and I don't trust anyone to give it back. He'll say nasty things about me, and no matter who I send will probably end up in a fight. Is there any way that I can give it to you and he can pick it up from you?"

"That's a good idea, Miss March. But I would rather that you come to the station and I witness you giving him the ring. To be honest, I met with Mr. Mailtlin. I definitely think he is the one who tore your house apart. But he does have an alibi. He claims that he was painting in his studio and we spoke to the model he was using, and she confirmed his story. That doesn't mean that he didn't pay someone else to do it, or that the model isn't lying. So I would like you both to come in and I would like to see his reaction when you give him back the ring. I want to see how he reacts. I will be with you the whole time, and I won't let him touch you. If he gets mouthy, you might just get your reason for an order of protection. Tell me when is good for you and I will contact him and set things up. Is this the best number to contact you once I have it all arranged?"

"Yeah, this is my cell phone. I'm completely free all this week. I don't have to work until this weekend. So whenever he can come in, I can too. Thank you, Detective Edwards. I'll wait to hear from you. Thanks. Bye." I pushed the end button. I took a few cleansing breaths and walked out of the bathroom.

Matt was leaning up on one arm, waiting for me. The minute our eyes met, he lit up with that rock star smile.

"You okay, babe?" he asked.

"I was just on the phone with Detective Edwards. He's going to set up a time for Michael and me to meet at the police station so I can give him back the ring."

"I don't want you to do that. I'll go give the ring back."

"Matt, the detective said that I have to go. He wants to see what happens when Michael sees me. He said if Michael does anything inappropriate, I would have reason for a restraining order. I have to do this myself. I took the ring myself, I have to give it back. I'll be surrounded by cops. What could he possibly do?" I asked hoping that I could convince myself as well as Matt.

"Can I wait in the car?" he tried with an anxious stare.

"Only if you swear to me not to get out of the car, no matter what happens."

Matt pulled the sheet down around his chest and crossed his heart. I smiled. I walked back to the bathroom and brushed my teeth and when I finished rinsing my mouth and looked into the mirror, Matt was standing right behind me. Our eyes locked and he reached past me to pick up his toothbrush. I just sat on the lid of the toilet and watched him. His arm muscles were flexing in so many ways, just with his brushing his teeth. Even his back muscles seemed to move in a delirious rhythm. Hell, I was getting wet just watching him brush his damn teeth. After he rinsed his mouth, he knelt before me, took my face in his hands, and brought me close to his lips. It was a sweet and gentle kiss, no tongue, just lips.

His soft lips had just a tiny bit of pressure while they touched mine. I opened my eyes and found him smiling at me. It was a worshipping kind of smile. I felt it – I knew it was crazy soon, but I felt his love right there in the way that he looked at me. I only hoped that he would wait to say the words to me. I wanted to be able to say them back to him, and I wasn't ready yet.

"I think we should get dressed. I have a little bit of work to do today. Shouldn't you be doing something?" I asked.

"Yeah, I have to get an outfit for this restaurant opening that I got an invite to this Friday night," he said casually as he walked back into the bedroom and started to look for something to wear.

I stopped short as I was walking behind him. "Which restaurant opening?" I asked with a dumb look on my face. That was the type of event I had this weekend. Friday night I had to open a new restaurant at one of the casinos. I knew everyone who was going to be there and I had indeed put in an invite weeks ago to all the Blacking Out members. But none of their assistants had answered.

Since the first time Ali and I had seen them play, I knew she had a thing for Jace Wicks and I was always trying to get him to one of my parties to surprise her with a meet and greet. But I thought it would never happen. The night Ali did in fact meet Jace, she thought he was only someone who looked like Jace and Jace let her keep thinking that. When she had told me that night that she met someone and was leaving, I was totally bummed because I knew Jace was supposed to be at the event. Little did I know that he entered, tripped into Ali and then left to meet her somewhere more private.

"Oh, let me think. What's the name of this place? Table for You. I think that's the name. Know anything about it?" Matt smiled and then winked at me.

"Why didn't you say something sooner that you were coming? You never officially answered my invite, you know."

"To be honest, I'm not really into the whole Vegas excess scene. So why would I fly here just to eat at a restaurant? We have plenty of great places in L.A. But I did hear that this party was being hosted by a very sexy beauty. I was hoping that if I went, maybe I could convince her to leave with me. So maybe you should check your emails more frequently. I responded that I would be attending. Along with the whole crew in tow."

"Are you coming because you want to come and have a good time, or are you coming to babysit me?" I was frowning at him.

"Is it so hard for you to believe that I want to be with you? I know you'll be working and won't have a lot of time for me, but just knowing we're in the same place will make me happy. A smile here and there from you, and dance maybe? Besides, the guys are coming in this weekend anyway. So you just got some more celebrity power at your event. Isn't that a good thing for you?"

"Of course I want you there and I'm beyond happy that you want to be there. But please don't get pissed if I don't have a lot of time to hang out. This is my job and I love it and I have to remain strictly professional. Understand?"

Matt walked toward me, with a pair of jeans and gray t-shirt in his hands. I was standing with my back to the bed. He gently pushed me back as I flopped on the bed. He quickly covered my body with his and kissed the shit out of me. When I was panting and lifting my hips into his hard on, he pulled away. "I can't wait until you're ready for me, Sarah. But I'll wait until you are. Just say the word, and I'll make all your dreams come true." I lifted to him and continued the kiss, and he ground his boxer brief wood to my wet pussy. Then as I was about to cum, he pulled off the bed and walked into the bathroom, and I heard the water of the shower start. I was panting and needy. My pussy was physically throbbing and I had been so close to the edge. I tried to open my legs and stop the deep ache. It didn't help. I tried to close my legs tightly and that just made it worse.

I didn't know what to do. I felt like I was going to scream bloody murder I was so turned on. I looked at the bathroom door. There was no way he'd be out in the next few minutes, right? I quickly stripped off my pajama pants and undies and opened my legs wide. I sucked my middle finger and made it nice and wet. Then I put my hands between my thighs and touched my clit. But I didn't need my saliva at all as I was dripping already. I circled my clit over and over, my breath hitching and my moaning soft. I knew I had to be quiet. I wanted to put my fingers inside me, but that would waste time; I had to cum before Matt came out of the shower. My stomach muscles started to tighten and my breath became harsh and small. I was so close. I circled my clit harder and faster, and then I came. I was floating and holding my breath and seeing colors dancing before my closed lids. I finally tried to slow down my breath and then opened my eyes.

There was Matt, standing in a towel, soaking wet in the bathroom doorway, mouth hanging down to the floor. I didn't know what one says when she gets caught masturbating, so the only thing I did was close my legs and smile. He backed right back into the bathroom and again I heard the shower on. I pulled my panties and pants on and felt like a fool. He probably thought I was a whore. But I had to speak to him, so I just sat back down on the bed and waited for him. It was only a few minutes later that the water stopped and then the door was pulled back open, again with a soaked Matt in a towel around his waist. The first thought that went through my head was that if I had seen him like this before playing with myself, I would have cum the minute my finger hit my clit.

"Matt, sorry if that disgusted you. It's just that you left me all horny and needy. But I can see that it bothered you." I cast my eyes down in shame.

I didn't even see Matt jump on me and throw me back. He attacked my mouth. His tongue pushed right into my mouth without any gentle kisses or coaxing. He was sucking on my tongue and moaning in my mouth. Then we were twirling our tongues together like it was the only thing keeping us alive. I stopped the kiss, all kinds of confused.

"Wait, why are you kissing me like this if you were so disgusted by what I did?" I asked as I searched his eyes.

"You think I went back in the shower because I was disgusted?" He rested his forehead to mine and let out a soft laugh. Then he pulled back and looked me in the eyes. "I went in the shower the first time to jerk off, because the humping almost had me cumming in my pants like a fool again. Then when I came out and saw you playing with yourself, I got hard all over again, and had to go back for round two. I have never gotten that hard that fast after I came before. That was the hottest fucking thing I've ever seen. I can't wait until I'm the one touching your pussy. I can't wait until that fucking ring is gone." He kissed me again and we kept rolling onto each other.

I lost track of how long we rolled around kissing each other, but we finally had to stop when we heard a knock on the door. "Yeah!" I yelled in a pissed off voice.

"Sorry to interrupt. But Jace just told me that we have to go to this fancy schmancy restaurant opening this Friday night and I have nothing to wear. I thought maybe we could hit the mall and go shopping. Or I could always go by myself," Ali yelled through the door.

I bounced off Matt and reached for the door handle, jerking it open. Ali was there with a huge grin on her face. "Of course I'm coming. You know, I have nothing to wear either." My excitement faded and Ali must has sensed why.

"Well it just so happens that Jace told me to buy you something for Friday night, a dress, handbag, shoes. He feels really badly about what happened at the mall the other day. He knows it bugged you out. So, let's get rolling. Get dressed. Raymond is waiting for us." Ali stuck her head in the door and looked at Matt who was standing near the closet in his towel. "Hey, sexy, Jace wants to know if you want to go to the studio with him."

"Tell him I'll be ready in ten," Matt answered giving me a huge grin.

"I'll be ready in five," I said and quickly shut the door. I ran to the closet where all my new clothes were hanging and grabbed for a pair of khakis and a black t-shirt. Then I threw on a pair of black chucks and looked for my bag. I made sure to keep Matt from seeing my back as I quickly dressed. When I whirled around to look for it, Matt was standing there with an amused look on his face.

"What?" I asked.

"I don't think I can ever get you out of those clothes as quickly as you just got them on."

I walked to him and wrapped my arms around his waist. "I wish you were taking them off. But the truth is I do need a dress for Friday's event. I'll see you later." I kissed him and found my bag, grabbed it and headed to the front hall.

"Sarah," Matt bellowed from the bedroom. I turned to him. "If the detective calls with a time and day, I want you to tell me, immediately. Okay?"

"Yes, sir," I saluted and joined Ali as we waited for Raymond to walk us to the car.

CHAPTER
SIX

Sarah

The ride was only a few minutes and Ali just sat there with a smug look on her face the whole time. Finally I had to know what was going on with her.

"What are you so smiley about?" I asked.

"I'm waiting to hear what the hell happened last night. I mean, we are right next door and you're not exactly quiet. Not that I'm judging. Jace kept throwing a pillow over my head so you wouldn't hear me. Spill," Ali ordered.

"We did not have sex, Ali," I said.

"Oh please!" she screeched.

"No really. We just made out and kind of dry humped like a bunch of teenagers. He won't sleep with me until I give the ring back to Michael. He won't let me suck him off, he won't touch me under my clothes, nothing. Trust me, I would tell you. And I must say, for all that he's trying to be a gentleman, I'm going to lose it soon." I swooned and flung myself hard against the back of the seat.

"Actually, I think it's very sweet. He wants to make sure you're really all his when you guys bump pieces. I think that's cute," Ali grinned.

"Yeah, it's fucking great. Is there a female equivalent to blue balls?" I asked.

Before we both stopped laughing, Raymond pulled

the car into the parking garage and we were on our way. We both agreed to head to Lola's Boutique. It was a great little dress shop in the mall. It was early, and since no one really gave a rat's ass who we were, it was easy and relaxing to shop. Raymond came into the store with us, but just shadowed us from a distance. It all seemed perfectly normal to Ali. She'd adjusted very quickly to working around Jace's fame and all the craziness that went along with it.

I stopped at a rack of red dresses. There was one I absolutely loved, but the back was too low. It wouldn't work. Next, on to a rack of black numbers. This was probably better, since I'd be there as a worker, not a partygoer. I fingered through them and picked three that might work. The sales woman asked me if I wanted to try them on, and helped me into the dressing room.

Ali was just in the other room, trying on a dark midnight blue dress. I tried on the first one, and it was a no go. The second one was just as bad. When I put on the third one, I couldn't zipper it up all the way. I poked my head out of my dressing room and thankfully the saleswoman was there. I asked her to help me out. She entered the room with me and immediately gasped when I let go of the dress for her to zip it up.

"I'm so sorry, miss. I didn't mean to..." she broke off, not knowing what to say or how to say it.

"It's okay. I was in an accident, that's all. I just take a really long time to heal. Can you finish zipping up the dress? I have to make sure the bruises are covered." She tried to smile at me in the mirror and pulled up the zipper. I could see the look on her face, and that the dress wouldn't work. I hung my head in defeat.

"I don't think we're going to find anything that will cover all those bruises, unless you wear something with long sleeves. But, wait, I have an idea." Just as she was about to head out of the dressing room, Ali called to me, asking me if I needed any help. I grabbed the saleswoman by the hand and stopped her from leaving, as I told Ali I was fine.

"Please don't say anything about this to my friend. She, um, she, she was driving when it happened and is very upset about it." I lied my ass off and thankfully the woman bought it hook, line, and sinker.

She left quickly, closing the door behind so no one could see me. She came back in moments later, with a black pashmina in her hands. "Let's try this. Now just see if you like it first. If you do, then I'll show you how to wrap it the right way." She moved the pashmina around my shoulders and waist in a pattern and then when she finished, told me to look at what she'd done. I looked around at all the reflections of myself in the dress, and the pashmina was covering all the bruises. The dress looked great, and I could move my arms freely and do my job. I became so overwhelmed I almost broke out in tears. I hugged the woman and asked her to show me how to do it on my own.

Ricki, the saleswoman, took plenty of time and helped me learn how to properly place and tie the pashmina. I was so grateful for her help. When I walked out of the dressing room, Ali was there waiting for me, with five dresses in her hand.

"That's all you're getting? You need to get at least two more, or I'll have to put some of these back and I don't want to put them back. Get shopping, March," she ordered. I turned to Ricki and asked for her help. By the time we were done, we charged a ton of money to Jace's credit card and I was thankful that Ricki would get a hefty commission.

We made our way to one of the department stores and headed straight to the shoe department. Apparently, Ali and I didn't scream money because it took the bitch of a sales girl forever to help us. Ali had picked out two pairs of Jimmy Choos and a pair of Louboutins. I had two pairs of Jimmy Choos. The girl said she could only bring out one pair at a time. Okay, so it took us awhile to try on the shoes and get everything set with colors and sizes. But we were finally very happy with our shoes and Ali handed the girl her credit card and said we'd take them all. As Ali and I started to chat about how we should get our hair and makeup done by Jace's assistant that night, the rude little bitch interrupted us.

"This credit card is in the name of Jace Wicks. I know who Jace Wicks is, and you are not he," she said in a bitchy snooty way that made me actually want to grab my bag and run home to cry to my mommy.

"I know it has Jace's name on the card, but I am an authorized signer. You just have to call the number on the back and give them my license number." Ali pulled her license out of her wallet and handed it to the girl.

She looked at it like it had lice. "I think you and your friend here should leave before I call the police. Obviously you somehow stole Mr. Wicks' credit card and I am just going to keep it and turn it back to the rightful owner." With that she grabbed the boxes of shoes and walked to the back room.

I was literally on the verge of tears. But Ali was having none of it.

"Hey, Raymond, we need a manager ASAP!" she screamed at him. He jumped to attention, and then stopped short and turned to her. "We'll be fine and we won't move." He nodded and off he went.

"Come on, Ali, we can just get shoes somewhere else. We don't need to make a scene," I begged and tried to make her follow me, but she was standing like stone. I walked back to her and pleaded for her to leave.

"Oh no, sweetie. This is going to be so much fun, you won't want to miss it." Just as she finished, bitch girl reemerged from the back room and pointed her obviously reconstructed nose down at us.

"I thought I told you two to leave." She picked up

the phone and called security.

Ali was just staring her down, hard. "Please, Ali, I really just want to go." My eyes were full of tears as I felt so shitty, and I had no idea why.

"Watch how much free shit we get out of this. Actually, we're going to hit the jackpot. Here comes security. Just stay calm and watch and learn," Ali whispered into my ear.

"What's the problem here?" the security man asked the bitch and eyed us like we were two diseased trouble makers.

"These two women have stolen someone's credit card and attempted to buy things with it. I am holding the card, but they didn't want to leave." Bitch sneered at us.

He grabbed Ali and me by our arms and all but dragged us with him, fuming about people like us and how he was calling the cops. I was terrified. I looked at Ali who had a huge smile on her face. Then it hit me. Let them call the cops. This was Jace's fiancée and he knew Ali had his card. Oh, Ali was right; this was going to be fun. The idiot security guard called the police on his cell as he was pulling us to the basement office. He practically threw Ali and me into chairs and then hand-cuffed us to the side of the chairs.

Ali was still smiling. Then Raymond walked into the security office.

She saw Raymond and simply asked, "Jace?"

Raymond answered, "Five minutes out."

"Who the hell are you?" security jerk asked Raymond.

"I'm their body guard," he answered.

"Yeah, sure you are. You stay here too. The cops are on their way." Raymond just crossed his arms over his chest and smirked at the jerk.

The police arrived and didn't bother to speak to us. First, bitch shoe girl came and explained that we stole Jace Wicks' credit card and tried to make purchases with it, and then refused to leave the store.

Just as she was going on and on about how she knew her job and knew from the moment she saw us that we were trouble and that we were probably going to try and steal the shoes, in walked Jace, Matt and an older well-dressed man who looked to be the store manager, stopping her dead. She was there with her mouth hanging open.

Ali moved to my ear and whispered, "Don't say a word to Jace or Matt, just watch." I dumbly nod.

"Officers, I'm Mr. Jace Wicks. What seems to be the problem?" Jace asked without looking at Ali or me. I was so confused. Matt wouldn't look at us either. What the fuck was their deal?

"I'd like to explain to Mr. Wicks, officer, since I am the one who has saved the day for him." The police officer shook his head indicating that bitch girl could explain. "I was doing my job and these two hooligans came in and demanded all these pairs of shoes. I thought they might try to steal the shoes so I told them they could only try on one pair at a time so that they couldn't steal them. I worked with them, giving them the benefit of the doubt that they could be real customers, and wasted an hour with them. They then told me they wanted to buy five pairs of very expensive shoes. The large overweight one handed me your credit card and when I looked at the name, I told her that I would not ring up the shoes. I quickly put them back in the stockroom so they wouldn't try and steal them. Then she made up a story that she was an authorized signer to your account and told me to call the credit card company. I quickly called security."

Jerk-ass security guard cut in then, "I quickly grabbed them so they couldn't escape and dragged them down here. I knew they looked like trouble, so I had to manhandle them a bit and cuffed them to the chairs. A few minutes later, the police showed up and there you go." He puffed out his fat stomach like he was the mac daddy for saving the world.

Jace had his hands behind his back the whole time nodding in all the right places as he heard their bullshit. Then he directed his attention to bitch girl, "So what happened when you called the credit card company?" he asked, sounding grateful to her and not the least bit pissed.

"Well, she handed me her ID and told me to call, but after all, look at her, why in the world would someone like that have your card? So I just told her to leave." She actually had the nerve to take a step closer to Jace and smiled up at him.

"So you didn't call and actually see if she could use my card?" Jace asked. Then he turned to the manager, "Is that the policy your store has?"

The manager was turning bright red and stuttered. "Actually, no. Miss Garbiel should have called the company and checked. Did you know that was our policy, Miss Garbiel?" He looked at her with a death stare.

"Well, yes, I know that is policy. But I mean, there's no way she would have your card. I mean, look at her," she answered with pure disdain.

Jace turned around and looked at us for the first time. He walked over to Ali and winked without anyone else but us seeing it. Then he pointed to Ali and said, "I guess this is the woman who tried to use my card. See, I am guessing it was she since she is my fiancée and I gave her my card and she was supposed to come shopping today with her friend" – then he pointed to me – "and buy whatever they wanted. You see, Miss Shoe

Girl, if you did your job and called the credit card company, you would all know that this woman is marrying me and has all access to my credit cards. Now would be a perfect time to uncuff my fiancée and her best friend and start kissing some major fucking ass so that I don't tweet about what absolute incompetent fuck wits are working in this shithole of a store."

The security guard practically fell over himself to uncuff Ali and me. The police gave the security guard a stern lecture about wasting the taxpayers' time and money and Miss Garbiel was getting a stern talking to from the manager. She looked at Ali who stuck up her ring finger and waved her huge engagement ring in the bitch's face.

The manager joined Jace and asked what he could do to remedy the situation. I turned to Matt who was standing by, trying his damnedest not to laugh out loud. By the time we were done shopping, we had the original five pairs of shoes, free, and three more pairs to boot. Not to mention some purses and sunglasses.

As we all started to pile in the car, Jace asked Matt if he could sit in the back with Ali. Jace got in and pulled her closer, apologizing to her over and over. She reassured him it wasn't his fault and that she was not upset about it anymore.

"What do you mean, anymore? That's happened to you before?" I asked Ali.

"Yeah. This is the third time it's happened. After the first time, I had this whole thing thought up with Jace and Raymond. The first time, I was so scared even though I knew I was allowed to use the cards. I was in tears by the time Jace made it to the store. Second time I was just pissed. Then I came up with this little show. Hey, I know you got upset back there, but I told you it would be okay." Then she turned to Jace and sweetly asked, "Hey sweetie, would it fucking kill you to have Jeff get me cards in my own name?" He just laughed and told her he would do it himself.

"You were upset, Sarah, why?" Jace asked. "You knew I told Ali to buy you guys whatever you wanted."

"I don't know. I've never gotten into trouble before. That shoe girl was a bitch from the moment we walked in the shoe department. Ali, with that little show, you got us like several grand in free shit."

"Several grand? Honey, you are a genius," Jace said and then kissed Ali with all his might.

Matt turned to look at me, and the look he gave me made my thighs close together. I was getting wet and wanting Matt more and more. I couldn't wait until I gave this fucking ring back and I could tap that shit. I gave Matt the look that said without words, *I want you more than anything*. He smiled back and knew it. I must have been sending out some serious signs to the universe, because just as I finished thinking about getting the ring out of my life, my phone rang, and the caller ID showed it was Detective Edwards.

"Hello, Detective Edwards. How can I help you?" I cheerily asked.

"Well, I think I can help you, Miss March. Your ex is trying to head out of town as soon as possible. Do you think you can get to the station in an hour, say six o'clock? He's going to meet me here then, and we can have the ring given back to him."

"That is definitely doable. Thank you so much, Detective. I don't know how to thank you enough for helping me out like this. It's the station on Cheyenne and 215, right?" I asked as my eyes were locked on Matt's.

"Yup, that's the one. When you come in the front, just ask for me. I'll let them know up front that I'm waiting for you. It might be a good idea if you could be there a few minutes early to try and get there before him."

"Will do. I'll see you soon. Thank you." I hung up and looked straight at Matt. "I have to be at the station in forty-five minutes. Michael's meeting me there so I can give him back the ring."

"Raymond, get us to Ali's now and then take us to the police station. We're all going go with you, Sarah," Jace said.

"Guys, you don't have to do that. You have all done enough. Now I made Matt promise to stay in the car. You don't have to worry about me. I can handle this," I said as my hands were shaking.

"Sarah, we want to be there with you. Hey, when I ran away from Jace because I thought he was cheating on me, you were the only voice of reason. I owe every-thing I have right now to you. What kind of friend would I be if I wasn't there to stand beside you? Look, if you truly don't want Jace and me to come, we won't. But if you're saying you don't want us there because you think we don't to be mixed up in this, that's just stupid. So what's it going to be?" Ali smiled at me.

"I guess we're all going. And, Ali, if you're not too uncomfortable, would you come in with me?" I looked at the car floor as I asked her, scared to see her face. I knew she would go with me, but I didn't want to put her in an uncomfortable situation.

"Of course I'll go in with you. Actually, I wasn't going to wait for you to ask. I was just going to get out of the car with you and hold your arm for dear life, and make you take me," Ali laughed.

Ali leaned over to me and hugged me so tightly that I could feel she was not going to let me go in there alone.

We pulled up to Ali's house and all scurried out to drop off the bags while I ran to the guestroom to get Michael's ring. I heard a loud popping sound coming from the kitchen and ran to see what was going on. Matt was pouring champagne into wine glasses as Ali, Jace and Raymond were all waiting for me to make my way into the kitchen.

"What's the champagne for?" I asked.

"It's for you. For being brave and strong and wonderful and for this being the beginning of a new part of your life. Here's to you," Matt said as everyone raised a glass looking at me and drank a sip of champagne. Matt held a glass for me, but I shook it off.

"I'll drink mine when we get back and this ring is gone from my hand. Let's go, guys. Let's get this done." I turned and started for the car. I sat in the back with Ali and was surprised when Matt got in next to me, leaving Jace and Raymond in the front. Ali had just started to direct Raymond as Matt gently took my hand in his and lifted it to his lips and kissed each of my fingers, and then my palm. Then he rested my hand on his thigh.

I had to keep saying in my head that I was strong and could do this. I had to put on the perfect game face for Michael. I couldn't look sad or miserable about my house or belongings. I didn't want to show him that he had ruined me. Because the truth was, he hadn't.

As we drove into the police station parking lot, Raymond pulled into a spot. I didn't know what was going through my head, but before I knew what I was doing, I climbed onto Matt's lap and took his face in my two hands, dragging his mouth to mine. He opened wide for me and moaned as I thrust my tongue deep into his mouth. He was wrapping his fingers into my hair and dragging me closer and closer to his body.

I leaned back and looked into Matt's smoking hot eyes. "I didn't break up with Michael for you. I did it because it was time and because I wasn't in love with him. But this, I am giving this ring back and ending all ties to him, for us. Just remember that, Matt." I kissed him once more and then told Ali that we needed to get inside. Raymond told me that he was going to walk us to the door and wait outside for us. Ali and I shook our heads in acknowledgement. Ali wrapped her arm through mine and we headed into the police station.

The police station was pretty busy with people running in all different directions. Ali and I walked to the front desk and I asked for Detective Edwards. The officer asked who I was and I gave my name. Ali suddenly took a stronger grip on my arm and I turned to see why. There was a pretty scary looking thug staring at her and licking his lips. I think she actually turned as white as a sheet of paper. I jerked her arm to make her stop looking at the handcuffed guy.

Detective Edwards came out from behind a locked glass door and motioned for Ali and me to follow him. He led us to what looked like a small interrogation room. At least that's what these small rooms with a mirror were used for on all those detective shows. There were three chairs around the table. Ali let go of my arm and stood in the back of the room, trying to stay out of the way.

"Just relax. He can't hurt you while I'm here. I promise. And I won't leave you alone with him. Just try and act as calmly as possible. Even if he tries to get a rise out of you, try to breathe and count to five before you answer him instead of just blurting out a response. Okay? We want him angry and mad and incriminating himself in the vandalism of your home. You can do this, Sarah, I know you can." The detective had calm and caring eyes. I actually believed him that I could do this.

There was a knock on the door and Detective Edwards signaled for me that Michael was here. I took a deep breath, looked at Ali who smiled at me with love and support, and I prepared to face this and end it.

Detective Edwards stood from his chair and opened the door to admit Michael into the room. When he saw Michael, he shook his hand and thanked him for making time in his busy schedule to meet with him. Michael just nodded and looked straight at me.

He looked like hell. His hair was longer than I remembered, and greasy as if he hadn't washed it in weeks. His skin looked almost yellow and his eyes were very red and bloodshot. He even looked like he had lost weight. It had only been about a week since I had seen him, and I couldn't see one thing that I had once loved in him. This man before me was a stranger. He looked right through me. Almost as if he had no idea who I was.

The detective told him to have a seat and he sat down across from me. I tried to look away because I didn't want to stare. But I couldn't understand the change in him. He had pure hate in his eyes for me.

"You look well, Sarah," he grunted.

"You too, Michael," I lied. What was I supposed to say? Well thanks, you look like shit?

"Are you sure this is what you want? You want to give me back my ring? 'Cause once you do, we're done. No changing your mind and coming back when that piece of shit rock star fucks you and then drops you." I heard a gasp behind me and assumed Ali was about to speak, but Detective Edwards had given her a look to stop her.

"I'm not ending our relationship because of Matt. Michael, you and I have been drifting apart for a while. Plus, we have been fighting nonstop. I just think we're going in two different directions. I will always believe in you and your art, and I only want you to be happy. But this between us, it's over. I won't come back and I will move on, just as you should." I took another deep breath and handed him his engagement ring.

He took the ring and twirled it in his fingers. Then he smiled and looked at me again with pure evil. "I heard your place got messed up. That's a shame. The police told me that everything was destroyed. That's too bad. What are you going to do about that now? Without my help?" he sneered.

"Ali and Jace went out and brought me all new clothes and stuff and I'm staying with Joseph. I'm really enjoying being with my brother and he loves having company. So it all worked out pretty well. I'm putting the house up for sale and the realtor told me the market's hot and I should make a good profit. So whoever did it actually did me a favor," I smiled.

Michael's eyes turned even darker and his smile turned into a total teeth bearing sneer. "I'm just happy that you weren't home when it happened. I'm so happy that you weren't hurt. That would be such a shame if something happened to you, Sarah. What would everyone do without you? Think of your parents and your brother. They would be so hurt if something terrible happened to you. Not to mention Ali. As it is, she's all alone and all she has is your family to hold on to. It's only a matter of time 'til Jace realizes that he can do so much better and dumps her fat ass. Who's going to be there to help her through? You? What if you're not there for her? Wouldn't that be horrible? Maybe you should just kind of walk away from them all now and make sure they don't get hurt too? 'Cause after all, little girl, it looks like someone has it out for you."

I took a deep breath and counted to five. "It does seem that way, doesn't it, Michael. But I'm a big girl. I can handle anything that comes my way. I'm lucky. I have so many people who love me and would do anything to keep me safe. I'm never alone. There's always someone to take care of me."

"Remember how I used to have to take care of you, Sarah? Does Matt know about that? Does he know how I had to take care of you? Does Ali know?"

I started to ring my hands under the table. Calm down, girl. Breathe. "I'm done here, Detective. Do I need to do anything else?" I looked to the detective and I just needed to get out. I couldn't breathe anymore.

"I think that we're all done. Is there anything else you need?" he asked Michael.

Michael still had his eyes on me. He shook his head no and then walked toward to door.

When he finally left, I dropped my head to the table and couldn't hold back the tears that had been in check for too long. Ali was right behind me, holding me, telling me how well I had done. Then Detective Edwards came back into the room and told me he now knew that Michael had destroyed my house and he promised me he would do everything to put him behind bars. He said that Michael never really outright threatened me, but he thought it would be wise to always have someone with me for a while until they could get some damaging evidence on Michael.

I nodded and wiped my tears away, and in a daze let Ali walk me back out to the parking lot. Raymond was waiting outside the main doors, and immediately took my free arm to walk me back to the car. I felt like Ali and Raymond were carrying me and I didn't care at all. As we rounded the corner to the car, Matt and Jace were outside of the car, waiting for us. And as soon as I saw Matt, he was sprinting toward me. Raymond moved aside so Matt could hold me up. He stopped to ask me what happened, but Ali told him to get me in the car. I couldn't answer. It was all too much.

Matt and Ali got in the back seat with me. As we drove back to Ali's house, she told everyone to just let me be and everyone was quiet. I just wanted to crawl into bed and forget this whole damn day. I practically jumped from the car to get into the house. Matt was right behind me. I walked straight to the guestroom and just flopped on the bed. The tears were gone, but my body was wrung out.

I felt Matt taking off my sneakers and peeling my

socks off. Then he was pulling my jeans off and I lifted my hips to help make it easier for him. Then he pulled me to a sitting position. He was reaching for my shirt. I had to stop him. "Wait, turn off the light first, please." My voice was so scratchy and weak. Matt didn't put up a fight. He hit the light switch and we were in pitch black. Then I heard Matt feeling his way to the bed. I felt it dip and he was next to me. I put my arms above my head and he lifted my shirt off and threw it to the floor. Then he unclasped my bra and threw it too. I lay back on the bed and lifted my hips to have Matt pull the covers over me.

"Do you want something to eat or drink?" Matt whispered to me.

"I just want you to lie in bed with me. I want you to hold me and make me forget this whole day." My voice was barely above a whisper.

I felt Matt leave the bed. I freaked. "Where are you going?" I almost yelled in fear.

"Baby, I'm just taking my clothes off to get into bed with you. I'm not going anywhere." I heard him pull off his shirt and then unzip his jeans. Shoes and socks, all tangled together on the floor. Then I felt the bed dip again as Matt went under the covers and had his chest to my back. He put his arms around me and pulled me closer to his chest.

He kissed my head and started to sing to me. The soft sound of his words made me weep. I tried to hide it from him, not wanting him to think that I was mourning Michael.

"It's okay, Sarah, let it all out. I'm here for you," he whispered into my ear sending a shiver through me.

I pulled back from him and turned so that I was facing him, even though I couldn't really see him in the dark room. "Matt, I have to tell you something." I took a deep cleansing breath and then continued, "I lied to you."

Matt raised himself up with his arm and was quiet for a few seconds, but it felt more like hours. "What did you lie to me about?" he voiced, trying to sound calm but failing.

"I know that I told you and keep telling you that I didn't end things with Michael because of you. But that's a lie. Things between Michael and me have been pretty horrible for a while. We had been able to keep our shit private and away from friends and family, only fighting in private. But when he started to fight with me around you and Ali and the guys, I couldn't take it anymore. The truth is that I knew the end was coming. I probably would have stayed a bit longer until the next big blow up, then ended it. But the night you and I talked by the pool, it all seemed so clear. I wanted a man who was, well... just like you. Then you told me that you liked me, and I realized that I could have not only someone like you, but actually you. That's when I didn't want to fight anymore. I didn't want to hide anymore. I just wanted normal and happy and, well, you."

"So you ended things with Michael just for me?"

"Not just you. Things were crappy between us. But meeting you was the final push. I wanted you to know to truth. I know it seems like a lot of pressure to be putting on you. But I always had to tailor things that I said and did with Michael, and if you and I are going to give this thing between us a real shot, I felt like I should tell you the truth about how I feel." I held my breath, waiting for Matt to take in what I had just thrown at him.

I felt him shift in the bed, and he was gone. The bed felt empty and cold in that one instant, but then the nightstand table lamp clicked on, emitting a soft yellow glow to the room. I pulled the covers all the way to my neck and looked at Matt, who was by the door. But instead of leaving, like I thought he was going to do, he climbed back into bed with me.

He took my face in his hands and kissed me lightly. Just a soft and light kiss on my closed lips. "You just made me very happy, Sarah," he said as his eyes lit up.

I smiled so brightly that my cheeks hurt, and my tears freely flowed. "I was so scared that you were leaving, that what I said was too much too quickly," I said as he still held my face in his hands.

"Not at all. Are you forgetting that I want you to move in with me? Talk about moving quickly. I want it all. I want everything for the two of us. I'm already there, and just waiting for you to catch up. Now I feel like we're so close to being on the same page. Just one thing. Please don't ever lie to me again. I would rather be scared, or hurt, or afraid, or whatever, than be lied to. Okay? Promise me, no lying." He held my chin firmly so I was level with his eyes.

"I promise. No lies," I swallowed hard, and hoped he didn't notice. I wasn't actually lying to Matt, I just wasn't sharing with him. I only hoped that I would never have to tell him the truth, or if it came out, he would forgive me and understand why I couldn't tell him.

"Roll over. Let's get some sleep. I have a surprise for you and Ali tomorrow. You're going to need your rest." Matt shut the lamp off and I cuddled up to his chest and fell asleep so quickly.

CHAPTER SEVEN

Matt

It felt so right sleeping with Sarah. I rarely slept the whole night with a woman. It was usually, thanks for the lay, and now I'm on my way. Ever since we started to become famous, I would never even think about bringing a woman to my house. Who the hell needed that? But here I was, wanting to have a house with a woman, wanting to come home to her, wanting to wake up with her. She was the one for me. She was close, very close to where I could tell her how I felt about her. But not quite there yet. A few more days together and she would know it, even without my words. But truthfully, I couldn't wait to say them to her.

Sarah was still asleep in my arms. She looked like an angel asleep and relaxed. I started to gently move her hair out of her eyes and just couldn't get enough of watching her. She started to stir, and when she moved and realized that she wasn't alone, she smiled brightly as she looked at me. Then her smile instantly vanished and horror filled her face as she grabbed the covers and pulled them all the way to her throat and jumped out of my embrace.

"Sarah, it's Matt. Are you okay?" I asked, moving back from her and trying to look into her eyes.

"Sorry, yeah. I know it's you. I'm just a little, um, shy being naked in front of you. Um, would you mind closing your eyes while I slip into the bathroom to get some clothes on?" she nervously asked.

"Sure. But you do know that I intend to see you naked, soon I hope," I said with a toothy grin.

"At ease, boy. I know. I just want to surprise you and want it to be special. Please," she urged.

I turned away from her and slipped out of bed in nothing but my boxer briefs and stood facing away from the bed and bathroom. I heard her jump from the bed and literally sprint to the bathroom and shut the door behind her, locking herself in. Okay, a little weird, but she was right. If I did lay eyes on her naked, there was no way we would be leaving the room for a few days at least. I had to do this right. I didn't want to have sex to Sarah for the first time in Ali's house. I wanted it to be either our house or, at the very least, a hotel room. That way we could do whatever we wanted and be as loud as we wanted. I already knew Sarah was a screamer.

I shrugged on my jeans from the night before and grabbed my phone walking to Ali's office. I turned on my computer and called the realtor who was offering the house that I wanted and asked him to meet me at the property at noon so I could get a good look at it. He agreed to meet me there and I ended the call and headed to the kitchen for coffee.

Ali and Jace were already eating and had left enough food for Sarah and me on the stove. Ali got up from her chair and made me a cup of coffee, while asking me how Sarah was doing. I told them she was fine. Then I asked Ali if she would come with me to look at the house at noon. I wanted to take Sarah, but I wanted to surprise her with the house, and had to make sure that Ali thought Sarah would like it. She agreed, and even said she'd keep it all quiet.

Jace told me he would keep Sarah busy by trying to have her book some interviews in town. All set then. Then Sarah walked into the kitchen and came right to me, hugging me and kissing my chest before getting her coffee. She made us both plates of breakfast and we all sat down to eat and talk.

"Matt, the guys are coming in tonight. They're going to stay on The Strip. Did you tell the girls your little surprise yet?" Jace asked.

"Not yet. It should be here any minute now," I said.

"Jace, Matt, I hate surprises. What is it?" Ali asked.

Just then the doorbell rang and Ali said she would get it. Within a few minutes, there were seriously loud screams of joy coming from the front door and then a few minutes later, Jace's assistant Jeff and my assistant Lucas were in the kitchen. Sarah launched herself into Jeff's arms and then hugged and kissed Lucas.

"Well, ladies. I hear we have a big night tomorrow. You know what that means. We need a spa day. Then tomorrow I am going to glam the shit out of you two," Jeff said in his overly flamboyant way.

"A spa day!" Ali squealed.

Sarah didn't look as happy. But I guess it was just so much to take in at once.

"Yes, I have everything booked for eleven. We start with facials, then mani pedis. Then we have body scrubs and finally massages. So finish up on the grub so we can get on our way. Sorry, Lucas, but someone has to stay here and see to the men. I'm one of the girls, so I'm with them," Jeff said and made a sad face at Lucas, who just shrugged his shoulders and sat down with us.

"Oh, eleven? I have an appointment with someone at noon," Ali said. "Is there any way to move back my stuff for a while, Jeff? I can meet you guys there?"

"No problem, sweetie. Come on, Sarah, finish up and let's get going." Jeff almost started to shovel Sarah's food into her mouth. Sarah being so good-natured just followed his orders and did as she was told.

It wasn't long until Jeff and Sarah were out of the house on their way to the spa with Raymond driving them. I asked Ali if we could leave early, so we could make a stop. She agreed. I ripped her out of Jace's arms, then we took her car and headed to the mall.

"Where in the mall should I park?" Ali asked.

"By Tiffany." Ali looked at me with raised eyebrows. I just smiled.

It wasn't long until we were walking around the jewelry store scanning all the beautiful jewels. "What are you looking for exactly, Matt? I can help," Ali said.

"I'm not sure. What should I get Sarah? Earrings, a necklace, a watch, a bracelet? I don't know. I just know that I'll see it and then I'll know," I said, still walking around row after row of glass cases.

I saw it. It hit me like a ton of bricks. It was a platinum chain with a platinum lock and key covered in diamonds. Ali must have noticed that I stopped; she came over to me and looked to where I was staring.

"Yup, you're right, that's it. Nice job, Matt," she said and ran her hand over my shoulder. We had someone help us and we were in and out very quickly, and then were on our way to see the house.

When we got to the community, there was a twenty-four hour manned guard gate and they didn't want to let us in, so I knew it was secure.

We were finally admitted and given printed directions on how to get to the house. Ali followed my directions and when we pulled up to the house, again, I just knew it. This was it.

The realtor was waiting for Ali and me when we exited the car. I hadn't said who I was; I had just given my name. But this guy obviously didn't put Matt Lewis together with the Matt Lewis of Blacking Out. When we got close enough for him to see me, his mouth hung open and he kept stuttering over his words. We shook hands and he told me he was a huge fan.

He walked us into the house and I was instantly impressed. I had seen the virtual tour online, but it did not do the house justice. It was amazing. The front hall was large and round with beige marble and a huge long chandelier hanging when you first entered. You walked further inside the house and there was a stairway that went from both sides of the hall to the second floor. The carpets were plush and cream colored. There was a small sitting area when you walked straight from the door to the back of the house, which had floor-to-ceiling windows and looked out to a lake. The living room was to the right, and huge with a fireplace in the middle. There was a chocolate brown L-shaped sectional sofa and two brown lazy chairs. A huge TV was off to the side of the fireplace. The kitchen was to the left. It was enormous with a breakfast bar made of brown and beige granite and all stainless steel appliances. There was also room for a small table in the kitchen with three windows surrounding the table that also looked out over the backyard. The formal dining room was beyond the kitchen and had a large rectangular dark wood table with twelve chairs in a dark burgundy.

We walked through each room, and as I went, I could envision Sarah here with me. When we made our way upstairs, things just got better. There was a hallway to the left that held four guestrooms with queen size beds and each had its own bathroom. Then you walked the other way down the hall. To the right was an office with a double desk, perfect for Sarah and me to work on. The door to the left led to the master bedroom. There was a king size bed in dark wood in the middle and a matching nightstand on each side. There was a fireplace tucking into the corner of the room and French doors that led to a terrace. The closets must have been impressive, because I heard Ali complain about how lucky Sarah was going to be to have all this room for her new shit.

The bathroom got me. There was a large walk-in shower, with a built-in bench and six-shower-head fixture. There was definitely enough room for Sarah and me and I could just imagine the things I would do to her in there. Also, a built-in hot tub sat in the corner of the room. Even though it was in the corner, it was big enough for two people. There were two sinks and even a small makeup table. The realtor asked if I wanted to see the backyard, but I didn't need to. I knew this was it. I had to have it. It was only a few minutes away from Ali and Jace. It was secure and it would be ours.

I walked to Ali, and she was smiling and just simply shook her head yes in agreement with me.

We made our way to the kitchen where I signed a one-year lease and handed over a check for the full year and security deposit. The realtor handed me the keys, garage clickers and all the paperwork I needed for the guard gate.

I dropped Ali off at the spa so she could catch up with Jeff and Sarah. Ali promised not to say a word to Sarah about the house. I took Ali's car and headed over to Sarah's house. I had to see it again. Why, I don't know. When I pulled up in front, I saw the For Sale sign on it and was happy that Joseph was true to his word and taking care of this part of Sarah's problem. The place was quiet and seemed to have a feeling of unhappiness about it. I walked around to check all the doors; everything was locked up tight. I went to the mailbox and it was kind of full. So I took Sarah's mail, and a package for her I found, and walked back to the car.

I put the mail and box on the floor and headed back to Ali's so I could talk to Jace about moving into the new house and try to figure out how to get Sarah to come with me. As I was driving, I noticed a strange smell in the car. It was weird, because it wasn't in the car when Ali and I were driving. I started to sniff around, and when I sniffed near the passenger's side, I smelled it more prominently. I pulled the car over to a quiet street and looked down at the mail. There were letters and bills, and underneath it all, the box. I picked it up and sniffed. Yup! That was the smell. It smelled like bad meat or something. It was addressed to Sarah, but there was no postage and no return address. I wanted to open it, but I knew this wasn't good. I called Jace and told him to meet me at the police station. I used Ali's GPS and headed to the station.

I broke just about every traffic law to get there and luckily didn't get caught. When I got there, Jace was waiting for me at the front steps. I showed him the box and we both went inside. Detective Edwards was there and came to get us right away. I explained what had happened and how I took the package and mail from Sarah's house, and showed him the box. He said that since it wasn't sent through the mail, we didn't need Sarah's permission to open it. He took us to a private room and carefully opened the package with a knife while he was wearing gloves. When the lid was opened, we all jumped back, knocking into each other. In the box was some kind of animal heart covered in blood. But there were also flies and maggots roaming over it. It smelled so much worse with the lid open, we were all covering our noses and coughing from the foul smell. Edwards immediately called for someone who came in and took the box away to run tests on it and see if they could get any prints or DNA.

"What are you going to tell Sarah?" Edwards asked.

I looked at him and Jace back and forth. "How do I tell her about this? She'll completely freak out and lose it. I can't tell her. We have to keep this a secret," I stated.

"I can't do that. I have to tell her, she has to know. This could have come from the same bastard that screwed up her house. I'm sorry, Matt. I know you mean well. But she has to find out. I'll give you until Monday to tell her. Then I'll have to come and talk to her." With that Edwards left, shaking our hands.

"I think we need Raymond to call in more backup. You sign the lease on that house yet?" Jace asked.

"Yeah, and I already paid the full year. Now I wish I hadn't. It would be easier to take her back to L.A. and leave all this shit behind."

"I think maybe we should all move in to the new place together," Jace said, looking around the room, not in my eyes.

"What's going on, man?" I asked.

"Not here, let's go back to Ali's," and he started to leave.

I met Jace back at Ali's house. When we got there, Raymond was nowhere around. Jace walked to the kitchen and pulled out a bottle of scotch. Then he poured himself and me a shot. Jace clinked glasses with mine and shot the whole thing back.

"There was a package for Ali left at the door today. I found it after everyone left. I brought it in the house and opened it. There was a dead rat in it. It had been sliced open with its guts hanging out. There was a note that said 'This is what I'm going to do to you.'

"Someone has it out for our girls and I'll be damned if anything's going to happen to them. I called the guys while you were out, and they're all on their way. I think we're safest at your new place. We're going to have to all bunker down there for a while. If you want, we'll wait until after the weekend. That way you and Sarah can have some time alone before we all overrun you. But I think unless we can convince the girls to come back to L.A., this may be the best way to keep them safe." Jace ran his hands over his shaved scalp.

"What the fuck? Maybe it's not Michael then. Why

would he want to hurt Ali?" I asked.

"I have no idea. But I will not let anything happen to her, or Sarah. I promise you, man, I'll take care of them both."

"I know you will. Same here, bro. How the hell do we tell them?" I asked and then shot back my scotch and let it burn my throat.

"We don't until after the weekend. This event tomorrow is big for Sarah. We let her have that. Then you take her back to the place and have the weekend with her. On Monday, after Ali is done with work, I'll bring her over to the house and we'll tell them both what happened. I'll keep the guys here with me over the weekend so you can have time with Sarah. Ali won't mind. But you have to keep your cell phone next to you at all times. If anything weird happens, call and I'll send Raymond to you. Deal?" Jace asked.

"Deal," I said and told him to hit me with more scotch.

We were both pretty fucked up when the guys got to the house. Jace brought them into the kitchen and told them everything. He then laid out his plan about having the weekend and then we'd all be in my house to watch the girls and try to get some work done.

"How are you actually going to let Ali go to work?" Ian asked, sounding very angry with Jace.

"They have a ton of celebrity kids at the school, it's very well locked up. I'll call her boss on Monday and let her know what's what. But if she wants to finish out the year, I'm not stopping her," Jace answered.

"Fuck that, Jace! You have to keep her safe. Fuck her job and what she wants. You have to have eyes on her all the time." Ian was screaming now.

"Ian, do you think I'm just going to let something happen to her? Fuck, man, you sound like you're the one engaged to her dude," Jace spat back.

"I know she's your fiancée. But that makes her our responsibility too, ass wipe," Ian screamed back at Jace.

"He's right, Jace. Ali and Sarah are part of us now. We take care of our own," Sam said more calmly than Ian.

"Look, Jace and I are doing the best we can. We're going to talk to Raymond and have him bring in more backup to watch over everyone. Until we get some more guards, we need you guys to help. That's why we needed you here. We all have the event tomorrow. Someone has to always be close to the girls at all times. I mean within arm's-length of them. I can't stick close to Sarah while she's working; it'll piss her off. So we're going to have to take turns watching out for her. Ali is a different story. She knows she needs protection from Jace's crazy-ass fans. So we can just keep Raymond on her all night. Sound good?" I asked.

All the guys agreed and went off to figure out where they were going to bunk down. Jace called Raymond and told him to pick up a shitload of food when he brought the girls and Jeff home. I had to move my plan up a bit with Sarah. I had wanted to take Sarah home tomorrow night, after the event. I wanted champagne and candles and music. But with all the crazy shit going on, things were put on fast forward. I went to find Lucas and asked him to drive me to Target so I could get a few things. I had quite a few shots and didn't think I should be driving. I needed to sober up and I needed to get things ready for Sarah.

Lucas and I had just pulled into the driveway as Raymond pulled up behind us with Ali, Sarah and Jeff. I kept my bags in the car and headed out toward the house to get the girls inside. Jeff and Raymond were carrying tons of Chinese food boxes to the house.

Ian had set stuff up for the group to eat while I was

out. Everyone was having a great time, being together and laughing and eating. Everyone except for Jace and me. We tried to hide our fear and pain. But I think if they really took a long look at us, they would see that our having fun was just an act.

The girls looked great. They were talking about the fantastic time they had at the spa and all the funny stuff that happened there. Then Sarah took over, talking about her big event tomorrow night and how she wanted all the guys on their best behavior. It wasn't long before my head was spinning out of control and I just needed to get Sarah alone and out of here.

I leaned over to her and asked her if she wanted to take a quick drive with me. She shook her head yes and we asked everyone to excuse us for a little while. Jace slapped my back and we headed out. I took Ali's car and headed out to our new house. I must have looked like a man on a mission to Sarah because I could feel her staring at me the whole way.

"Hey, Matt, are you all right? You're gripping the steering wheel like a madman."

"I'm sorry, babe. I just have a lot on my mind. Did you have fun today?" I asked her, and faked a smile on my face.

"I had a great time. Thank you so much for everything. I am getting so spoiled by you. You have to stop all this, Matt. What are you going to do next?" she laughed.

"Actually, I do have one more surprise for you." I held out my hand and she took hold of me.

CHAPTER
EIGHT

Sarah

I had no idea where we were going. But as long as I was with Matt, who cared? We pulled into the very exclusive neighborhood. Matt gave his name to the guard and we were whisked through the gates. Matt steered the car around a few streets and then he stopped the car in front of a beautiful cream and terra cotta house. Matt pulled into the driveway and even opened the garage. He slipped the car inside and then shut the garage behind us.

"Where are we?" I asked Matt.

"Come with me," Matt answered and held out his hand.

I took his hand and let him lead me through the house. It was breathtaking. We quietly walked from room to room and I was just in awe.

I was standing in the living room when Matt walked over to the fireplace and turned it on.

"Please sit and relax. Here's the remote. Would you mind waiting here for a few minutes?" Matt asked. "I have to get something from the car."

"Matt, whose house is this? Why are we here?" Sarah asked again.

"All in due time, baby. Just sit here and relax until I get back, okay?"

"Sure," I said and took the remote from Matt. I

flipped on the TV and scrolled through the channels to try and find something good to watch. My favorite secret show came on. It's the one where the bitchy women are getting married and treat everyone like crap. I love this show. I love how stupid these people are. Just because a woman is getting married does not mean she can be a cruel ugly bitch. But her friends and family all put up with it. It's funny as well. I didn't know how long I was watching the show and laughing my ass off. But eventually, Matt was back.

He walked up to me and simply held out his hand for me. I took his outstretched hand and let him lead me upstairs. I hadn't seen this part of the house yet. I just guessed that it was time to see the whole place.

"Matt, this place is beautiful. Whose house is this?" I asked again. There was a small hope that he was going to say that it was his.

"It's ours. What do you think?" he asked with a smile on his face, but concern in his eyes.

He had just walked me into the master bedroom, which was covered with candles and rose petals. The fireplace was blazing and a soft Dave Matthews song played from an iPod in the corner.

"What do you mean, ours?"

"I signed a lease for a year. I want you here with me, Sarah. Move in with me."

I looked at Matt. I must have had a look of shock on my face because I sure felt like I was almost frozen still. "Um, Matt. Don't you think it's a bit soon? We've been together like a week and a half."

"I want to be with you, Sarah. I know what I want, and it's you."

I was not this impulsive person. I needed everything planned out. I also wasn't one for change, which was one of the reasons I stayed with Michael for so long. But then I thought about my relationship with Michael, which had been a mess for so long. Maybe it was time to go outside of my comfort zone, jump into things and just see where this all took me. I knew deep down in my heart that Matt cared about me. I knew he would never intentionally hurt me, and he would never do to me what Michael had. I wanted to be with him. The moving-in thing was just logistics. Go for it, girl.

"I want you too, Matt. Yes, I'll move in!" I was squealing like a teenager and jumping into his arms. When we pulled back, his eyes were burning with desire. I brought my lips to his and he moaned into my mouth. His hands started to run up and down my back. I held his neck tightly. I pulled back from him. He stood rooted to where I left him. Then I slowly walked around the room, blowing out the candles he had lit, over and over, until they were all out. There was just the slight light from the fireplace. I walked back to stand a few feet away from Matt, but straight in his line of view. I pulled my top over my head and threw it to the floor. Then I unzipped my khakis, let them drop to the ground, and toed out of them. I was in nothing but my bra and panties. I unclasped my bra and slowly pulled the arm straps down each shoulder and then my breasts popped out as the bra fell. I was very well built. I had D boobs, with a tiny waist and hips. My short legs were toned and muscular. My stomach was flat and my ass was a firm bump. Matt's eyes were roaming up and down my body. Then I started to turn my back to slide off my panties, but quickly realized what I was doing. I slowly stood still, trying to calm down. Then I leaned over and slowly slid down my thong.

I stood in front of him, stark naked. He didn't move, didn't say a thing. Just looked at me. I walked toward him and took the hem of his shirt in my hands and started to tug it up and over Matt's head. He held up his arms and I reached up on my tiptoes and got off Matt's shirt. His chest was beautiful. He had an eight pack. I had never seen an eight pack before in my life. Matt also had gorgeous tattoos covering his left shoulder and his right abdomen. I lowered my lips to his right nipple and took it into my mouth. I sucked and pulled it with my teeth. Matt gasped and put his hands into my hair. I then went to the left nipple and gave it some attention.

Then I slid my hands down to Matt's jeans. I ran my fingers right along the edge of his jeans. I popped the button open and slowly unzipped the zipper. I took hold of each side of his jeans, and tugged them down until they hit the floor. He stepped out of them. There, before him only in boxer briefs, I slid to my knees. His huge bulge was before me. I moved my nose toward his hard dick and sniffed him. Then I tugged his dick free of his confining underwear and his cock sprang free, almost hitting me in the mouth. I took my hand to the tip and saw the tiny bead of precum. I swirled it around the head of his penis as his hips started to thrust and then as his eyes met mine, I licked my finger into my mouth.

"Baby, you are so fucking hot," Matt gasped out as he grabbed me and pulled me to his chest. He was kissing me and fucking my mouth with his tongue. He was slowly walking me back to the bed. He had me to where my legs were against the bed. "Lie down for me, baby," he whispered.

I didn't want him to see my back, so this was the best thing right now. I lay down and my chest was heaving with need and anticipation. Matt stood over me, just looking down my naked body. Then he shook his head. "I don't know where to start. I want your mouth, your breasts, your pussy. I want it all, now. I want to feast on you."

"Come and get me. I'm all yours, Matt. All yours," I said and arched my back making my tits stick straight up toward him.

Matt crawled up the bed toward my chest. He took my breasts in each of his hands and started to massage them and pull on my nipples. Then he took one in his mouth and started to suck my nipple, and pulled at it with his teeth. I groaned and wrapped my fingers into his hair, pulling him deeper to my breast. "Oh, Matt, more, more please," I moaned to him.

Matt switched breasts. I was wiggling on the bed from all the feelings coursing through me. Matt's hand started to move between my legs and I gladly opened them to give him better access. But just as he was poised at my thigh, he stopped moving his hand. I couldn't take it.

"Matt, please keep going."

"Going where?" he smirked.

"Touch me please," I moaned.

He took his hand and rubbed my arm.

"Not my arm. Touch me lower," I said very breathlessly.

"Tell me where to touch you, baby."

I had never been one for dirty talk. But I wanted Matt so much, and right now I needed him. "Touch my pussy. Please, I need to feel you touch me." I practically had tears in my eyes from need.

Matt laughed low in his throat. Then he brought his hand back between my legs. "I have to see you, baby. I have been dreaming about this." He crawled lower until he was at the edge of the bed. He was right before my open legs, right over my pussy. He slowly flicked his finger over my wet folds. I bucked up from the bed. Matt grabbed me and brought me back down. Then he laid one of his arms over my thighs to keep me flat on the bed.

"Baby, you're so wet. Are you always this wet, or is it only for me?" his husky voice asked.

"Only you, Matt, only you could make me this wet."

I was turning back and forth from desire.

Matt took his finger and brought it to his mouth and made sure I watched as he licked it. "So fucking sweet. I knew you'd taste fantastic." Then he brought his fingers back and found my clit. He flicked it and massaged it until I was about to see stars. My breath was ragged and I was having a hard time staying still. My stomach muscles tightened and I roared as I came. I was panting and still riding the wave of ecstasy when Matt refused to give me any time to come down. He forcefully plunged his tongue into me, and started to work my pussy with his mouth. He was fucking me with his tongue, so strong and deep. Then he pulled back and put two fingers into me and continued to torture me with his mouth. His lips were sucking on my clit as his fingers pumped into me.

"Oh, Matt, please don't stop, I want to cum again," I yelled.

"I'm not going to stop. I want to taste your cum. Cum for me, baby." As soon as Matt finished speaking, he returned to his assault on my pussy. As soon as his tongue hit my clit, I was done. I screamed out Matt's name and shook like mad.

"Matt, please, get in me. I need you inside of me. Now!" I yelled.

Matt smiled the sexiest smile I had ever seen and slowly kissed his way up my body. When he finally made his way to my face, I grabbed him and kissed him long and hard. I loved the taste of myself on his tongue. It made me so hot. I could feel Matt's hard dick pressing against my lips. I pushed my hips closer to Matt to try and force him into me.

"Wait, babe. I need a condom." Matt rolled off me and grabbed for his jeans. Then he took out the square foiled packet and opened it with his teeth. He took himself in his hand and started to stroke himself to make sure he was hard enough to put on the condom. It was hot to watch him touch himself like that.

"Don't put it on yet. I want to watch you do that some more. Stroke yourself for me. I want to see what it looks like when you think of me and play with yourself," I said feeling like a little sex kitten.

"Since the first night I saw you, you have starred in all my hand jobs," he answered.

"Did you imagine my hand, my wet hot mouth, or my wet tight pussy, Matt?"

"I imagined everything with you. I had you in the shower. I had you in my bed. You were sucking me off before I went on stage. Everything, baby. Since the first moment I laid eyes on you." Matt was having trouble speaking in between ragged breaths.

"Come here and take me, honey. I want you so badly," I purred.

Matt reached over to me and pulled my legs to the edge of the bed. He had me facing him, flat on my back, and he took my legs and hooked them over his hips. Then he opened my pussy with one hand, and guided his rock hard dick slowly into my opening. He was very big, both in length and girth. I wasn't used to it. He took a moment to let my insides stretch to accommodate his size.

"Baby, I don't know how long this is going to last. You're so fucking tight, I can't take it."

"I don't care. We have all night, we have every night from here on out." I lifted my hips to move him more into my channel. He groaned and entered me quickly with a hard push and I gasped and yelled at the beautiful pain of his size. He filled me up. It felt incredible.

He would take himself almost all the way out and then pound back into me. Over and over, and I was climbing. My moans were filling the room. I couldn't even hear the music anymore. Again and again, I felt him throb in my tight pussy. I was so close, and then he stopped his slow torture and just started to rock into me hard, over and over. After two thrusts, I was cumming and screaming out his name. He followed me with a scream of my name and then one more push into me as he emptied himself. He leaned over onto my chest and we both tried to catch our breath. I pulled his head as close as I could get it and took his mouth. He answered my need to claim him with my mouth, claiming me right back.

Then he pulled out of me to get rid of the condom in the bathroom. I quickly made my way under the covers and sheets and watched him stalk back to the bed. He got into bed with me, and wrapped me close to him. I faced him, making sure he couldn't see my back in the light of the fireplace.

"Are you okay?" he whispered to my ear.

"I'm so much better than okay. I feel fabulous and safe, and cared for, and I owe it all to you." I kissed his cheeks. "I know this is all happening between us so quickly, but it all feels just so right. I just want to get some things straight with you, if this is going to continue to work," I said into his crystal blue green eyes.

"Name it, baby, it's already yours."

"I'm not sharing you, Matt. I don't want to hear, she was just a groupie, or it meant nothing, baby. I don't share. No sex, no oral, no kissing, no touching, nothing."

"I don't know whether to be happy you feel so jealous, or angry that you actually think I'm such a prick. Seriously, have you been blind to everything? Can't you see how I feel about you?" Matt was angry and whipped back the sheets and headed out of the bedroom. Yes, butt naked.

As he whipped back the sheets, I instinctively flinched and scurried away from him. Looking like a deer caught in headlights, I pressed myself against the back of the bed.

Luckily for me, he didn't notice my moves and just thought I was getting out of the bed. There was a split second there when I thought, oh no, here we go again.

I wrapped the sheet around myself a little tighter, tears tickling the sides of my eyes. I just fucked up everything about this amazing night. What a dumb shit I am. What do I do now? I threw on my clothes, no bra or undies, just the top and bottoms and went in search of Matt.

I found him in the kitchen, looking out from the windows to the lake in the backyard. I knew he could see my reflection in the window, so I slowly walked toward him, giving him a chance to dodge me if he wanted to. He didn't. I wrapped my arms around his waist and went on tiptoes to kiss the back of his neck. "I'm sorry, Matt. I know you wouldn't hurt me like that. But you have to just forgive me, and give me some mistake room. My relationship with Michael was so much more of a mess than anyone knows, not even Ali. I caught him cheating on me, often with his models. He always gave me the same line – it was nothing, just his artist juices having to really take in his model so he could properly portray her on the canvas. I bought it over and over again and always took him back. Why, I have no idea. I've never told anyone about that. I always felt like such a stupid fool. Then I just started to think, maybe I'm just not enough woman, and he deserves to have his little affairs to make up for what I lack. I couldn't tell anyone, because how do I tell even my closest friend that I suck? I know now that's not a loving relationship. But I'm still fucked by it, and still have shit confusing my head because of it. So, if you want to be with me, you have to be able to understand, I really am a mess and need you to just let me learn with you and be able to forgive me. I don't say shit like this to hurt you, or compare you to Michael. I just don't know anything else."

Matt wrapped his arms around me and held me closer to him. "I hate that he fucked you up like that. I hate that you didn't even tell Ali. She would have understood and helped. She would have helped you get out a lot sooner, you know. I promise you, I won't ever do anything like that to you. You're all I want, all I need. I didn't mean to leave. I guess what you said hit too close to home. I used to be like that. Not for a long time now, but when the band first started to get popular. I hate to say it, we were all like that. We fucked all the dumb groupies, let them give us head. Whatever to get our rocks off. It was cool thinking that all those girls saw us as rock gods.

"I met a girl a few years back, Kara. She won a meet-and-greet pass from a local radio station. She was beautiful and really into our music. What I loved was she played guitar too. I asked her to meet me after the show. We dated for a bit. I would fly her out to our shows to be with her. It lasted a few months. Then one night, after not seeing her for about two weeks, a groupie came into our green room after the show and she looked like Kara. I wasn't supposed to see Kara for another two weeks because of the touring schedule. I took the girl into the bathroom and was fucking her when Kara walked in. She used her money to fly to the show and surprise me. She wanted to kill me. I told her it meant nothing, that I just missed her and the girl looked like her. She was crying and couldn't even look at me. I realized that what I did was shitty. But then I realized that if I really gave a shit about Kara, nothing would have made me fuck that other girl. So even though she was willing to take me back, I ended it. It wasn't fair to her when I knew I'd probably do it again. But after that night, I never truly dated anyone. I've had people who are friends with benefits that I used to see here and there to blow off steam and get my rocks off, and I've done the rock star one-night-stand thing. But I haven't gone on what I'd call a real date in years.

"With you, it's a whole different ballgame. I only think about you. Even when we're together, it feels like I'm too far away from you. This is completely new for me, Sarah, but I know I would never do anything to fuck us up. But you have to understand, there will be times we have to go on the road or go do a show. You have to know I'm nothing like I used to be, and nothing like Michael. I won't do anything to ruin this, but there is press, and paparazzi. They could always do things to make it all appear worse than it really is. You have to have faith in us, faith in how I feel about you. Can you do that?" Matt looked with imploring eyes.

"I have faith in you, Matt, in us. I've seen all you've done for me, and you still barely know me. I promise. If anything makes me upset, or if I have something to question, I'll ask you about it instead of just acting like a fool and walking away. Okay? But you have to have patience with me. Can you do that?" I asked.

"I'll do anything for you." Matt kissed me. "Want to go to sleep now? You have a big night tomorrow and I think Jeff wants to do your hair and makeup. So you're going to need your strength for him." Matt and I both laughed. We held hands and walked to our room together. I loved the room, but it needed some pictures of family and friends in it. It needed a bright painting, or better yet, maybe a big mirror that we could see from the bed. That would be interesting. I had to have Ali over to help make this place more like home for Matt and me. But that could wait. I was sore, and happy and sad, and had just too many other things to worry about right now. I needed sleep. While Matt walked to use the bathroom, I slipped out of my clothes and slid under the covers and got comfy.

Matt came back and joined me in bed. A tangle of legs and arms and kisses, and we were both fast asleep.

I woke up to the smell of coffee and bacon. I must have been dreaming. Matt had just signed the lease. How could we have breakfast? I opened one eye and looked toward Matt's side of the bed, no Matt. I quickly put on my top and pants, and used the bathroom before heading toward the kitchen.

I stopped in my tracks when I saw the most incredible sight. Matt was standing in his boxer briefs cooking at the stove. He was cooking eggs, bacon, and French toast. There was coffee brewing. There was even fruit in a bowl. Was I still dreaming? I actually pinched my arm to check. Nope, awake.

"Seriously, you cook too? What the hell have I done in this lifetime to deserve this?" I asked.

Matt turned with a wide smile on his face when he saw me. "Come here, baby. I made you breakfast. Hell yeah I can cook. Do you think my mom wouldn't make sure I could treat a woman right?" he asked with a wiggle to his eyebrows.

I walked to Matt and kissed his lips and gave him a big hug. "What can I do to help?" I asked.

"You can set the table," Matt said as he got the food ready on platters.

I set the table, put the pot of coffee on it and poured a cup for Matt. We both drank it black, so that was easy to remember. We sat down and dug in. Everything was wonderful. I had to get his mom's number and call her to thank her for her good job. Not only for the food, but Matt was a perfect gentleman and so wonderful. I knew it was because of his parents being so involved. It made me think of my own parents. I really had to call them to let them know I was finally free of Michael and I was fine. Ugh, I would also have to tell them that I was moving in with Matt. I didn't know how that would go over.

They were always very supportive parents. I was an adult and they wouldn't say anything against it. But I could picture their worried looks that it was too soon for me to be moving in with Matt. I wasn't in the mood for that look. I could still put off that conversation for a day or two.

When we were done with breakfast, I told Matt that we had to head back to Ali's so I could get my clothes and computer and get ready for tonight. Matt said that I also had to start packing up all my stuff to move it into the house with him.

"You know, there are some things we need here. We don't have to get it all today, but stuff like water, juice, and more groceries. Then we need laundry detergent and soap and toilet paper and stuff," I told Matt

"I don't know about you, girl, but I'm a Target man. Wanna do that on the way to Ali's?" Matt asked. "Then I'll drop you off to get ready, I'll take the stuff back here to put it away and I'll meet you at Ali's later when I have to get dressed?"

I shook my head yes. I loved Target. This was going to be so much fun. A half hour later, we were pulling into the parking lot at Target. Matt put on his sunglasses and tried to change his hair around a bit. It was short in the back and a little longer on the top, in a gleaming black. He tried to part it down the middle and looked like a total dork. I couldn't hold back the laughter, so he just messed it up and hoped for the best that no one would recognize him.

We each took a cart and started with the non-food stuff. We needed cleaning supplies, dish detergent and garbage bags, stuff like that. Matt even picked up a few sets of sheets. Then he took a load of towels too. He also dropped a ton of toothbrushes and toothpaste, and soap and shampoo, in the cart. I didn't know guys needed all this shit.

Then we bought a TV for our bedroom. I really loved to fall sleep to TV. Matt even bought a DVD player and some movies. We actually asked someone to hold both our carts, and had to get two more for the food. Matt was buying tons of stuff. Bags and bags of chips and soda and water, peanut butter and cheese, and tons of frozen food. I didn't ask him who he thought he was feeding; I just went with it.

We were just about done when Matt walked to the electronics section and bought some sort of game system, and a bunch of games. I didn't even know what he bought, so I hoped he didn't think I was going to play it with him. Over a thousand dollars later, we pulled our four carts to the parking lot, and loaded up the car.

We were at Ali's before I knew it and had no idea how Matt was going to unload all this stuff himself. But just then Jace came running out toward us.

"Hey, Sarah. I'm going to go over to your place with Matt and you girls can have fun here with Lucas and Jeff. We'll be back later, okay?" Jace asked.

"Sure, thanks a lot. I have no idea why Matt bought so much stuff, but he will definitely need your help getting it all in. I'll see you guys later," I said. "Please don't be late. I have to be at the restaurant at five. Some-one has to drive me, okay?" I rounded the car to Matt's side and kissed him good-bye.

CHAPTER
NINE

Matt

I was glad that Jace and I cooked up this whole idea. We were meeting at my new place with the band, Joseph and Sarah's parents. We had to put everyone on the same page about the girls. We were going to tell them tomorrow about the threats and have them all move into my place. I had to meet Sarah's parents and explain my intentions toward Sarah. I only hoped they would listen to me before kicking my ass.

Jace and I got to my house and we started to unload and set up some stuff. We were still getting food put away when the doorbell rang. Time to face the music. I walked to the door, while leaving Jace to put the rest of the food away.

I opened the door and Joseph was standing there, looking like he was going to kill me. He walked past me and then I saw two very warm and friendly people smiling at me. "Please, come in. I'm Matt Lewis. It's such a pleasure to meet Sarah's parents." I shook both their hands and ushered them into the kitchen. I don't know why, but my family always discussed serious business in the kitchen. So that's where I led them.

Gillian and Sam March followed me to the kitchen and I then asked them to take a seat while I got us all some waters.

"Mr. and Mrs. March, I'm Jace Wicks, Ali's fiancé. It's such a huge pleasure to finally meet Ali's parents.

Thank you so much for all you've done for her." Jace shook their hands and sat down at the kitchen table next to Gillian.

"Honey, come give me a hug. You have made my baby so happy. She loves you so much. We have loved Ali like she is our own. Just take good care of her, you hear me?" Gillian said and hugged Jace again.

"And you, Matt. Joseph has been telling us how much you've been helping our Sarah. Are you just one of those really good guys, or should we know something that we don't already know?" Sam asked and smirked at me.

I sat down across from Sam and Gillian. "Mr. and Mrs. March, I know this is probably going to sound crazy, but from the first moment I saw Sarah I knew she was special. I stayed away because she was with Michael. But then he started treating her very poorly while we were all at Jace's place in L.A. I stood up for her, and want you to know I always will. I actually leased this house so she could have a place – neither she nor I want her back at her place after what happened. So she's going to be living here, with me. I'm sorry you're finding out like this, but a situation has arisen that has forced me to move very quickly when it comes to Sarah."

"That's why we asked you to come here today. Something else has happened, this time involving both the girls," Jace added.

"What the hell happened now?" Joseph yelled.

"Someone sent a box to Sarah; they left it at her house. I went by there yesterday and found it. It smelled rancid, so I just drove it straight to the detective who's been working her case. He opened it, and it was an animal heart covered in blood and bugs. Then Jace found a box at Ali's house; it had a dead and dismembered rat in it. Both boxes contained threatening messages for the girls. The police are investigating both matters. But we haven't told the girls yet," I added at the last minute and watched for their reactions.

"What do you mean, they don't know? Why wouldn't you tell them? Are you fucking crazy? They need to know they're in danger!" Joseph screamed at me and got a little close to my face.

"Man, relax. Tonight your sister is running a big launch. I didn't want to have her freaked out. It would really kill her to screw this job up. We already have the whole band here in Vegas. They're all going to be there and all of them know to keep eyes on the girls, no matter where they are. Jace already travels with a bodyguard, Raymond. And Raymond is bringing his wife who can be in the restroom and other places where we can't follow the girls. As soon as tonight is over, we're all moving in here."

"We both would prefer to move the girls back to L.A.," chimed Jace. "I can't speak for Sarah, but I know Ali won't just quit her job and leave the kids in the middle of the school year. So we have to make provisions here. Matt's house has better security than Ali's. We're going to move in tomorrow. Matt figured we'd have you all over tomorrow morning for a breakfast and then break it to the girls with you all here. They might be more willing to listen to the new security details if they have the three of you already aware and on our side. That's why we wanted to lay it all out to you beforehand."

"What do you have in mind?" Sam asked.

"The band, the body guards, Ali, Sarah, Jace and I all lay low here as long as the investigation is ongoing. They go nowhere without guards, even work. They're not allowed to be here alone either. We also want to change their cell phone numbers and only have family, the guards and the band to have those numbers. I already have new security being installed in a few hours. There will be cameras all over this place and a state of the art security system." I was looking between the three of them, hoping to get them on our side.

"Well, this is pretty frightening, and I'm in a bit of shock right now. I'm not sure what to do and probably can't even think straight. It seems like you two have thought of everything. I have to say, I'm happy that Sarah and Ali have the two of you. I think I'm fine with everything you've said. I'll do whatever you want me to do to keep my girls safe. What time do you want us here tomorrow?" Gillian asked.

"Damn, mom, you're taking this all too well. What the fuck?" Joseph screamed.

"Watch your mouth, Joseph. What am I supposed to say? My two daughters are in danger, and these two men and a police detective are trying to do everything to keep them safe. I can't think of anything else that they haven't already thought of. I want my girls safe. And Jace is right. Ali loves teaching and won't just leave her kids. We have to wait this out, and hope whoever is doing this screws up, and they get caught. Until that happens, I have to believe they'll be fine. Otherwise, what do I have?" Gillian turned to Jace and me. "I trust you boys. Just take care of my girls, okay? Just take care of my girls." Gillian started to cry but rose from her chair and put a kiss on my cheek and hugged me, and then did the same to Jace. Then she sat back down and turned to Sam.

"I agree with Gil. What can we do to help? What can we do to help our girls?" Sam asked.

"Just be here tomorrow, around ten, and we'll explain everything to the girls," I answered.

I turned to Joseph. "Man, I know you love them. I know all about when Ali was in high school. I know everything you've been doing for Sarah. You can hate me because of what I do, or what I look like, or just because you don't like me. But I love these girls. I swear to you, I wouldn't even think twice before taking a bullet for either of them. I love your sister. I'll do everything to keep her safe. I need you on our side, Joseph. After all, aren't we on the same side, the side where we keep the girls safe?"

"I know you care for her, man. I can see it. I saw it the moment you looked at her house, and saw what some asshole did to her. I know you moved heaven and earth to get to her. I know from Ali that you're a good guy. I'll do whatever you guys and your security team say to keep the girls safe. But if you fuck up and a hair gets hurt on their heads, I'll fucking kill you. That goes for you too, Jace." Joseph said it all calmly, but with a real chill of what would come if we screwed up.

"Joseph, if God forbid anything were to happen to either one of them, I don't think we would be able to live with ourselves. But you can feel free to come at us. Okay?" Jace said and held his hand to Joseph.

Everything went even better than I thought it would. Sarah's parents and Joseph would be at our house tomorrow morning, along with the guys and the new security team. So now we just needed to get through tonight without anyone getting hurt. It felt like there was a ticking bomb inside of me. I just couldn't wait to get back to Ali's and see for myself that Sarah was fine. I knew she was being watched by Raymond and that Raymond's wife Ella was on the way. Ella would follow the girls closely.

All my stuff was at Ali's. After Jace and I had everything sorted from my little shopping spree, we headed back to our girls.

Jace and I had to laugh when we pulled into the driveway. The music was so loud I thought the house might fall down. It was so good to hear them all laughing and screaming and singing and partying. This house, right here in Las Vegas, was filled with the most important people in my life. Only my parents were missing. It was crazy to think how well the guys took to Sarah and Ali. When Jace and I called them to tell them what was going on, they didn't hesitate to tell us that they were hopping on a plane with their stuff and would be staying with us until we wanted them to leave.

Jace and I walked into a crazy house. Miles and Alex were dancing around in the living room. Lucas was running to the bedrooms with glasses of champagne, singing too. Jace and I just shook our heads and laughed and I went in search of my woman. I was almost to the guestroom when we all stopped because we heard Ali and Sarah scream bloody murder. I went running, and felt the others on my heels. I stopped when I got to Ali's room and saw that the girls were screaming because Ian had his head shaved into a Mohawk. The girls were already dressed and their hair and makeup were done. Sarah looked so fucking hot, I couldn't control the wood that was quickly growing in my pants.

When she saw me, she slowly walked to me, holding her glass of champagne. "Well, sexy man, what took you so long to get back here?" she asked and started to kiss my neck.

"I was putting everything away. Look at you. You're so fucking hot. I'm probably going to jail tonight. Will you bail me out?" I asked.

"What the hell are you talking about?" she responded.

"I know that every guy in the place tonight is going to try and pick you up, and I'm going to have to punch them all, and then I'll get arrested and you'll have to come bail me out," I said as I wrapped my arms around her waist.

She took my arms down from her waist and took my hand and led me into the guestroom. When we were both inside, she locked the door and leaned against it. "You know, Matt, I have been replaying last night in my head all day long. And I have to say, I am very, very, horny. I was hoping that you'd get here while I was in the shower so you could join me. But you were so late, and I have to leave soon. But I think we do have some time…" Sarah winked at me and then started to get to her knees in front of me. But I stopped her.

"Oh no, baby. You are too fine right now to be on your knees. After all, this is your big night." I brought her back to her feet and then backed her against the door. I slid to my knees. I lifted her dress to her stomach and saw that she was wearing a thong. I dipped my fingers into the side of her thong and slowly brought it down and had her step out of it. It was so wet. It made me even harder than I already was. I wanted her, I wanted to take her. But I also didn't want to mess up her hair or makeup. We were getting short on time so I had to move quickly. I hooked her right leg over my shoulder. I spread her lips apart with one finger and slid my tongue over her slit while one hand firmly latched onto her ass. I moaned loving the taste of her wetness. She was moving with each stroke I gave her. She was riding my mouth. I then pulled back a bit and plunged two fingers into her and rubbed the top part of her pussy wall. I knew I hit the right spot because after three rubs, she shuddered and came in my mouth. I licked it all up as she shook holding onto me.

It wasn't enough. I had to be buried in her. I took her leg down and then bent her over the bed. I started to carefully lift her dress, but she flinched and immediately grabbed it from me, raising her dress just enough that I could see her ass and pulling it tightly around her so I couldn't move it any further. Her ass was calling to me, so I massaged her round globes. I unzipped as quickly as I could and grabbed for a condom. I suited up and then teased her entrance with my hard dick. I rubbed it over her opening and she was pushing back into me, silently begging for me to enter her. But I wanted to hear her say the words, so I just kept the torture for both of us.

"Matt, please, fuck me. I need to feel your dick in me, now!" She was whimpering and that was all I needed.

I slammed into her and both of us moaned. I was hammering into her over and over. It didn't take long for her to tighten up around me, getting herself close. When I felt her gripping around my dick, I couldn't hold back. I shot so hard I couldn't even breathe. We were both gasping and trying to catch our breath.

I leaned off Sarah, and then pulled her up. I looked at her, the lust and love in her eyes got to me. At that moment, I knew I had her. I saw it. She didn't have to say the words, and I didn't need to hear them. I could actually feel it and I glued my eyes to her.

"Honey, are you okay?" Sarah asked.

"Yeah, baby. I'm fine. You just take my breath away. You are everything, Sarah. Always remember that, everything," I said to her and then I had to kiss her, lightly and lovingly.

"Better get dressed, sexy. We need to head out," Sarah said as she finished undressing me and then walked to the bathroom to start the shower.

"Can you please pick something out for me to wear? I have no idea what to wear to this kind of thing. Plus, I don't want to embarrass you," I said and walked toward the shower.

"You could never embarrass me, honey. You are amazing, Matt," Sarah said to me as she walked to the closet and picked out black jeans and a white button down shirt with a huge cross in black on the back. It was one of my favorite shirts. I was glad she liked it. She also took my black boots from the closet and set them down for me.

I showered as fast as I could and then dried off and

got dressed. Everyone was already out in the living room waiting for me. When I got there, everyone seemed to be happy and laughing at something that Ian had been saying.

"Well, thanks for joining us handsome," Ian laughed at me.

"Nice hair, dick. Trying to scare the girls away from you even faster?" I asked.

"Hey, watch it. I'm the one who did his hair," Ali said looking amused.

"I think he looks hot," Sarah said.

"See, I look hot. Even your girl thinks so," Ian smugly answered.

Raymond came in from outside and told us that the bus was ready to roll. Jace had hired a party bus so that we could all leave to go to the opening together and get home together. We locked up tight, and headed to the bus.

The ride to the restaurant felt like it took forever. There was just a bad feeling that I had about tonight. I could tell that Jace was feeling the same way. Even though he kept a smile on his face, I could see it in his eyes. He was terrified for Ali. He kept looking at her like he was going to lose her at any second. I felt the same way. We both had just found our girls, and someone wanted to hurt them. I only hoped my feeling was wrong, and that tonight would be uneventful and over soon.

CHAPTER
TEN

Sarah

Something was bothering Matt. But we were around everybody, so I wouldn't be able to get it out of him now. And I had to do my job tonight. As soon as we got home I'd get it out of him. Home, our home. I loved that thought. I couldn't wait to move my clothes in tomorrow. I wanted to try and get some photos of everyone tonight. I hired one of the best photographers for the event, and she was a friend. I had to ask her to get me some good stuff so I could add them to the house.

"Okay, listen up, everyone. This is my job. So, no one embarrass me by being drunken fools. Okay?" I said and gave all the boys a stern look.

"Yes, mom, we'll be good," Ian said.

We arrived at the hotel and we all made our way to the restaurant. I pulled out my folio and started to track the guest list. I told the guys that they had to keep themselves busy for a while. The party hadn't started yet, but my job did. I needed them to make a grand entrance later in the evening. Matt didn't want to leave me, but I agreed to take Ella with me.

I put on my headset and got things started. I had to taste everything before it left the kitchen and make sure the booze was ready to flow. I saw Nell McLean walk in and I smiled.

"Hey, girl. Thanks for the job tonight. Give me a little info as to who is heading in tonight," Nell said as she hugged me.

"Hey, Nell. I am so happy you could work this event for me tonight. I'll give you a rundown in a minute, but I have a favor to ask you. I'm seeing someone, and you might have heard of him, Matt Lewis, of Blacking Out. The whole band will be here tonight, along with Ali's fiancé who happens to be Jace Wicks. If you could get me some killer shots of them having a good time together, I'd really appreciate it. I'll pay for the shots."

"No you won't. It will be my pleasure. But tell me, are *all* the guys from Blacking Out coming tonight?" She sounded giddy.

"Yeah. Are you a fan?" I asked.

"I am a huge fan of Ian Buchanan. But don't tell anyone, especially him, that I just told you that. I hear he is the player to end all players. But I would love to see if he's as hot in person as he is on TV and stuff," Nell said with a wicked smile.

"He is definitely hotter in person. I hope you like Mohawks, because he just cut his hair today. Find me when you see him and I'll introduce you."

"Thanks, I'm going to go get set. I'll catch you later." Nell walked back to the front entrance of the restaurant to set up her camera and light stand.

I grabbed my checklist and started to go over the events for the night. The wait staff was all ready and I had them lined up for inspection. They all looked great. The food was starting to get ready. The bar was fully stocked. The D.J. was set up and we had gone over my playlist of songs for the event.

Before I knew it, a few hours of prep had passed and we were ready for the official opening and the guests to be admitted. There was already a nice line outside the doors. I ran to get the chef and owner, Jim Mallori. He and I went to the outside of the restaurant. He gave a small speech and then officially opened the doors to the restaurant. The party was on.

I had told the guys to wait until about nine to make a grand entrance. The first people to come in usually were family and close friends, followed by other chefs and restaurateurs. Then writers and critics. The celebs had to make a grand entrance.

It wasn't long until I heard gasps and screams and knew that the band had arrived. I couldn't help but let out a little giggle, as I still had that childlike giddy feeling when I was hanging with the band. Somehow, when they were all together, I always imagined that they would all just break out in song and give me a small intimate concert. I know, crazy. But whatever.

I saw Ali first, who only allowed a few shots with Jace and then came toward me, leaving the band to get photos together.

"Sarah, this place is great and it is packed. Great job! So you know, last time I came to one of your events, I got a fiancé. What do I get at this one? Or rather, maybe you'll walk out with a fiancé tonight?" Ali said with a wink.

"Yeah, as if we're ready for that. Hey, I'm already living with him. One step at a time. Did the guys get crowded out in the casino?" I asked.

"Like you have no idea. You think the mall was bad? That was nothing. Imagine, they're all together tonight, so people were going nuts. It was okay though. As soon as the first scream broke out, I dropped Jace's hand and ran to Raymond. Jace is pissed at me, but he'll deal. I'd rather he has all the fun of people screaming in his face and trying to rip his clothes off. I'll just stay quietly to the side for that shit. Oh, where's the bathroom? I really have to pee."

"I do too. Come on, let's go."

I led Ali to the restrooms. After using the loo, I was washing my hands when I realized that my pashmina was slipping and you could see my back. I listened for Ali who was still in her stall, and made a mad dash to fix the pashmina in place. I was so intent I guess I didn't hear Ali flush.

"What the fuck, Sarah!" Ali choked out.

I looked up into the mirror and met her eyes. "Ali, please, it's not what you think. Please, can you just help me set this the right way, and we'll talk about this later?" I pleaded.

"Um, fuck no. Get in the stall with me, Sarah. So help me God, now!" She held the stall door open and I walked in to where she was. "Turn around, Sarah, and hold the front of the dress so it doesn't fall on the floor." I did as Ali said. I was too scared and weak to argue or put up a fight. Especially when it came to Ali. When Ali was hard, I was soft. When she was strong, I was weak. When she was sick, I took care of her. We were each other's yin and yang. Right now, I just listened to her.

I heard her choke as she pulled the zipper of my dress down and examined my back. She lightly touched the bruises, so lightly that I didn't even flinch. It was as if she thought she could heal them with her fingers. Then she raised the zipper. She didn't say a word. I just hung my head in shame.

She put her hands gently on my shoulders, turned me to face her, and the tears were freely flowing down her cheeks. She wrapped me in her arms and she shook and cried holding me. "I'm so sorry, Sarah. I'm so sorry that you didn't think you could tell me. That you couldn't confide in me. What did I do to make you think you couldn't tell me?"

"Ali, I was ashamed. I didn't want you to know I was one of those women. After the first time, I believed him when he said he wouldn't do it again. So I stayed. Then it happened again, and again, and I just felt like a fool and was too embarrassed to tell anyone." I was crying now too.

"We have to tell the detective. He has to know so that he can watch Michael more closely. Oh shit!" Ali looked freaked,

"What?" I asked.

"The guys are going to lose it. They'll probably end up in jail after they kill Michael." Ali said it calmly, but I knew she was dead serious.

"Ali, you cannot tell Jace or Matt. No!"

"Sarah, how can you not tell Matt? Wait, how did you two have sex and he didn't see these?" Ali looked confused.

"I made him keep the lights off, and I stayed on my back or made sure my back was never visible. But we can talk about that later. Ali, seriously, they will go find Michael and beat him to a bloody pulp. Neither of them needs that publicity, Ali. You have to think about them. You know what would happen. Plus, Michael will just turn around and sue the shit out of them. Do you really want all of that? Look, I'm sorry I didn't tell you about this. I promise we'll do a girl day and I will tell you everything. But please, promise me you won't tell any of them?" I begged.

Ali took a calming deep breath. "Okay. But you do realize you are totally putting me in a shitty place right now. If Jace and Matt find out about this, and that I knew and didn't tell them, they're both going to kill me."

"All the bruises should be gone soon. Truthfully, I don't think I ever want Matt to know about this. I feel so stupid and weak and like such an ass about it. Please. Just give me time to figure it all out. Okay? Promise me." I looked her straight in the eyes.

"Okay. But we need that girls' day this weekend. Got me?" She meant business.

We made our way out of the bathroom and by the front podium stood the guys. They all looked incredibly hot. And it made my heart swell when I realized that they were all there just for me. They all smiled when they saw Ali and me walk toward them.

Matt wrapped his arms around my waist and pulled me into a kiss. It felt so good to have him there with me. I felt like the night just might be perfect. All the guys kissed and hugged me and I told them what we had to eat and drink, and slowly they all made their way toward the food and drinks. But Matt stayed by my side.

"Are you busy, or can we hang for a bit?" Matt asked.

"You can always hang with me. I think all the celebrities are here so I just have to make sure everyone is having a good time. Oh, wait, where is Ian? I want him to meet a friend of mine," I said looking through the crowd for a Mohawk.

"Please tell me you're not trying to set Ian up with a girl. He is not a one-woman kind of guy, babe," Matt snickered.

"Neither were you, dirtbag. No, I'm not setting him up. She just happens to be a fan of the band. Come on, I want a picture together." I took Matt's hand and guided him through the crowd toward Nell.

"Nell, I want you to meet my friend, Matt Lewis. Matt, this is Nell McClean." I introduced them and they shook hands.

"I'm actually Sarah's boyfriend. Nice to meet you, Nell. Would you mind taking a few pictures of the two of us?" Matt asked and gave his million-dollar smile to Nell. She was not immune to it. She actually blushed and started to snap away as Matt wrapped his arms around my waist.

"Sorry, I didn't mean to insinuate we were just

friends," I said, feeling like I had hurt his feelings.

"Just letting everyone know that we're both very taken," Matt responded and kissed my ear.

After a few shots, Jace and Ali were nearby and I asked Nell to take a few more shots of all of us together. That's when the rest of the band caught up to us.

I introduced Nell to everyone. When Ian shook her hand, he looked like he was going to swallow his tongue. Nell played it totally cool and looked at Ian with indifference. That seemed to make Ian even more interested in Nell. I even heard him ask her out for drinks when the opening was done, but she declined. Well, well. Someone who was actually not running after Ian. That was something new for him. I looked at Ali and smiled as we watched Ian follow Nell around the restaurant like a little puppy. Apparently the play-hard-to-get approach really works.

Just then I heard a page over the headset that there was a problem at the check-in desk and could I please make my way to the front of the restaurant. I asked everyone to excuse me, that I had a problem at the front. I went walking, giving the message over the system that I was making my way there now. I was almost to the door of the front when I stopped short.

There, at the front door, was Michael. Fuck.

"Michael, what are you doing here?" I asked, trying to sound calm and even-toned, but I think my bulging eyes gave me away.

"You invited me, remember? You thought that the owner would possibly want to look at some of my work. But it seems as if I'm no longer on the guest list, and neither is my date," Michael said, indicating the beautiful model standing next to him, leaning on his arm. She was a model that I had caught him with once. I knew he did this all to try and throw me off my game and make me fuck the night up. I wasn't biting though.

"Samantha, you can admit Mr. Mailtlin and his guest," I said to one of my assistants.

"I'm actually his girlfriend, not just his guest," the bitch practically spat at me.

"My apologies. Please, enjoy your evening," I said and turned around to walk away, and eventually rammed into Raymond. I grabbed him by the arm and dragged him to a corner.

"Raymond, you have to get the guys out of here. Michael is here, and if Michael and Matt are in the same room, shit will go down and it won't be pretty. Please, find Ali and tell her that Michael and some girl are here to screw up my job."

Raymond shook his head and went running through the crowd to find Ali and Jace.

I went in search of Nell. I needed her. There she was, taking pictures of the crowd as Ian was right on her heels.

"Nell, can I ask you for a favor?" I whispered in her ear.

"Yeah, what do you need?" she asked.

"I need you to keep Ian away from Michael. You remember what Michael looks like, right?" I asked.

"I'm on it, sweetie," she said and then turned to look at Ian.

"So listen, sexy, why don't you show me the way to the bar and we'll have a drink and get to know each other a little better?" Nell put her arm through Ian's and walked him to the back bar.

I was scanning for Ali, Matt, and Jace. But I couldn't find anyone. I did see Ella and she looked a little out of sorts. Then I realized why. Ali was making her way out of the bathroom with Michael's ho right behind her. The ho was yelling at Ali. Ali turned around and raised her hand to hit the ho, but Ella intervened and grabbed Ali's hand and pulled her back. Oh shit.

I went toward Ali, but hands stopped me and pushed me back into a dark corner. I knew it wasn't Matt. But it was dark and I couldn't see who it was at first. Then I heard the slow laugh. Michael had me against a wall, in a dark corner, where no one could see me or help me. Maybe it was better this way. At least Matt couldn't find me and get into a fight.

"Well, sweetheart. Do you miss me? Are you done playing around with that rock star asshole? Ready to have me take you back?" Michael whispered as he licked my ear.

I felt like I was going to vomit. How could I have taken his shit for so long? Now the feel of him on my skin made me want to throw up. "Michael, it's over for us. I am with Matt and I'm happy. It seems like you're pretty happy with what's her name. So why are you here? Why are you doing this?"

"I'm the one to tell you when it's over, sweetheart. You do not get rid of me. Do you hear me?" Michael roughly grabbed my face in his hands and was squeezing my face hard. I knew I would have bruises soon.

"Please, Michael, please let go of me. You're hurting me!" I pleaded as my eyes started to water.

"You know this is your own fault. You always do this. You act like a fucking slut and make me angry and then what else can I do but hurt you?" He released my face and when I thought I could get away, I tried to run. But Michael grabbed my wrist and swung me, flinging me hard against the back wall. I turned my face in time not to have my nose hit the wall. He then pushed me harder against the wall, using his forearm. Then he pulled back and hit me with a closed fist against the back. I yelled at the pain shooting through my back.

Then he turned me around and back handed me

across the face, splitting my lip open. I felt the pain radiate through me and the blood flowing down my lip. I put my hands to my lip to try and stop the blood from flowing all over the floor, but then Michael had my hair in his hands and was going to throw me against the wall again. I felt my body begin to slump toward the ground after the latest blow against the wall. Michael grabbed me by my hair and hauled me up to a standing position, and he raised his hand again to slap some more. But I heard a loud scream of fury and then Michael was pulled back.

I turned to see Ali on Michael's back. She was kicking him and clawing at his face, screaming everything under the sun at him. I was just standing there watching, frozen in shock, not knowing what to do. I didn't know if she was winning and didn't need my help, or whether Michael was going to hurt her. I stood in a daze.

Then I saw Ian running toward us with Nell close behind. I screamed to Nell, "Stop him, Nell, please!" She jumped on Ian's back to stop him, and her wiggling made him drop to the floor where Nell was wrestling him to keep him down.

Then I saw Raymond barely holding Jace back as he came barreling to get to Ali. When Jace was just a few steps away, Michael grabbed Ali and threw her to the floor and kicked her in the stomach, over and over again, and he was not stopping. Raymond immediately released Jace and I saw a wild man going at Michael. Jace was not holding anything back. His arms flew wildly back and forth, back and forth, fists clenched in rage, pummeling the shit out of Michael. As Michael fell to the floor, Jace jumped on top of him, grabbing his head and pounding it to the floor while pinning him down with his knees.

Then Matt showed up and yelled to Ella to get me to the hospital. Ella moved me as I was trying to get to Ali. With Jace directing his fury toward Michael and Matt worried about me, no one was picking up Ali from the floor. I told Ella to get her, and she turned and saw Ali on the floor. She went over to her and helped her up. That's when Nell came over to help me too. With Ella practically carrying Ali, the four of us walked out and didn't even look back at the guys. We made it to the front lobby and our party bus was there waiting. Ella helped Ali and Nell assisted me. Ella barked at the driver to take us to Summerlin Hospital immediately. That was the hospital closest to Matt's and my house.

I looked over to Ali and she strained to offer a weak smile. I walked to sit next to her and wrapped my arms around her and started to cry.

"Why are you crying? I think I did some serious damage to the fucking dickwad," Ali said in a low hissing voice. She was having a hard time breathing and looked ashen, and I started to quiver.

"This is all my fault. I'm so sorry he hurt you, Ali. Thank you for rescuing me," I sniffled and continued to cry.

Ella's phone rang and she picked it up. It must have been Raymond. She told Raymond that we were safe and on our way to Summerlin Hospital. Then she cursed and said that she'd bail them out as soon as we were all stable.

"Who got arrested, Ella?" Ali whispered in pain.

"All of them. I'll bail them out after I make sure you guys are settled at the ER."

"No, you stay with them," Nell said. "My brother is an attorney. I'll call him and have him pick me up at the hospital and then I'll go with him and get your men out. Don't worry about them. Ok?"

"That's too much to ask of you, Nell. You did so much tonight. How can I ever thank you enough?" I asked Nell, bawling all over again.

"Sarah, we're friends. This is the kind of shit that friends do for each other. I'll just make sure you guys are okay, then I'll go. Let me call my brother. The poor thing has no life anyway, so he'll be home bored. This is actually a gift for him. Plus, he is a big fan of the guys." Nell dug her phone from her camera bag and started to dial her brother. "Hey, Adam, I need your help…. No, I'm not in trouble, but my friends are. You know how you love the band Blacking Out? Well, Matt Lewis' girlfriend is a friend of mine and, well, tonight at the event I was working at, a fight kind of broke out. The guys all got arrested. They need some help. I'm on my way to Summerlin Hospital…. No I'm fine. The girls got hurt so I'm with them. Come by there and pick me up and I'll go with you to bail the guys out. I'm sure they have the money themselves. And to let you know, I was a witness. The fight was not their fault. They were protecting their women. Just come and get me at the hospital and we'll go get them. I'll explain it all on the way there…. Thanks, bro. See you soon…. Love you, too," Nell said. "Okay, he's on his way. Ella, did they say which station they got booked into?"

"I think they said the twentieth precinct. Trust me, Jace and the boys have the money to get bailed out, but let's try and see if your brother can have the charges dropped before they have to go to a hearing," Ella said.

"If anyone can get them off, it's Adam. He is a pussycat of a man but a tiger of a lawyer," Nell said.

Just as everyone started to be quiet, we pulled up to the Emergency Room entrance. Ali and I got off the bus with Ella and Nell's help. Nell said that she was going to wait outside for her brother Adam. Ella walked us to the entrance and helped us sign in.

I didn't know why we were so quiet. I knew I was worried about the guys, especially Matt. But it was more than that. I was quiet because I had no way to erase all the night's events, and how it all revolved around me.

Me and my continued stupidity. I should have just told Michael to leave, that he couldn't come to the opening. I should have stayed with someone once I knew he was there. I should have stayed with Matt. I should have torn Ali off Michael. It seemed like I went through tons of what I should have done. But what it came down to was that everything was my fault. The guys were all in jail, because of me. Ali was hurt, because of me.

Ali, Ella and I just sat in the waiting room of the ER. Matt didn't call me. Jace didn't call Ali. Maybe they were in jail. Maybe they just figured the call Raymond made was enough. But it wasn't. We didn't know if the guys were okay. We didn't know if they needed medical treatment. A nurse came out and called me to follow her.

"Wait, can you take my friend first? She got hurt more than me. She's having trouble breathing, and I'm scared her ribs are broken or her lungs are hurt. Please," I pleaded.

The nurse took Ali and I asked if I could go back with her. Ella told me she would stay outside to wait for word from the guys.

They started to work on Ali as I sat next to her. They took her clothes off and started to examine her. Then Ali turned her head to look at me and so softly, in more of whisper, said, "I love you, Sarah. You're my sister, you know that right? Kiss Jace for me and tell him I love him."

"You tell him yourself when he gets here, okay, honey? You're going to be okay, sweetie." She held out a shaky hand to me. I took her hand in mine and held on to her, crying onto her fingers. "You are going to be okay, Ali. I need you. I can't get through this without you. Please stay strong for Jace."

"Miss, we'd like to take you to your own room now so we can look you over. You're probably going to need either stitches or glue for your lip. Come this way."

I gave Ali's hand a final squeeze and kissed her cheek as I left with the nurse toward my own curtained room. Then I was asked to change into a hospital gown.

The nurse looked me over. She saw the bruises on my back and asked me the protocol questions. Who had been hurting me? How long had it been going on? Did I fear for my life? When she asked that last question, I said yes. I told her there was a Detective Edwards who had been working with me, and I asked her if she could call him for me so I could finally report the pain Michael had been inflicting on me for a while. She said that first I needed to have some stitches for my lip and then she would call the police. I asked her about Ali and she said that she wasn't sure how she was, but she saw my lips tremble and felt badly for me. She told me she would go see how Ali was and would be right back.

I sat there, at the edge of the hospital bed, and let the thin gown fall off my shoulders. There was no reason to hide the marks any longer. These marks were what ruined everything tonight. What if Ali wasn't okay? What if I lost my best friend, my sister? It was all my fault. The nurse came back in during my pity party.

"You're friend…" she started, but I stopped her.

"She's not just my friend, she's my sister," I said.

"I'm sorry. You're sister is going to be okay. It looks like just bruised ribs, but she's having trouble breathing so they're giving her oxygen treatments. But she'll be okay."

I nodded. She put some numbing medicine on my bottom lip and then a doctor came in to get to work sewing up my lip. I looked at the table and saw the things laid out. Oh fuck! They were going to put a needle in my fucking lip. I wasn't looking forward to that. I felt the room spin, and that was all she wrote.

CHAPTER
ELEVEN

Matt

Jail isn't that bad when you're a rock star. The only sucky part was that I couldn't call Sarah. Raymond called Ella and she said that she'd be there to bail us all out. But that was over two hours ago, and we were still stuck with no phones. Jace was pacing back and forth. I didn't blame him. Even I was freaked out after seeing Ali on Michael's back, trying to kill him. Then to see her hurtled to the wall and then the floor had me totally wrecked. And Sarah. She was bleeding from her mouth and her face was swollen. But it was the look of sheer fear when she saw Ali that was killing me. I had to get to her and let her know that we were there for her and Ali. All the guys were ready to lose it. At least the police were smart enough to stick Michael, or as we were now commonly referring to him, douche bag, in another holding cell, far away from us.

"Jace, I know you're worried about Ali, but you know she's a strong chick. You know she's fine. You just have to try and relax," Ian tried to tell Jace.

"You didn't see the way he threw her. I'm not so sure she's okay. She looked white as a ghost. I'm pretty fucking terrified." Jace finally sat and hung his head.

"I can't believe that fucking douche bag actually hit the girls," Miles finally said.

"I'm still trying to understand why Sarah made Nell stop me," Ian said.

"She didn't want us to fight. She knew this would happen. And here we are," I said.

"Do you think we're really going to get booked and have records? That's pretty fucking badass." Ian looked proud that we were all in jail.

"Hey, dickhead, this is *not* good for us. Fucking idiot," Alex said and then started his turn to pace.

"I'm just saying. We're a rock band, now we have more street credit for being in prison," Ian added.

"Did you stop to remember that the girls are hurt and we aren't with them? Did you think that maybe the record label wouldn't be thrilled with our new convict status? No, you just fucking think you'll be able to pick up more chicks because of this," Alex said and looked disgusted.

"Sorry, guys. Guess I wasn't thinking," Ian said sheepishly.

We all stood up and jumped to attention when we heard a door open and someone walking toward us. It was a police officer. "Gentlemen, you've been sprung. Time to get out of my jail. Let's go." He didn't have to tell us twice. We were all running toward the open door. We had no idea how it all happened, but we followed the officer and were so happy to be out of the stinking cell.

"Nell, so are you our angel who rescued us?" Ian asked and walked toward the wonderful sight of a familiar face.

"Actually, this is my brother Adam. He's a lawyer, and he was the one who got you all out. Now I just spoke to Ella and I need to get you guys to the ER ASAP. Jace, Ali has bruised ribs but is having a hard time breathing. Matt, Sarah was doing okay, but then she..." Nell looked down at the floor and didn't continue.

"What, Nell? What the fuck happened?" I yelled.

"She apparently has a concussion and she lost consciousness. They said that the next twenty-four hours are crucial. They really need her to wake up. So let's rock and roll and get you there. Okay?" Nell tried to sound positive.

I felt Jace take my arm and bring me out of the station to a waiting car. I felt myself being put inside, and I felt the car move as we drove. But it all seemed like it was a dream. I knew that Nell told me Sarah was in trouble, and then my mind just shut down. How could I already lose her? I just got her.

I was lost in my thoughts and didn't realize that the car had stopped and that Jace was trying to pull me out. I felt like my body couldn't move. I had him dragging me along behind him. I knew I had to get myself together, but as we walked into the ER, I saw Sam and Gillian, both crying, and Joseph with his head hanging down. That's all it took to freeze me on the spot. Was she already gone? They looked panic stricken.

Jace had to put his hand around my shoulder and move me. Gillian saw me and came running to me and wrapped me up in her arms, crying on my shoulder. "Oh, Matt, thank God you're finally here. You have to go talk to her. You have to make her come back. She'll come back to you. I know she will."

"Gillian, tell us what exactly is going on," Jace stated calmly.

"Oh, Jace, they had to sedate Ali to help her breathing. No ribs were broken, but they said she is badly bruised and having a hard time. Joseph, come here, help Jace. Bring him to see Ali while I tell Matt what's going on."

Joseph came over to Jace, but Jace said he wouldn't leave until he heard what was happening with Sarah. So Gillian went on. "Sarah's unconscious. She won't wake up, Matt. We've been talking to her and she just won't wake up."

"Can I see her?" I asked in whatever voice I could push out of my mouth.

"I'll take you to her," Gillian said and then linked our arms and walked me to an elevator bank. We rode to the third floor. I didn't even realize that Jace was still with me until we got to the restricted ICU unit. The nurse said that only one of us could go in at a time. I looked at Gillian and Jace, and they told me to go in and that they would wait for me.

I pushed the door and it felt very heavy. It felt as if it would swing back, hit me and crush me. But I had to move on, I had to see her. Before I could see her in the stark white hospital bed, I could hear the sounds. The sounds that told me things were bad – machines beeping and blipping. Then there was the smell. The smell of disinfectant, not Sarah's perfume or her body lotion. I have never really been challenged with losing someone. I mean I lost my grandparents, but they were old and I was much younger. I didn't know this feeling of utter helplessness. I loved Sarah and I couldn't fix this. I couldn't be in control. I'm always in control. But I couldn't make her wake up and be with me.

I walked to her slowly, hoping that I was in a dream and that I would wake up before having to see her in such a state. But no, it was no dream. I walked until I was at the foot of Sarah's bed. She had tubes coming out of her mouth and both of her arms. My knees almost gave out just seeing her looking so frail. I walked to the side of the bed and pulled the metal chair closer to Sarah's bed. I took her hand in mine. It felt so strange that her hand was just hanging and it wasn't molding to mine.

I brought her hand to my lips and my eyes watered. As the tears flowed, I was kissing her hand over and over again. It felt like forever until the tears were all drained. Then I could speak.

"Baby, you have to wake up. I need to talk to you. I have so much to tell you. Where to start. Other than the brawl we all got into, your restaurant launch was a huge success. We kicked the ever-loving shit out Michael. He's got a broken nose, and I think collar bone, and we busted his lip and I think that Alex might have even bit him at some point. Ali's is going to be okay they said. Jace wants to see you. But I want to see you more than anything. You've gotta wake up. I want to see your eyes open. I want to see you smile at me. I want to take you home and hold you in bed with me. I want to hang the pictures that Nell took of us tonight in our bedroom. I want to tell you tell you that... I love you. Not because you're here and hurt. I wanted to tell you that I loved you for days, and I was just a chicken shit. I thought you would think I was crazy, or that I was rushing you. But I love you, baby. I love how strong you are. I love how you took Ali in and made her your sister and gave her a family, just like I did with Jace. I love how you stood up to Michael when he was a shit. I love your family and how close you are to them. We're just the same, you and I. I need you. I need you badly. Please come back to me. Please."

"I'm sorry to interrupt, Mr. Lewis, but I need to speak to you outside for a minute," Detective Edwards interrupted.

"I'll be right back, baby. Don't go anywhere." I kissed her hand again and went to the lounge following the Detective.

"I'm sorry to hear that Miss March is in such bad shape. I need to ask you a few questions. You see, when Miss March was taken back to the ER, the nurse who was attending to her saw bruising all over her back. When the nurse asked her some questions, she told the nurse that Michael Mailtlin had caused the bruises and that she was fearful of her life because of him. Are you aware of any of this? Or could her bruises have been a result of the brawl I heard you guys were in tonight?"

"Wait, what the fuck are you talking about? Michael had beaten her in the past? When? Where were the fucking bruises?" I was so confused and just spitting out question after question at the detective.

"Matt didn't know about the domestic violence. No one knew except for Ali, and she just found out tonight while we were at the event." I heard Jace speaking and turned to look at him. "That was why Ali jumped him when she saw him hit Sarah. She had promised Sarah she wouldn't say anything, but I think when she saw Michael hit Sarah, she just snapped and had to stop him before he hurt her anymore. Detective, Ali, my fiancée, told me about Michael literally moments before we both saw Michael attack Sarah," Jace said.

I was still in shock. How was this the first I was hearing of this? Michael used to beat Sarah? She had told me so much, why not that? I felt like I was sinking lower and lower into the floor.

"I think it would be good if I could talk to your fiancée, Mr. Wicks. I already spoke to the nurse. In fact, before Miss March passed out, the nurse took some photos of Miss March's back. The bruises appear to be punch marks, closed fist punch marks, and other marks as well. We're going to need a full statement from Miss March when she wakes up. But until then, since she did tell the nurse, we are able to charge Mr. Mailtlin with domestic assault. I called the precinct and he hasn't been released yet. They know to keep him there until I get done here and then I'll book him on the new charges. If you need me, here's my number. I will talk to the nursing staff and make sure that Mailtlin is kept away from Miss March while she's here. That is if Mailtlin actually makes bail. I think I should see your fiancée now, Mr. Wicks."

"They have her in a room, but being her fiancée

doesn't really count. I haven't been able to see her since they moved her. Any way you could help me out here? Think you could get them to talk to me about what's going on?" Jace asked.

"Come with me, Mr. Wicks. I'll see what I can do for you," Detective Edwards said and patted Jace on the back.

"Hey, man, you want me to do anything for you?" Jace asked me.

"Yeah, call Mom and Dad. Tell them I need them here." I didn't say any more. I just walked back to Sarah's room.

I held her hand again and started to sing to her. Even though we were her favorite band, she loved Linkin Park too. *Iridescent* was her absolute favorite song, so I started to sing it. I hoped that her favorite song, and my voice, would pull her out of the hold the coma had over her.

I don't know how many times I sang to her. I only knew my voice was getting scratchy and I just wanted to sleep. My eyes felt heavy and they were definitely bloodshot from my tears. I didn't want to leave. The nursing staff came in and said that I could sleep in the ICU waiting area in the lounging chairs. They needed to make some checks on Sarah and required me to leave for them to do their job. They promised to run and get me if there was any change. I walked to the ICU lounge and saw that Sam and Gillian were already there, in two loungers moved close together so they could be holding hands.

I stayed still for a few moments and just took in the sight of them. They were awake, holding hands and talking to each other in low voices. What must they be going through? To have your daughter in a coma, I hoped to never feel their pain. I had only known Sarah a short period of time and was losing my mind. Sarah was their daughter – what did their pain feel like? Then it hit me: maybe I didn't belong here with them. Why was everyone so sure that Sarah would want me here? She didn't think enough of me to tell me about being beaten. Maybe I did love her just so much more than she would ever be able to love me. Maybe it would be best for all of us if I just left, and walked away now.

I turned to leave the ICU lounge, and stopped as I almost hit right into Jace. "Don't even fucking think about it, man," he whispered to me but gave me a face of sheer anger.

I nodded for him to follow me, and we went down the hall to the elevator bank. "What do you mean?" I asked.

"You are not leaving. You are not going to turn this around and make it about you. I understand you're mad that she didn't tell you what Michael did to her. But I can see why she didn't. Everyone looks to her as the calm, cool, independent one. She didn't want anyone to know she had flaws. Do you love her, Matt?"

"Of course I do. You know that. But I feel betrayed. I feel like there was this huge piece of her that she didn't tell me about." I rubbed my hands through my hair.

"Bro, I didn't even tell my fiancée who the fuck I was for months. Did she walk away from me? No, she loved me and she forgave me. You two have been to-gether barely a few weeks. Maybe she was going to tell you. But I can tell you this – if you walk away now, and when she wakes up she asks for you, and you don't have a really fucking good reason for not being here, waiting for her, you will never get to do that over. And I have no doubt in my mind that she will completely shut you out. And so will I. You don't walk away from the people you love, Matt. No matter what mistakes they make. Maybe you never had to learn that lesson because you've always had your parents and always had it easy. Or maybe you only think you love her, and you really don't. But fucking get your shit together fast and figure it out. I'm going to sit with Sarah for awhile. Ali's recovering, and they won't let me see her until she's feeling better and moved to her room." He walked away from me, then stopped and added, "Oh, Mom and Dad didn't want to wait until the first flight this morning. They hopped in the car and are on their way here. They should be here in another four hours." Then Jace turned back and headed for Sarah's room.

I just stood there, too confused to move one way or another. I decided to hit the elevator button and go get a cup of coffee.

"Get on that elevator and I'll fucking kick your ass until you're lying in the bed next to her." I turned to see Joseph fuming at me. His hands were clenched into fists at his side. He was breathing hard and his face was red with anger.

"I was just getting coffee for your parents and myself. You want one?" I asked.

"You sure that's the only place you're going?" Joseph eyeballed me.

"You know, she didn't tell me either," he continued. "Before you came along, even when there was still Michael, I was always the first one she called for anything. When she needed help changing a tire, when the washer was overflowing, when that idiot made Ali cry. It was always me. But I had no clue about her getting hit. I heard what Jace said to you. He's right, you know. This isn't about any of us, or how we feel about being left out of it. It's about helping her and getting her back." Joseph turned around and walked toward the ICU lounge and just left me to my decision.

I went down to the cafeteria and got four cups of coffee and a ton of creamer packets and sugar and stuff. Then I headed back to the ICU lounge. Joseph was there with his parents. I made my way to them, and Gillian and Sam both gave me a loving smile when they saw me. I silently handed everyone a coffee. Sam pulled a lounger closer to the little group and motioned for me to sit down. I had no words for them.

"You know, when Sarah was little, she came home from school crying one day. Oh, I think she was around six or seven. She said that the teacher was talking about love, because it was close to Valentine's Day. The teacher asked all the kids to talk about something that they loved. Ali was sitting right next to Sarah. Sarah went first and said that she loved her mom and dad and her big brother Joseph. Then she said she also loved her nanny and papa. Next it was Ali's turn and Ali said nothing. The teacher again explained to Ali saying something like, love is when you care about someone. It's what your parents say to you, that they love you when you're sad, or scared, or at night before you go to sleep. Ali said to the teacher that her parents had never said that to her before. Sarah started crying in class, and the teacher said she didn't stop the whole day. Even when she came home, she cried. She thought it was so sad that no one ever told Ali that they loved her. So we talked about it with Sarah for awhile. The next day Sarah came home with Ali, and said that she told Ali she loved her and promised her she would never stop loving her." Sam was laughing at his recollection.

I wanted to tell them about Jace's and my story and how it was so similar. But words were still failing me at the moment. I just thought about the story and smiled, knowing that Sarah was that good a person. She took care of Ali because she didn't think anyone else was.

"I remember when she got into trouble at school for fighting with Marsha Brandi. Remember that, Joseph? Matt, Joseph was dating this girl, Marsha. He was over the moon for her and she was crazy about him too. Sarah was dating a boy named Cliff. He was captain of the football team, the basketball team, class president. Everyone loved him. Well, one day, the two couples were watching a movie together at our house. Sam and I were out. Cliff went to the kitchen and Marsha later followed. Well, Sarah never trusted Marsha. So she followed Marsha without her knowing. Sure enough, she heard Marsha coming on to Cliff, and Cliff – he was a good boy – he told Marsha no and told her to stop constantly coming on to him. Well, Sarah lost it. Sam and I had just come home and opened the door from the garage leading to the kitchen, and Sarah was on top of Marsha, pulling her hair and screaming at her. It took all four of us to get her off of Marsha. Joseph broke things off, but so did Sarah. She said that even though he didn't do anything wrong, she thought that Cliff's being around Joseph would hurt Joseph. She really liked Cliff, but she loved Joseph and wanted to take care of him." Gillian smiled remembering her story.

"I remember when she called me because Ali was with that asshole, Mitch," Joseph started. "I was out on this hot date with this girl I had been asking out for weeks. She finally agreed to go out with me. We were in the car at Hill Point Park. Just watching the stars of course. And here comes Sarah on her bike, looking for me. She is banging on the window. My date Kris assumed she was my angry girlfriend and started crying because she thought she was going to get beat up. I rolled down the window and Sarah was totally fuming. She told me what Mitch had done to Ali and that we needed to drive to the Hamptons and get her. I dropped Kris off without a second thought while Sarah went home to wait for me. I picked her up and we headed to the Hamptons to get Ali. The whole way Sarah was talking about all the vile things we should do to Mitch once we got there. She wanted to dig a hole and put him in and cover him with honey hoping that a bear would eat him. She said that we should tie him up and throw him out of the car naked on the way home. She had a very wild imagination when it came to sticking up for Ali. When we pulled into the driveway and were walking to the door to get Ali, she stopped me and asked me if I was going to hit Mitch. When I said yes, she said good, and to make it a good shot. Then she took Ali in the car and took care of her the whole way home." Joseph was smiling and there was a sheen to his eyes.

Then it was my turn. "I remember the first time I saw her. She had been gone all afternoon shopping with Ali. She didn't realize that the whole band was in Jace's media room. She had just bought a New Year's Eve dress, and got her hair done. She walked into the room to show it all off to Michael, not realizing we were all there. She made this grand entrance, and my mouth dropped when I saw her. It wasn't just how gorgeous she looked. She's just one of those people. You know, the kind of person where you can see their goodness shining through them. I couldn't stop thinking about her all day and night. It was after midnight, and I couldn't wrap my head around how easily obsessed I was with her. I went to my backyard to jump in the pool for a swim and to try to clear my head, then I heard her crying in Jace's backyard. Our houses connect, so I walked to the gate and asked her if she wanted to be alone or whether she wanted someone to talk to. She looked up at me, with her eyes shining full of tears, and even in her sadness gave me an adorable smile. I knew I couldn't have her because she was with Michael, but I also knew I was done for." I had forgotten that I was speaking out loud until I looked up from the floor and saw Gillian, Sam and Joseph all with tears flowing, looking at me.

I started to lose it, shaking while trying to hold back tears. Gillian was in front of me, kneeling on the floor, holding me.

"Can anyone join this cry fest, or do you need an invitation?" We all looked up to see Jace walking toward us, looking shaken up.

"Jace, what's wrong with Ali?" Gillian asked and ran to him.

"The doctors said that she will be fine. She's just sedated to help her breathe. She bruised up really badly, so they think she might have some underlying bleeding problem. But they don't think there's any internal bleeding. She just needs to wake up on her own now."

"Wait, who's with Sarah now?" Joseph stood to go to Sarah. "I don't want her alone."

"Ian's with her and talking to her. He's a member of the band. Actually, Matt, maybe you should go back to her. Last thing I heard Ian telling her was how smoking hot she is," Jace laughed, restoring some kind of light-heartedness to the situation.

"Yeah, Gillian, Sam, do you mind if I go back to her now?" I asked them.

Gillian stood by me and hugged me and whispered in my ear, "Bring my daughter back." And then I went back to Sarah.

As I opened the door, I heard Ian talking to Sarah and waited to hear more of what he was saying. "You know, Sarah, you and Ali have shaken everything up. In a good way though. First Jace with Ali. Now you and Matt. We all love you two like mad. You're the sisters we never had and we truly love you already. Maybe not as much as Matt loves you. I'm gonna tell you a little secret. He was going to tell you tonight. He has been in love with you since he first laid eyes on you. But he was a pussy and was scared you'd run from him. So he's been waiting and waiting for the perfect moment to tell you. Wouldn't it be great if you could wake up and hear him say it to you? You really have to come back to him. He really loves you. He's never been like this before. If you love him too, you need to come back and tell him. If you love me more, you can wake up and tell me you love me. Isn't that right, Matt?" Ian leaned over to see me at the door and smiled.

"Dick. Telling my girl you love her," I said as I

walked beside her and held her hand and kissed her forehead.

"I do love her, not the way you do. I love her like the sister she is to me. Hell, I kicked fucking ass for her tonight. And I'd do it all over again and more. Bring her back, man. I'll catch you later, Sarah. I'm leaving you in good hands though." Ian slapped my back and walked out of the room. The only noise was the beeping of her heart monitor. I turned on the TV knowing that Sarah liked noise. She always slept better when the TV was on.

"Hey, baby, you should get up and see this. It's that tattoo show you like. The one where people have the fucked-up tattoos and the artists cover them up with something awesome. Come on back to me and we can watch." But there was nothing but the beeping. "I know that you know I love you. If you're not coming back because that scares you, just come back and tell me, and I'll back off. If you want me to leave, I will. If you never want to see me again, I'll go. I'll do whatever you want. Even if that means letting you go. I just want to make sure you come back to everyone who loves you and needs you. But if you want me to go after that, I'll go. No matter what you want, I'll do it. I'll love you, even if it's from afar." I stopped talking, because Sarah's hand flexed in mine. "Sarah, can you hear me?" Nothing. Now I didn't know if I had imagined it or whether she had actually squeezed my hand.

"Sarah, I need you. Please come back to me." Again, nothing. "Is it what I was saying? Do you want me to leave, Sarah? Do you want me to leave you alone? Do you want me to get your parents? Or maybe Joseph or Ali? Do you want someone else here with you?" There it went again. She flexed her hand. I jumped back. She was squeezing me, because she wanted me to leave. But at least she was squeezing my hand. I let go of her and ran to the nurse's station to tell them that she squeezed my hand twice. A team of them ran to Sarah. I ran to the lounge to tell everyone. But I didn't tell them that she did it when I told her I would leave.

Half an hour later, the doctor came to tell us that he saw no change in Sarah. That her muscles could have just jumped. Gillian and Sam were with her now and Joseph was going home to get everyone fresh clothes. I was with Jace. Ali was still sleeping back in her room. I finally broke the silence that was hanging between us.

"She squeezed my hand when I told her I would leave her. I told her how I felt and begged her to come back, and she did nothing. Then I told her that if she wanted me to leave I would, and she squeezed my hand. I feel like shit. How would you feel if you told Ali you loved her and she wanted you to leave her alone?"

"Matt, Jace." We looked up to see my mom and dad. I stood up and they ran to me and grabbed me in a huge hug, both of them. Then they finally released me and hugged Jace. They asked us what was happening and Jace filled them in on everything.

"Jace, go back to Ali and be there when she wakes up. We'll take care of Matt for a while. But come get me when Ali's up so I can go see her. Okay, sweetie?" Mom asked Jace

"Okay, mom. Thanks for getting here so quickly. Love you guys." Jace hugged them both once more, and then headed back to Ali's room.

"Why aren't you with her, honey?" Mom asked.

I just shook my head and dropped my head in defeat. After minutes of silence and teary eyes, I told my parents what had happened.

"Son, she was squeezing your hand to let you know not to leave her! She knows you love her and she's probably in there fighting to get out of the coma. But when she heard you say that you'd leave, she freaked and was trying to get you to stay," Dad said.

"Dad, for once, don't be on my side. Just see it for

what it is," I said in an angry voice that I had virtually never used toward my parents.

"Sweetie, I think Dad is right. I mean, I know your father loves me. If I heard him say it, I would be happy and want to be with him. But if I thought he was leaving me behind, I would lose it. You have to get back in there and talk to her before she really thinks you left. If she loves you, like I know in my heart that she does, and she thinks she lost you, what would make her ever come back? We love you so much. But you need to go to her. Suck it up and be strong for her now. Then come back to us, and if you fall apart we'll hold you back up. But get your ass back to her. Now!" my Mom said and basically shoved me.

I went back to Sarah's room and knocked. Sam answered the door and smiled a weak smile at me and let me in. Gillian smiled at me too and continued to talk to Sarah, telling her that I was there and that she and Sam would go get some breakfast and be back. But she was leaving me in loving hands. They both patted my back and left me alone with Sarah.

I was so lucky to have Sarah's parents be like mine. It was unreal that I had only been with their daughter a few weeks and they were leaving and allowing me to be by her side. They knew I loved Sarah. I took the seat Gillian had been sitting in and moved it closer to Sarah and held her hand in mine. I kissed each finger. I stood over her and looked closely at her face. Her lashes were long and deep brown. They wouldn't flutter open. Her pulse was moving in her neck as I looked at her exposed flesh. I leaned in, and kissed her neck, smelling her and then licking her. I felt like I had to mark her and make her mine again.

I was mad at myself for being able to walk away from her. Fuck that! Even if she wanted me gone, I wasn't budging. I loved her, and she'd better learn to love me. I sat back down, holding her hand, and started to talk to her again.

"Sarah, I love you. You mean everything. I want you to wake up and tell me you love me. I want you to make your way back to me, baby. You know, I was thinking, we need a vacation. Maybe we could even go away with Ali and Jace too. Maybe Hawaii. I fucking love Hawaii. There's this house in a town called Kahala that Jace and I always rent. It's right on the beach. We always go there to unwind. We have never brought girls there. I think you and Ali should come with us. We could lie on the beach and get tans. There's also a pool. And we could go snorkeling at this beautiful bay with all these colorful fish. There's tons of great restaurants. Oh, you and Ali would have a ball at the Flea Market. Jace and I always haggle with the people there. The bedrooms are incredible. They have floor-to-ceiling windows and each room has its own private balcony. We could do a little nude sunbathing. I could feed you breakfast in bed. We could go for long walks on the beach as the sun sets. What do you think?"

I kept going on and on about Hawaii and how much I loved her and needed her. Before I knew it, I fell asleep and Jace was shaking me awake. "Man, go to the lounger and sleep for a while. I'll talk to her." Jace was holding Sarah's other hand.

I shook my head okay. I went to the lounge and saw Sarah's parents and mine having coffee together and talking as if they had known each other their whole lives. Gillian saw me coming first.

"Matt, honey, why don't you lie down and get some sleep?" She practically pushed me onto the lounger, and I was out before I could argue.

CHAPTER
TWELVE

Sarah

I was in such a great dream. Matt was saying that he loved me and wanted me. I think he even said he wanted me to be his wife. A dream come true to me. I know it's crazy; we've barely been together. But when you know you have the perfect man, the perfect partner, why wait? The talking was great, the support amazing, and the sex unbelievable. I kept trying to say yes, but my mouth felt so heavy and thick. I didn't know how to get the words past my lips. I felt him holding my hand and it sent heat through my whole body. I could feel my veins getting stronger and healing when he had my hand. Like his strength was feeding my body with love and support and making it heal. The only thing I didn't like was when he said he'd leave. I had to work as hard as I could to try and speak. But that wouldn't work, so I had to use all my energy to let him know not to leave, and I moved my hand. But he wasn't getting it. He thought I wanted him gone. What an idiot. I loved him – why would I want him gone?

Then there were doctors and nurses talking about me. I tried to tell them it was rude to speak about people as if they weren't there. But they didn't listen to me. Didn't they know I could hear them?

I felt sleepy and I zoned out for a while. I just wanted to hear Matt. I loved the way he was singing me my favorite song. I wanted him to come back. Why did he keep leaving me here in my dream? It was my dream after all, so why couldn't I just think him back in? Wait, who was this? Oh, it was Ian. He's so funny. He kept telling me that Matt loved me. I knew that. In fact, it was starting to annoy me that everyone kept telling me that Matt loved me. I knew he loved me; I heard him loud and clear. What did they all mean by coming back to him? Did I leave Matt? How could I do that? I loved Matt. Oh boy – did I forget to tell him that I loved him, and then he left me? Oh no. Where was Matt? I needed him.

I was screaming in my head, and I heard it. But it was like no one would hear me. What the hell was I supposed to do to make them hear me? Maybe I should have listened to them more. Maybe they would have told me how to end this dream and get back to Matt.

Oh, Matt was back. He kept telling me to come back to him. But how was I supposed to do that? I felt him holding my hand. Oh that felt nice. Wait, what was this? Oh, God yes. He was licking my neck. Oh that felt so good. I wanted to moan his name out loud and tell him don't stop there, keep licking me, come on, honey, keep going, lick more of me, take me in your mouth, kiss me. Why was he waiting to do more to me? It felt so right and so good, like my body was floating and little electric currents were running up and down my spine when Matt touched me.

Oh no, he was pulling away. Then I heard Jace. He sounded so sad. Why was he sad? Did something happen to Ali? That's right, Michael hit her and threw her on the floor. I hoped she wasn't hurt. Jace was telling me he loved me and that Matt was a wreck. Why was Matt a wreck? He kept telling me to open my eyes and come back to Matt. I had to open my eyes. I could do that. Let me see. I tried and tried, but I couldn't seem to find enough strength to get my eyes open. It felt like there were weights over my eyes. Why couldn't I get them off? Why couldn't I open my eyes? I had to concentrate, like I did with moving my hand in Matt's hand. I had to think it, and then give all my energy to opening my eyes. I tried again but just couldn't do it. I just wanted to cry. Maybe if Matt came back I could find the strength. Where was Matt? I wanted to open my eyes, and I needed Matt.

Mom and Dad came: *I love you Mom and Dad, please stop sounding so sad. I love you guys and I'm trying to open my eyes. I really am, I just need you to get me Matt. Mom, please get me Matt, please.*

Oh for the love of God, would someone listen to me please? I needed Matt to come back in here. If Matt really loved me, wouldn't he come back to me? Why didn't he come back? I didn't like the bed. I liked the bed that Matt and I had at our new house. *Our* house. I loved the sound of that. I just wanted to go there now. Maybe if I could open my eyes with Matt here, he'd take me home. I just wanted to watch movies in bed with him. I loved just bumming around with Matt and watching movies. I could totally go for In-N-Out right now. Oh, yes, fast food in bed, with Matt, and movies. Does anything sound more perfect?

Well, the whole Hawaii thing that Matt was talking about sounded pretty cool. I would love to go with Ali and Jace too. A week on the beach, with the warm sun, and I'd be totally into the nude sunbathing thing with him. I missed seeing Matt naked. I wanted to see him stripped naked in front of me, just the two of us, lying on huge plush beach chairs. That would rock. Oh, I could make us Mai Tais and we could drink and tan and get funky in the sun and the sand. *Oh, let's go Matt. Let's head there now. Matt, please come back so we can go. Matt, please come back.*

Ah, there was Matt. I loved the timber in his voice. I loved how he told me he loved me. *Hold my hand Matt, please*. He listened. That was better. I felt so much better when he was touching me, even if it was just holding my hand. Why was I so stupid to try and play like we didn't belong together? Maybe it was quick, but I didn't care. I wanted him, all of him, I wanted to marry him. I needed to be joined to him, forever. Maybe I should just ask him to marry me. That would totally be a great idea. He loves me, I love him and we're living together. So, why not just get married?

No, Matt, don't leave. Please, no. I'll try to open my eyes. Just get the fuck back here, MATT!!!

Matt

The nurses were kicking me out so they could move Sarah and perform another scan on her brain and see where the brain activity level was at. I asked if I could stay, but they wouldn't let me. I was going to the lounge to see how everyone was doing.

It was almost a full twenty-four hours now since Sarah slipped into the coma. The doctors kept telling me that the sooner she got out of the coma, the better. But things could stay this way for a very long time. I lay down on the lounger and just prayed. My parents always taught me to pray every night and I never told a single soul that I still prayed every night before going to sleep. Lately all my prayers were about Sarah, and tonight was no different.

I thanked God for giving me my parents, and my band members, my brothers in arms. I thanked him for Jace having Ali. I thanked him for letting me meet Sarah. Tonight I begged him to bring Sarah back to me. I told him I was sorry for almost walking away from Sarah. I didn't mean to just give up. I just thought maybe I wasn't enough to make her happy. But even if I didn't deserve her, I wanted her and I didn't want to walk away. But I needed help. I needed to be strong and I needed to have her back. God, please just bring her back to me and I will take care of her.

Sleep came very quickly. I dreamt of Sarah. I dreamt of us at the Kahala house. We were on the lanai on the second floor. We were staying in the green and white room. The bed was big and covered in a plush green and white Hawaiian quilt spread. The walls were covered in white wallpaper with giant Hawaiian leaf prints. We were on the lanai on the two plush lounge chairs. I covered them with big purple towels. She was lying on her stomach, and her head was turned to face me. I was on my back and staring at her. We were both looking at each other, both slathered in oil. I had to force myself to look in her eyes, and not at her beautiful plump ass that was rising in the air.

She smiled at me. "I love you so much. I hope you never forget that, Mr. Lewis," Sarah purred.

"I'll never stop loving you, Mrs. Lewis," I smiled back at her and then glanced down to her hands, and saw her wearing my wedding ring.

Screams shook me out of my sleep. I heard someone screaming my name. It was Sarah. Holy shit, it was Sarah. I started sprinting to Sarah.

I pushed the door open, and all hell had broken loose. Sarah was there, thrashing in her bed, screaming my name, and the nurses were trying to keep her still and calm her down. I took in the scene for a minute and then rushed to her side and literally pushed two nurses out of the way so that I could get to my girl.

"Sarah, I'm here. Please calm down and open your eyes." I had no more words, because her face was grimaced in pain and tears were falling down her cheeks even with her eyes closed shut. I grabbed her hand in mine. I started to kiss her fingers. "Baby, calm down. Please calm down and open your eyes for me. I need to see your eyes. Please, Sarah, open your eyes," I pleaded.

She stopped moving all at once. Then she turned her

head to me and slowly fluttered her eyes open. She had to flutter them several times until she could clearly see me. Then her lips spread a slight smile as she focused on my face. I could feel the wetness on my cheeks as I also began to smile.

She tried to speak but couldn't. She pointed to the water cup next to her bed. I went to grab it for her, but the nurses said to wait until they checked her vitals.

I sat next to her as the nursing staff worked on Sarah and finally she was able to speak.

"You left me, why?" she whispered in a raspy voice. Then she turned her face from me and began a howling cry as her whole body shook with wails and moans of hurt and pain.

"Sir, I think you should leave. I think your being here is upsetting her," the nurse said and I could tell that she was right. For some reason, because I wasn't there when Sarah woke up, she thought I had left her.

I lost hold of her hand when she started to cry. I lifted myself up from the hospital chair and started to make my way to the door leading out of her room.

"Again he's leaving me. All they all do is leave. I thought you loved me, but you're leaving. Fine, leave, you asshole!" Sarah shrieked. I was stunned silent and stone cold.

"Sarah, I was passed out cold in the ICU lounge waiting for you to wake up. I didn't leave you. What's wrong with you?" I yelled back. But my yelling seemed to have actually calmed her. She was no longer rolling around and crying and moaning. She was just looking at me with hate and anger in her eyes. What the hell did I do wrong?

"You wanted me to come back and you said you would leave me alone. You only wanted me to come back so you could leave," she spat out at me, fuming and breathing hard.

We had a full audience with the nursing staff and two doctors. "Miss March, I am Doctor Philips. I need to examine you. I promise that this gentleman will not leave, but merely wait outside the door until I am done. If you wish to speak with him after I'm done, I will personally bring him back to talk to you. Is that okay with you?" Dr. Philips calmly asked Sarah.

"Fine, but don't let that son-of-a-bitch leave," she warned the doctor and he shook his head in agreement. Then he turned to me and told me to wait outside with his nurse, and she put her arms on my elbow and walked me to the outside of Sarah's room.

"You know, I couldn't help but notice that you're Matt Lewis from Blacking Out. Maybe if things don't work out with screaming girl, you could take me out," the nurse had the gall to say to me and then thrust her tits, which were totally fake, into my chest.

"Are you fucking kidding me? My girlfriend has been unconscious for the past day, and she wakes from it thinking I'm leaving her. So I am having what you might call a bad day. Now, I was raised a gentleman, so I would never hit a woman. But I could walk down the hall to my future sister-in-law's room and tell her what you just said about her best friend and she will gladly kick your ass from here to tomorrow. Now fucking get yourself off me." I was pissed, beyond pissed.

Her face fell into a pouty frown and she let go of my arm and headed back to the nurses' desk.

A few minutes later, the doctor, Dr. Philips, walked out of the room and told me that it seemed that Sarah was going to be fine. But of course they would have to keep her in the hospital for a few days to observe her and make sure she didn't slip back into unconsciousness. Shit. I didn't know that once she woke up, she could go back into a coma.

"Well, what do we do to make sure that she doesn't go back into unconsciousness? Is there any medicine, exercises, anything?" I asked him.

"We can only watch her, and to be honest, she should be kept calm. So please, no matter what, try and keep her calm. Okay? She wants to see you now. Please, try and keep her calm. While you go in to speak with her, I'll head to the lounge and let the rest of her family know what's going on."

I nodded and pushed my way into Sarah's room. She was on her right side, facing the window. It was dark outside, around four in the morning. There were stars poking through the window blinds. I heard sniffling coming from Sarah.

I stood behind her and moved her hair from her face. I wanted to be close to the door in case she got upset and I had to run for the doctor. When she turned her face into my hand, I felt weak in the knees, like my legs couldn't support my full weight.

I crossed to the other side of the bed and pulled the chair close to her bed and looked at her. Her eyes were red rimmed and puffy, as was her nose.

"Sarah, I have to talk to you. I need to know you'll listen to me and be as calm as possible. Can you do that?" She nodded yes. So I continued, "I know about what Michael did. At first I was mad at him. Then I got mad at you because I thought you didn't trust me enough to tell me. You didn't tell me because you thought I would think differently about you. You stupidly thought I would think less of you. But I wish you would have given me the chance and trusted me enough to tell me yourself. But now, I'm just depressed. I'm depressed that you heard what I said about leaving. But it wasn't that I don't care about you. I thought maybe you didn't tell me because you didn't care enough about me to tell me. And then you didn't wake up. It was the worst thing I ever went through. And then I thought, why am I willing to leave even if she wants me to? I love her. You don't leave the woman you love. You stay and drive her crazy and spoil her and then she finally falls in love with you. I'm madly in love with you, Sarah. Totally and crazy-ass in love with you. I was only going to leave if you didn't want me. But forget about my stupidity. I love you, and even if you tell me to leave, I won't. I'll do everything I can to win your heart. I love you, baby. Please tell me you want me?" I felt like a little kid who was asking Santa for the most important and special Christmas present ever.

"I love you too, you fucking idiot. How could you not know that I love you?" She still wasn't smiling at me, but I heard the love in her voice.

"I know I'm a fucking idiot. I know I'm also the luckiest fucking idiot the world has ever seen. 'Cause I have you. I do have you, don't I?" I asked.

"Yeah, you have me. Now get the hell into this bed and hold me. That's all I've been thinking of. I was thinking of how I want to be home in our house together, in bed, curled around you."

I climbed into the bed next to her, making sure that I didn't pull out her IV. I held her tightly.

"So are you really taking me to Hawaii? Can we swim with the dolphins and nude sunbathe?" she asked.

"Holy shit! You heard all that? Baby, that's incredible. No one knows what goes on with coma patients. And now you're saying that you heard everything I said? That's amazing. You have to tell the doctor when he comes back to check on you. What else do you remember me saying?"

"You kept telling me that you loved me and that you wanted me to come back to you. So, did you just say that to make me come back?" She looked away toward the door, afraid of my answer.

"Sarah, I am so in love with you. I said it because I

meant it. I really love you, baby. You don't have to say it back until you're ready. I hope it doesn't freak you out too badly. I mean, I know it's soon. But I know what I want."

"I love you too, Matt. I know it's crazy. I know it's soon. But I know it's love too." We were wrapped around each other, sniffing each other, trying to get into each other's skin. We just couldn't get close enough.

CHAPTER
THIRTEEN

Jace

All this waiting was killing me. The nurses kept telling me that Ali was fine, but they had no idea why she wouldn't wake up. That's what was really eating at me – that they didn't know why she was in her current state.

I had been sitting between Ali and Sarah's room for the past twenty-four hours and neither of them would wake up. I heard the door open and in walked what I assumed was a doctor.

"I understand that you are Ali's fiancé. I know this is hard right now, but I think since we have some of the test results back, I can go over some things with you. It seems that your fiancée has a bleeding disorder. Did you know about this? Do you know if she was aware of it?" the doctor asked.

Just then, before I could finish telling him that neither Ali nor I knew, Ali started to wake up. I jumped up from the chair so quickly that I knocked it over.

"Ali, can you hear me? Ali, it's Jace."

The doctor took over and started to flash a light in her eyes, further awakening her.

"Ali, this is Dr. Stevens. Can you hear me? If you can, please shake your head."

Ali shook her head and then started to try and speak, but her throat must have been dry because it looked as if putting the words together hurt her mouth.

"Ali, do you need water?" I asked her.

She shook her head yes and I went running toward the nurses' station screaming that Ali needed water. A nurse ran to get me a cup with ice chips and water. Then I was running back to Ali's room. She was trying to sit up with the help of Dr. Stevens. I practically knocked him over to get to her. She just smiled at the doctor and I made sure she was all situated.

I held the water cup out to Ali and she took it from me with shaking hands. I helped her hang on to it. She took small sips and then was chewing on some ice. The doctor continued to ask Ali questions and she answered by shaking her head.

"Ali, I have some news to tell you. Were you aware that you have a bleeding disorder?"

Ali simply shook her head no and looked back to me. I could read her mind. So I asked the questions she couldn't yet.

"Is it serious? Was there any bleeding internally?" I asked the doctor.

"Lucky for you, Ali, you did not have any complications because of the bleeding disorder. But I want you to see a specialist who can better explain your disorder and some important facts. Like when you go to the dentist, you will need shots to make sure you can stop bleeding. The same with surgeries, and even childbirth. I'll write the name of the best hematologist in town.

I sat down next to Ali and we held hands, waiting for further instructions from the doctor.

"Baby, look at me. It's going to be okay. I know this sucks. But we can get you the best doctor and figure this whole thing out. Okay?"

Ali shook her head in understanding, and gripped my hand so tightly. I loved her so much. Why were we waiting so long to get married? I wanted to marry her right this second.

"I think you're going to be just fine. I'll leave you two alone for a bit. If you need anything, just ring for the nurse." With that the doctor left the room and I was alone with Ali.

"Baby, can I get you anything?"

"You can crawl into this tiny bed somehow and hold me," she said in a low voice.

I practically jumped into the bed with her. I was holding on to her like my life depended on it. I waited until Ali was calm and settled. She told me she was so tired and wanted to close her eyes for a little while. I told her I was going to go update everyone that she was awake. She nodded her head, closed her beautiful eyes and was happily sleeping.

Thank the Lord that Ali and Sarah were both awake and fine. Finally things were looking up. I walked to the ICU lounge and everyone was there and I told them all that Ali was awake and would be fine.

I loved Ali, and every time that I looked at her bruised face, I wanted to rip Michael apart all over again. Literally tear his fucking lungs out. Because Ali had this blood thing, her bruises were dark purple and vivid.

"Look man," Matt said, "I was going to talk to the doctor about whether or not I could take Sarah to Oahu to rest and recuperate. It might be a good idea if you asked too. I kind of told Sarah while she was unconscious that you guys were coming with me and she's all excited. Maybe Ali could rest there too and I think it would be good for all of us."

The idea was a good one. Matt and I always rented this one beautiful house when we needed a retreat from the crazy-ass rock star world. Maybe Ali and I could rest up there with Matt and Sarah. I knew Ali would love the place.

I shook my head and told him I would ask the doctor when she could be released and when she could fly and travel. Matt and I went to the nurses' station and asked if we could speak to Ali and Sarah's doctors. They came right away and said that Ali could leave tomorrow and Sarah needed to stay two more days. We told the doctors our plans to go to Hawaii and they both said it would be fine, but to keep the girls calm.

We left the girls alone a little longer and went to the ICU lounge to find the guys, Joseph, my parents and Sarah's parents. I relayed all the information and then had to tell my parents about the packages the girls got. We then asked Gillian and Sam when they thought we should tell the girls.

"Well, when they move Sarah out of ICU I think we need to split up to tell them. If we tell them together, they're going to get angry and feed off each other. This way, with us there and telling them alone, we stand a chance that they will just listen to your plan about moving into the house together," Gillian said.

"Oh, yeah, change of plans. We're going to head over to Hawaii for a week. When Sarah was out of it, I told her I would take her, and when she woke up, she said she wanted to rest there. She wants Ali and Jace there too. So at least we're getting them away for a while," Matt said.

"I think that sounds like a great idea. The girls will be safe away from all this. But you'd still better bring some security. At least Ella and Raymond," my mom added.

"We talked some stuff over, and we're going to stay here at your place, Matt," Alex chimed in. "That way, if someone tries to deliver another 'gift' or tries to get to the girls, we'll be there to catch them. You go on to Hawaii and take care of our girls."

"I thought they were *our* girls," Jace countered.

"Hey, man, once you brought them into our lives, they became all our girls," responded Ian. "They're our sisters now. Joseph is going to move into your place too, Matt. He will be at the house while we go to the studio to lay some tracks down. Then while he's at work, we'll be at the house. We already talked to Raymond and he's going to set up cameras along with a new sensor alarm system. Now tonight, you take Ali home so you can pack her up, Jace. We'll take care of everything here while you get them back on their feet." Ian was smiling, feeling in control of the whole situation. He had just gotten back from looking in on Ali.

To be fair, we all saw Ian as the slacker of the group. But I guess that was because we never gave him a chance to be in control of stuff. He was doing just fine and I felt confident leaving the guys behind to set stuff up with the album and the houses.

"Sounds like all we have to do is take care of the girls," I said and slapped Matt on the back. "Okay, who's gonna come with me to tell Ali?" I asked and scanned the crowd of people.

"I think that Gillian, Sam, Joseph and Ian should go with Matt to tell Sarah. This way, Ian, you can tell her how you've gotten everything squared away while she's away. Doug, Alex, Miles and I will go to Ali's room. Jace, you bring her back there so we can tell her. Okay, everyone, stay strong and let's take care of our girls," my mom Gloria said and stood up like she was about to win the war.

Matt went with the others to tell Sarah about the packages and about the Hawaii plans.

She was surprisingly calm and cool about it. She was certain that it was Michael. She said she felt that Michael blamed Ali for introducing her to Matt and that's why he was going after Ali too. It did make sense and I agreed. But we needed proof. I was so glad that the guys all came together on their own to stay behind and help us out. I didn't want to have to ask them to do it, but I did want someone watching the house for any other problems that might occur.

The next day, when Ali was discharged, she went by to see Sarah before going back to her house. They talked about their "gifts" and neither one seemed too freaked, which was good. I told them that we would be taking a private jet to Hawaii, but the girls were having none of it. They were both scared of the smaller plane and wanted to fly first class on commercial. I had to talk to my assistant about getting things booked. I knew the house would be free. We hadn't told anyone that Matt had bought the house two years ago. To be honest, he didn't want everyone to use it whenever they wanted to. So I just let people think that we always rented it out. Matt would tell Sarah, once he found out whether she liked the place. If she didn't, I would buy it from him. Hawaii was a very special place for me, and I needed to have a place there when I needed to recharge.

I had a feeling the girls were going to love it. I just wanted to give Ali whatever she wanted while we were there. The girls were busy talking about what they should pack. Matt and I would be lucky if we actually had so much as a duffle of shirts and board shorts.

"Oh crap, I don't have a single bathing suit," said Sarah. "I don't have a pair of sandals either. Crap."

"Have no fear. I'll do shopping for you tomorrow. I'm still on medical leave from work, so I'll take Ella with me and get you some new stuff. You're gonna need cover-ups, and hats. Oh, you need a beach bag. Oh, and we need to go wax before we leave. Not to mention new mani pedis since dipshit fucked up my nails. When are you out of here anyway?" Ali asked Sarah.

"I'm out in another two days. So we're going to have to get me all prettied up that day. After all, we leave on Thursday. You sure you can go out tomorrow to shop for me?" Sarah asked Ali.

"Let me think. I can stay home with a house full of guys, none of whom I can have my evil way with. Or I can take Ella with me and go blow some serious cash. Yeah, I'm right. Leave everything to me. I'm gonna head out now. I so want to take a shower and get into my own bed. I'll come by to show you the goods tomorrow and I'll sneak some food in to you. Love you, girl." Ali and Sarah hugged.

"I love you too," said Sarah. "Thanks for everything, guys." Then Sarah hugged me. Matt told me he'd have Lucas get everything settled and call him with all the info once it was done. Everyone was happy, and Ali and I left.

Matt

"So, sexy, we're all alone. What should we do now?" Sarah was biting her lips and looking me up and down.

"You've gotta be kidding me, sweetie. You were in a coma a few hours ago. We are not doing anything until the doctor clears you. So stop biting that lip and giving me that look." I kicked off my shoes and crawled into bed with her. I held her close to my chest and played with her hair.

"I'm so excited that we're going to Hawaii. Thank you for this trip. I can't wait to feel the soft trade winds blowing on my face. I'm dying to walk on the beach at sunset with you. And I can't wait to just sleep late and wake up whenever we want. Drink fruity drinks and dance until we can't stand it, just us. I can't wait." Sarah was getting sleepy. I could hear her voice getting lower.

"I just want you all to myself. I'm glad I get to be

the one to take you there for the first time. It's so beautiful. Almost as beautiful as you." I kissed her hair and heard her breathing evenly. I took out my cell phone and, as quietly as I could, called my assistant Lucas and asked him to get everything ready for Sarah, Jace, Ali and me. I wanted the house opened and cleaned, the fridge and freezer stocked, and flowers everywhere. I wanted a car waiting at the airport and the driver needed to have leis for Sarah and Ali.

I needed someone to shop for the girls and have their closets full. I snuck to see Sarah's ruined dress, along with her panties and bra, so I could peak at the sizes. I told Lucas to call Jace's assistant for Ali's size information.

I had him set up a time for me to take everyone to swim with the dolphins. I also needed a car left at the house so we could go around the island. Lucas took all my directions and never stumbled. Lucas also needed to call ahead to the airline to have someone waiting for us when we left Vegas and Honolulu; this way we could be held in a private waiting area before we boarded, so people couldn't bother us.

I knew Ali was now used to all the attention being with Jace, but it was still too new and confusing for Sarah. I wished the girls would just let us charter a plane, but they didn't want to. I was so bone tired when I finished all the arrangements with Lucas and just fell asleep with Sarah in my arms.

CHAPTER
FOURTEEN

Sarah

It was amazing to wake up next to this man. I loved him. Not a heart-pounding gooey feeling love, but an I-can't-breathe-without-this-man kind of love. Like I'd miss him even if I went to the bathroom to pee. This was so overwhelming, but in a crazy good way. I knew everyone would think this is crazy. But I didn't care. I knew this was what I wanted, and what Matt would want too. I knew he was just scared that I'd freak because it was so soon. But after all that I'd been through, I didn't want to be away from Matt. I wanted us to start right now.

As I looked at him, I started to devise my plan. I had to get Ali and the guys to help. I needed to find out Matt's size in clothes, and get them ordered and delivered without his knowing. For me, I'd just buy something when we got there. I had to find a florist for leis and I wanted flowers down the aisle. I had to book the minister and a Hawaiian band to play. I just had to make sure we got the guys on the plane at the last minute so they didn't spoil the surprise. Oh, and I had to book rooms for everyone. My mind was running a mile a minute. I loved Matt, but I needed him out of here so I could get all this shit done. I needed Ali too. She already knew what I was planning, and loved the idea and was going to help me. She'd be here any minute so we could get stuff going. She decided to send Jeff, Jace's assistant, to shop for us so she could be here and help me. But how would I get Matt to leave without hurting his feelings?

"Good morning, Miss March. We have some breakfast for you. How do you feel today?" a pretty sweet nurse asked me as she brought my tray into the room, before she proceeded to drop it straight on the floor when she saw a shirtless Matt slung over me. I knew it wasn't that a half-naked man was on top of me that made her drop her shit. It was that she saw who he was.

"Oh shit, that's Matt Lewis! Oh God, I'm so sorry."

"Don't worry about it, sweetheart. She's my fiancée and even she still can't believe it's me. So no worries. I'll clean this up if you could just get my girl another tray please." She vigorously shook her head and left as Matt kissed my lips and was stretching on the bed next to me.

"Fiancée?" I asked and gave him a questioning look, very happy at the sound of the word.

"It was the only way they would let me in. I had to say we were engaged. Does that bother you?" he questioned, looking as if I might run for the door at any moment.

"Actually, I like the sound of that very much." I leaned over to kiss him. He made the kiss a quick one so that he could start to clean up the mess that was supposed to be my breakfast. Just as he had all the food thrown away, a maintenance worker came in to clean the mess, and right on her heels was the nurse, once again drooling after Matt. I was seriously about to pull her fucking hair out of her scalp. Matt told her he was my fiancé, yet she was still looking him up and down.

I guess this was something I was going to have to get used to, but I really didn't want to. I knew how hot Matt was. In fact, I had always hoped I would meet him through my work, since I've always had a crush on him. Ever since Ali and I went to the first Blacking Out show, Ali had had a thing for Jace, and I always had a thing for

Matt. I guess it was lucky for us that the crushes didn't run the other way.

Naughty Nurse, or Shannon, as her name badge said, was busy telling Matt that he didn't have to pick up anything, and that she was so sorry to be so stupid and drop the tray. I love how she just said, the tray. Not your fiancée's tray or anything acknowledging me. Bitch!

Luckily Ali came in at that precise moment to save Matt and me. "Hi there, Shannon. Do you mind getting your hands off my brother and checking his fiancée to make sure she's okay? Thanks so much," Ali said with a curt nod and fake as all shit smile.

"Oh, yes, sure. Good morning, Miss March. How are you feeling today?" she asked as if she really cared, while checking my temperature and then blood pressure.

I was going to take a page from Ali's book. "I'll be doing a lot better when the doctor releases me and I can be back home with my fiancé. Right, honey?" I raised my eyebrows up and down, giving him a sexy smile and he returned it. Much to the dismay of Shannon.

"That's right. I can't wait to get my baby home with me where she belongs. Our place isn't the same while you're stuck here." Then he came to kiss me full force on the mouth. Was he doing it as a show to have this bitch leave him alone and make me feel better, or did he really feel that way? At the moment I didn't care. I just wanted bitch Shannon gone.

"Okay, we know you two love each other. But Sarah and I have work to do, so could you go back to the house and get Sarah some stuff, and maybe pack for the trip, Matt?" Ali had her computer and a notebook and pens ready to go.

Matt came over to me and kissed me, telling me he'd be back after he showered and got some stuff together for the trip. I missed him the minute he was out the door, but at least Nurse Shannon followed him out, so she was gone.

"Okay, I've been up all night going over stuff. I talked to Lucas, and he says that Matt uses this couple there to open the house and get all the stuff ready for when he goes to the island. I got their number, so I could ask them who to use for catering and music. Turns out their daughter is a wedding planner. I had Lucas and Jeff work on a contract with her. She won't tell anyone about the wedding, no media, no Matt, no one. She's only allowed to communicate with you, me or Lucas. I also found different outfits for you to look at for Matt, and there was even a commercial on TV late last night about a new wedding dress store that opened at Downtown Summerlin. I have their site up and they have stocked dresses. So you might be able to get your dress before we leave and I'll just pack it with my stuff. They have grooms' attire too, so we might be able to get Matt's stuff there and I'll pack it with Lucas' stuff. He and Jeff are going to come with us to Hawaii, but they're going to stay in a hotel. So they can have Matt's stuff and yours if you want." Ali was climbing onto the bed with me, and handing me papers to look through.

"This is it! This is what I want Matt to wear. Ali, you're a genius! How did you find this so fast? It's exactly what I pictured." The outfit was so simple, but I could totally picture it on Matt's handsome body. It was a pair of white linen pants and a white linen shirt, with a row of green intertwined vines going down the right side. There were light brown leather flip flops on the model. I even wanted the shoes. Ali had spoken to Lucas and gotten Matt's sizes. But before we called the bridal store to order it, I went through their web site looking for my dress. It was the very last one they had, and the one I knew I had to have. It was white lace that went around the neck and came down in a plunging neckline, actually moving both breasts apart, and then dropped at the waist and fishtailed out the back for a train. It was perfect and I had to have it.

Ali agreed with me and we were getting all weepy thinking that we were planning my wedding, like we always hoped we would do, together. Ali started to call the store and even thought to add a pair of white leather flip flops for me to wear. I told her she could pick any color dress she wanted, as she would be the maid of honor. But I wanted her dress and Jace's outfit to match in color. She decided on a sand color dress that came to the knee and flared, with a sweetheart neckline. Great for her big tits. Ali picked out a pair of sand linen pants for Jace, with a short sleeve linen sand shirt for him. They had his and hers sand colored flip flops to end the outfit. This was going to be perfect.

As we were thinking about the color leis we should order, Ali got an efax that the wedding planner Kailani signed. She would not tell anyone; she would help us and was waiting for our call.

I immediately grabbed for Ali's phone and called her. She was so sweet and understood that this whole wedding was going to be a surprise for Matt. We talked about wedding flowers to line the aisle – we decided on purple roses and irises. I wanted the chairs to the aisle to be white and a purple and white runner to make the way to the arch that would be white as well, with the same purple flowers twined around the top.

I decided to let her take care of the Hawaiian entertainment, as I had no idea who or what was a good idea. I wanted Hawaiian food for the dinner afterward. I decided on Kailua Pork Quesadillas, Shrimp Teriyaki Skewers, and a Sushi bar for the hors d'oeuvres. Then we would have a salad with local greens. The choices for entrée would be pan seared Mahi Mahi in a butter soy sauce reduction or a grilled filet. The wedding cake was to look like a sand castle and have yellow cake with fresh strawberry filling, and a layer of chocolate cake with banana pudding filling.

I wanted to walk down the aisle to the song Kailani

suggested called *Come To Me*, by the Goo Goo Dolls. She told me about the song and then Ali and I found it online and listened to it. There wasn't a dry eye to be had in the room. Matt was going to love it, I hoped. Everything was going too well. I was scared that somehow I wouldn't be able to keep it all a secret from Matt. The only thing to do now was have a way to get him out of the house for the whole day so we could have Kailani and her crew set up, and then I'd propose to Matt. Oh, rings.

"Ali, what do I do about the rings? I want one with black diamonds to propose with, and then we'll need wedding bands. How can I get that when I'm stuck here for another day, and then we leave?" I was freaking out. I needed rings.

"I'll go to Tiffany on my way home. I have Jace's credit card – consider it our gift. Well, my gift at least until he finds out about all this. I have a perfect idea. You and Matt want to go snorkeling, so you go with Matt. I know from listening to Jeff and Lucas that you have to go really early because they only let a small amount of people into the Bay. Then after that, we'll set up with Kailani a side-by-side massage on the beach and then you can have your hair and makeup done while he gets like a facial or something. That way, your hair and makeup will be done without him knowing. We'll tell him you're getting one too, and then you're all ready to propose. What do you think?" Ali was beaming from her bright idea.

"That sounds unreal! Oh you are so good with this stuff. Ali, can I ask you, seriously, are you all right with all this? I mean, you and Jace are engaged, and I'm kind of jumping in front of you to tie the knot. Are you sure this is okay with you?" I felt badly about not taking her feelings into consideration until right now.

"Seriously, girl? I am so happy to be helping you with this and I'm so happy that you and Matt will be getting married. I love Jace, and I'll marry him when it's our time. Right now, it's your and Matt's time. I love you two so much and I'm so happy to be a part of all of this. You should know that I love you and only want you happy, Sarah. I'm honored to be your maid of honor. Ha ha, you're going to have to be my matron of honor, because you'll already be married." I could tell that Ali was being truthful. She did not care that I was stealing her thunder. She truly wanted Matt and me to be happy.

I looked through different rings for Matt and me. Ali loved what I picked and quickly headed out to get the rings and be out of the way with all the plans before Matt came back.

I was a bit tired, so I closed my eyes and just fell into a very happy sleep. As I slept, I dreamed that Matt and I were getting married.

But then I had a strange feeling that the air was getting hotter and wetter. I suddenly felt sick. I tried opening my eyes, and as my eyelids started to peel apart I vaguely saw a male figure, Matt I assumed, who was holding my hand and telling me how sorry he was for hurting me. Then Matt morphed into Michael, and I realized Michael was in my room. Michael was looking at me, trying to lick my neck with his tongue. I felt the sickening wetness and wanted to pull away from him, but he was holding me so tightly.

"Open your eyes and look at me, Sarah. I'm so sorry. I won't hurt you again. But you have to take me back. You have to take me back and leave Matt, or I can't be held responsible for what I am going to do to him. Do you want me to hurt him, Sarah?" The voice was egging me on.

I was just too tired to open my eyes further. I felt drugged, almost like I was back in my coma. I couldn't bring myself back to life. I couldn't wake up and get out of the fog. Then I heard a crash and the din of furniture moving around, and then I started drifting back to life. I didn't know how long it took to get me out of the fog, but I was fluttering my eyes open. That's when I saw that Matt was there, looking enraged. When I looked to where his eyes were focused, I saw Michael giving him the same bad look back. Security was there, holding both of them. The doctor was next to me, asking me how I felt.

"Matt, what happened?" I heard my voice come out as a low whisper while my eyes were fixed on Matt.

"Motherfucker here was choking you so you would pass out and he was trying to get you out of here, but I came in and saw him, and ripped him off you." Matt was struggling with security.

"Did anyone call the police? I have a restraining order against him," I said and felt for the first time that my throat was indeed hurting. It felt heavy and thick.

"They're on their way, Miss March. I have them coming. But they said to hold all the people involved until they get here." Again, things got worse. Michael somehow managed to go slack and look like he was passing out, and when the security guard released his hold, Michael slipped out and jetted from the room and the hospital.

Everyone was too stunned to do anything but look after his fleeing form; everyone except for Matt who went running after him but got caught up between a couple rushing in to have a baby. So Matt either had to knock them down or let Michael escape. So Matt let Michael go. I couldn't believe this was all happening. I would never have pegged Michael for such a psycho. I didn't know how to feel about this, and I didn't know how Matt felt. He was so quiet once he got back into my room.

"Matt, I think we need to talk about this." I tried to straighten up in my bed, to try and look like I had some control over the situation.

"I promise, Sarah, I will not let him near you again. I hate to do this to you, but you are going to be shadowed from now on, until he's completely behind bars, or dead." Matt was pacing back and forth running his hands through his hair. "How the fuck did he get into this room?" Matt screamed uncontrollably at the hospital staff.

"Matt," I interrupted, "I don't want this to be problem for you. I love you, but this is getting crazy now. How much money is it going to cost to have a guard follow me all the time? And what does that even entail? Do I get to go to the bathroom alone? What about taking a shower? What about my job? What about talking on the phone? It's like he's crazy so I have to be in prison." I was so confused by my emotions. Was I crazy to think I could, or should I even try to, pull off this surprise wedding for Matt? I knew he loved me, and I knew he was just trying to protect me, but what about him? I hadn't even told Matt that, while I was out of it, I heard Michael threaten him. Maybe I had to just walk away from Matt. Maybe that was the only way to keep him safe.

I needed my mom and Ali like now! "Matt, I really want to talk to my mom and Ali. Could you get them here as soon as possible? I just really need them." I snuggled down in my hospital bed.

Matt came to the bed and took my hand in his. "Why can't you talk to me, baby? I'm here for you. I'll listen to whatever you have to say. That's my job. To listen, to take care of you, to protect you." Matt kissed my hand and looked at me with his piercing eyes.

"I know. And I love you for everything you do for me. But I just need a good girlie cry over this, and you are most definitely not a girl. Please, sweetie. And after they get here, you can have the fun job of getting me sprung. I don't feel safe here, and I just really want to go home. After getting attacked here, I think the hospital will be more than willing to let me leave."

"Okay, I'll call Gillian and Ali and get them here for you. Do you want anything else?" Matt asked with such goodhearted love.

"Just you, and to go home." I kissed him. I fought back the tears. Was this the last time I would kiss him?

Ali and Mom were here before I knew it. Matt had filled them in on what Michael had done. So luckily I didn't have to go over that mess. They sat down with containers of ice cream and waited for me to tell them why I wanted to talk. We had done this talk thing before. In fact, when my parents decided to move from New York to Vegas, we had a family talk, and Ali was invited to join. My parents knew they couldn't leave Ali and me behind. Ali and I decided to finish off college in New York, and then move out to Vegas. We lived with mom and dad for a while until we got our own place. Then when I started to see Michael, Ali decided to find her own place and move out.

Over the years, one of the three of us would invariably call the other two and inform them we needed to talk. Whatever was going on got dropped, and we brought ice cream to the talk. Here they were now as part of our standard ritual, and I was about to drop the bomb on them.

"I think that in light of Michael being a complete and utter psycho, I have no choice but to break things off with Matt," I said and started to scoop ice cream into my mouth without meeting either set of eyes that were burning into me at the moment.

"Mom, excuse my very vulgar language that I am about to spew at your dumb-ass fucked up daughter. Sarah, what the fuck is wrong with you? Are you crazy? You're in love with him, and he's in love with you. You were planning a goddamn wedding with him, now you want to just break him and walk away! Fucking really?"

Ali was actually standing over me, screaming and fuming.

"Sarah, I have to say, everything that Ali just said, well, ditto," my mom stated more calmly.

"I love him, Ali, but Michael threatened me that if I didn't stop seeing Matt he would go after him. Don't I have to keep him safe? Think about it logically for a minute. If the roles were the other way and Matt had a crazy ex, and she threatened me, you know he would distance himself from me to keep me safe, and you would all be on his side saying how great he was for thinking of me and keeping me safe. So shouldn't I do the same thing?" I asked.

"Sarah, he is a big boy, and you have no idea how much he loves you. When he thought you weren't waking up because you didn't love him, he was a mess. He was actually in tears, honey. If you leave him, do it because you don't love him and you want him to find true love. But do not leave him and hurt him and break the man in pieces because you think he doesn't want to put up with a little bit of madness. Honey, I love you, but I refuse to take your side on this. I have watched this man cry over you, talk to you and sing to you until his voice was gone, and fight to the death to keep you safe. I will not let you walk away from the right man because the wrong one poses a threat. Matt can take care of himself, and you. Now stop this crazy nonsense and tell me what the hell Ali was talking about when she said you're already planning a wedding!" Mom was beaming with happiness.

"Sorry to intrude and eavesdrop, but I heard what you all were saying. Sarah, I have to tell you, I know my boy better than anyone. He was most certainly in love with you the first moment he laid eyes on you. And while I am a mother, and appreciate that you want to walk away to keep him safe, you would in fact crush him, permanently. Your mother is right. If your feelings aren't wholly into this relationship with Matt, then I understand. I hate it, but I understand. But to leave him just because you worry about him? He is a man and can take care of himself, and you. Now, what your mom said, tell me about this wedding! Which I hope is still on, because I want a daughter. I want you as my daughter," Gloria said and was sitting next to my mom, and the two of them were happily holding hands.

"I know it sounds crazy, but being in a coma, and knowing that there was a chance that I might never have woken up, it changed things for me. I know I love Matt, and I know what kind of guy he is. He wants what he wants, yesterday. He's been purposely slowing himself down to not scare me away. So, while we're in Hawaii, I am going to propose. I was going to fly everyone out in a few days and hopefully he will say yes. Then I'll lead him to one of the bedrooms where he'll put on his clothes, and in the meantime, everything will be waiting in the backyard. We'll get married. I know it all sounds crazy, but it's just what I want. But still, now I'm not so sure about the whole thing, after Michael threatened Matt."

"I think it sounds perfect, honey," Mom said and hugged me. "Just tell us when we leave."

"I'm with Gillian. When do we hop a flight? Where do you want us to stay? Who other than us knows about this?" Gloria was full of questions.

"Lucas is making all the hotel and flight arrangements. But you have to make sure Dad, Joseph and Doug don't say a word. I need this to be a surprise. God, could you imagine if he says no?" I started to fill with fear.

"Sarah, how could you even for a second think Matt wouldn't say yes? I think he's dying to ask you, but is scared that it's too soon. The boy is gaga over you, honey, and you know it. Now stop thinking all negatively and let's tell them everything we've planned so far,"

Ali said as she dipped into her ice cream.

I had Mom, Ali and Gloria with me for three hours, and when Matt came back he was wheeling in a wheelchair with a purple plastic bag on top of the chair.

"What is that for?" I asked him.

"This is a new set of clothes for you, and some toiletries in case you can't wait to shower at home. And then you are out of here, girl. The doctor will be in to go over the aftercare in about fifteen minutes, so let's get going. Then I'm taking you home." Matt was beside me, handing me the bag.

When I looked inside there were a pair of black yoga pants, a white t-shirt, a white bra and black panties. There were socks and a new pair of sneakers. There was a toiletry bag from Bath and Body Works, and a hairbrush. He thought of everything. Yes, I loved this man.

"I do not want to take a shower here. I just want to jump into these clothes and go home with you." I tried to stand, but Matt was right beside me helping me get out of bed.

"Well, honey, I think Matt has everything in hand. I'm going to head home. Your father and I will be over to your place to see you tomorrow. Ali, do you need a ride?" Mom asked Ali.

"Nope. I'm all packed and heading over to their place to stay for a while. I'll go home with them. Matt, do you want me to help Sarah into her clothes?" Ali probably didn't want him to see my back yet.

"I can do it. But you can help me stand her up. Thanks for taking care of her while I was gone. Gillian, if you or Sam need anything, let me know." Matt kissed mom's cheek and was right back at my side to help me get dressed. "Mom, are you and Dad staying in town for a while, or heading home?" Matt asked his mom.

"I was hoping to see your new house and then we'll

probably stay the night before heading home in the morning, if you don't need us anymore?" Gloria asked and her eyes were happy as she looked at Matt.

It didn't take long with everyone helping, and the doctor was right in to talk to me. There were no real restrictions other than avoiding extremely strenuous activity, but if I lost consciousness again, or had a huge headache, Matt had to call an ambulance and have me right back into the hospital. That was it. I was glad there were no serious restrictions, because I wanted to live it up in Hawaii. Not to mention, I needed to have my way with Matt as soon as we got home.

CHAPTER
FIFTEEN

Matt

Ella and Raymond were outside of Sarah's hospital room when we wheeled her out. The nurse who wouldn't stop staring at me was unfortunately the nurse who had to wheel Sarah out to the car. She was still looking at me the whole time. I had never hit a girl before in my life, but this one was asking for it.

We got to the car, and Raymond and I secured Sarah in the backseat.

"Do you want anything special for dinner? We were all waiting to see what you wanted," I told her.

"I want Italian food from Terra Rosa. That sound good for you guys?" Sarah asked.

"Whatever my baby wants, she will have." I kissed her lips softly, scared that she would break.

I was happy when we got her home. I actually carried her up to our room, with much protesting from Sarah. I asked her if she wanted to take a shower and then change again, as there was still some old blood crusted on her hairline and near her mouth. She happily started stripping and walking to the shower. I had Ali help me get all her brands of toiletries and stuff. Even her favorite perfume was awaiting her. She noticed and just turned to smile at me in the mirror, before closing the door to finish getting undressed. That's when it hit me: I had never seen Sarah fully naked with the lights on.

I waited until I heard the shower, and a moan escaped her lips, then I quietly opened the door and slipped into the bathroom. I opened the shower door so silently that she didn't even turn around. That's when I saw her back. There were not only bruises, but also what seemed to be whip marks. I gasped, and then Sarah turned around. Her lips started to shake and quiver and she slid down to the floor and cried. I didn't even take off my clothes, but walked into the shower and picked her up from the floor and held her close to my chest and tried to ease her crying.

"I know that douche bag probably said this to you once or twice, but I promise I will never do anything like that to you, ever. I would rather die than hurt you, baby. Please, talk to me. Tell me what you're thinking and why you're so upset."

"I never wanted you to see what he did. I didn't want you to realize that I was such a weak and stupid woman. I believed all his bullshit and I kept going back to him, like an idiot. I never wanted you to know that. I thought I deserved what he did to me. Every time I went back and he'd hit me, I thought I must have deserved it, because I went back."

"What could you possibly have done to have deserved that, Sarah? What reasons did he give you to hurt you?" I had to know what this sick asshole had done to my girl, physically and emotionally.

"He told me that I wasn't supportive enough. I was hurting his creativity. I didn't understand what a genius he was. I would catch him with his models, and I would yell and scream and break up with him, and he would come back and tell me that I was lucky he wanted me, and that I wasn't enough woman, that he needed more than just me. I believed him. It scared me, especially thinking it might be true. It won't be long until you need other women too. But I guess I can just deal with it if that's what you need to do, Matt." Sarah looked at me like a little broken china doll.

"Sarah, I will never fucking, ever, cheat on you. How could you think for one second you're not enough woman? I have been jerking myself dry since the first time I looked at you. I will never get enough of you. Don't think for one second that I'm going to go outside of this relationship. It's just the two of us. Do you hear me?" I lifted her face to make sure she knew I meant every word I had said.

Now I knew I had to kill Michael. He fucked with my girl's body and mind. No one fucks with what's mine. Especially not her.

She pulled back to look at me. How could he take this strong, smart woman, and hurt her so badly mentally that she felt like a fraction of what she truly was? I knew the real kick-ass smart, strong, amazing Sarah was right inside. I just needed her to remember who she was and forget all the bullshit Michael had fed her.

"I think it's time I tell you something, Matt. I've had a huge crush on you ever since the first Blacking Out show Ali and I went to. What was a crush has turned into love. I love you, Matt. Look at you, you're all wet."

"I don't care. I love holding you close to me. When I do, I feel like I can protect you from everything. I love you, Sarah. No matter what happened in the past, you have to know that I am nothing like Michael and I love you with everything that I am."

"I do know that, Matt. Can I ask you for something?" Sarah was looking away from me.

"Anything, baby." And I meant it. I would give her everything I had to make her happy.

"Will you take me to bed, and take me?" She seemed so nervous asking me to sleep with her, as if the bruises on her back would change the way I felt about wanting her.

I didn't answer her, but lifted her from the shower and picked up a towel to drape over her. I carried her to the bed and sat her on the edge. Then I walked back into the bathroom and picked up another towel and a bottle of her favorite body lotion. I walked back to her and went down on my knees. I dried her from bottom to top. Then I dropped back to my knees and started to cream her luscious body from her toes to her neck. I held my hand out to her, and she took it. Then I held her up to me, and turned her around so I could apply the lotion to her back. I was as gentle as I knew how to be. I was making a puddle on the floor with my wet clothes, but I wanted to take care of her first.

Then I picked her up, careful not to get her wet, and laid her back on the bed with her head on the pillows. I stripped off my clothes in front of her, making sure she saw how hard I was for her, that nothing could change how I would always feel for her. I took the towel and dried myself in a few fast motions. Then I palmed myself and started to stroke myself at the foot of the bed.

"See what you do to me, baby? See how hard you make me?" I wanted her to see that the bruises were behind us, and that this was a new start for the two of us.

She shook her head in understanding. Then she spread her legs and popped up her knees, so I had a full view of her pussy. "Can you see how wet I am for you, Matt. How I can only get wet for you? Only you," she said and then started to pull on her nipples and lick her lips.

I crawled up the bed to her. I held myself up so that our bodies weren't touching yet. I had my arms on each side of her head. Then I pressed my lips to her and with my kiss asked for entrance into her mouth. My tongue whirled around hers. I was pushing my tongue in and out of her mouth, fucking it with my tongue. She was moaning and tried to lift her hips to my hard cock to tease me into giving it to her. But not yet. Tonight was all about showing her just how much woman she was.

I shook my head at her and pinned her hips down to the bed. Then I quickly slid back, sitting on my knees, and I spread her legs wide open to me. I looked at her glistening sex and I could swear I saw it actually throbbing with need. I knelt down and lifted her legs over my shoulders. I used one hand to open her lips and plunged my tongue into her channel. I was grinding my tongue as deeply into her as I could go. Then I pulled out and started to plunge her again. She was lifting higher and higher off the bed, but I didn't let up, I just held her and her pussy in place. Then I pulled out and licked her from the front of her clit to her ass. I pumped two fingers into her and lifted them to the top of her wall and moved back and forth, then clamped my lips onto her clit. I was working her hard and fast, rubbing and licking and flicking her. She was moaning and gasping for air, then I heard a huge intake of air from her and I felt her pussy clamp down on my fingers as a rush of her amazing liquid rushed at me and covered my fingers and tongue. I moaned at how hot her reaction was to me. I never had a woman cum in a rush like that before. I kept going at her, again and again repeating what made her cum. I wanted her to come apart on me.

She came again in another warm and wet rush over me. She was now begging me to stop, that she couldn't take any more. But I was not done with her. I had to show her how she could make me cum like crazy. I moved to cover her with my body and when our naked flesh hit together, we both let out a loud scream. The feeling of her naked tits against my chest made me want to cum on the spot. She felt incredible, all soft and silky and warm. I leaned down and kissed her nipples. I wanted to take them in my mouth, but I had to feel the inside of her pussy now. I knew it was wet and warm and tight, just what I wanted.

I let the tip of my penis make its way into her pussy. She took in a sharp breath. I just let it sit there for a minute. If I pushed in farther, I'd be done before I began. I loved this woman with everything I was. Feeling how I could make her wet and warm put me higher than ever. She tried to push into me, but I grunted out no, not yet. I had to get myself under control. I repositioned my arms right around her face, and leaned down to kiss her. I meant it to be a soft and slow kiss, but she pushed her tongue into me and started to moan and lick and bite my lips.

"Baby, I need you so fucking much. Please push into me. I need to feel you inside of me," Sarah was panting.

"Fuck, I need a condom, baby, I'm so sorry I forgot." I started to pull out of her but she held my ass tight.

"No, I'm on the pill. We're good. I know I'm clean. You?" she asked and I nodded that I was too. "Then you have one minute to start fucking me or I'm gonna flip you and ride you like you've never been ridden before," she stated through gritted teeth.

I pushed slowly into her and we both moaned. She was like a tight fist holding my cock. I loved the feel of her around me. I slowly pulled out and then pushed in again. I was going slowly so as not to hurt her. But I couldn't take it anymore. "Baby, I can't go slowly right now. Later I will, but I need you hard and fast. You okay with that?" I looked into her eyes so I could see the truth rather than hear it from her. And she was ready and waiting.

I pushed all the way hard and strong until I was buried into her. I moaned her name, like a prayer. Then I pulled almost all the way out and started to pump her hard and fast again, and again. I was rocking into her with everything I had and she wrapped her legs around my waist and told me she was about to cum. I felt her clamp down on my cock as she screamed out my name, and that was all it took for me to cum, roaring her name as I emptied myself into her pussy in hard spurts.

We were both trying to catch a breath, looking into each other's eyes. "Was that too rough?" I asked her.

Sarah shook her head no but I started to freeze with fear that I hurt her. "I am so much more than okay. I am so in love with you and I never want to be out of arm's length from you." She reached up and kissed me long and hard.

I finally rolled off her and lay down next to her. I held her hand and kissed it, and then rested it over my heart. "I love you, Sarah."

"I love you too, Matt."

"Can I get you anything, baby?" I turned to look at her.

"I would like my Italian food now. Want to go join the others?" Sarah was already getting out of bed and putting on her yoga pants and t-shirt and socks. She had totally forgone the panties and bra, which was making me hard all over again.

I rolled out of bed and put on a pair of cargo shorts and a t-shirt and followed my girl down the stairs. The boys, Raymond, Ella and Ali were all eating around the huge dining room table. When we walked in, Ian got up from his spot and pulled the chair out for Sarah and started to help serve her dinner, which someone had warming in the oven for her. Mine was sitting out on the table, and there were bites taken out of it. The guys were assholes. They were all laughing because they knew they sucked and I was gonna be pissed that they ate my food.

"Oh, stop fucking around with him. Matt, I got you two orders because Jace said they always eat your food to piss you off. The other one is in the oven keeping warm," Ali said and opened another bottle of wine that she set on the table.

"Thank you all for being here and staying here. I

know that other than Ali, you guys haven't known me a long time. And seeing as how you've been treating me, I can honestly say I love you all. I thank you all and I want to raise my glass to toast you. To family," Sarah said and raised her glass of wine that Ali had poured.

Everyone else raised a glass in agreement. We were all clinking glasses and enjoying our meal. Soon, the guys finished up and went into the living room to play video games. Jace asked me if I wanted to join them, and I looked over to Sarah.

"Go play with the boys, sweetie. The girls will stay in here and talk about how amazing you are in bed," Sarah teased me. I went inside with the guys. Sarah, Ali and Ella stayed in the dining room and were drinking and laughing.

We were all sitting on the L-shaped couch. "Hey guys. I just want to say thanks for all this. I know this house isn't as big as the one I have home in L.A., where you all have a room. I appreciate you all bunking up and staying here. I hate to sound like a puss, but I even feel better knowing we're all here and there are a few pairs of eyes on Sarah and Ali." I was playing with the rim of my beer bottle.

"No worries, man. We love them like our sisters. Just remember all I'm doing when I need help with Nell," Ian said.

"Nell? Seriously, man? I thought you were trying to hit that, but she took you down at the party," Jace snickered.

"She did that because Sarah asked her too. She wants me; she just doesn't realize it yet." Ian looked smug.

"Ian, you're a male whore. There is no way I am going to help you fuck one of Sarah's friends and then dump her." I was serious. I wouldn't be a part of hurting a woman. Ian was always leaving a trail of broken hearts wherever he went. We always had crazy ex fuck buddies trying to get into our hotel rooms, or back stage at our concerts.

"I'm with him. Nell is a nice girl. Not the fuck-her-and-leave-her kind," Jace said.

"How the hell do you know what she's like?" Ian asked.

"If she's friends with our girls, she's not for you. Unless you suddenly realized that you want a relationship?" I asked and sipped my beer.

"Well the rest of you motherfuckers are all pairing up. Maybe I do want something more than a roll in the hay with Nell. I don't know. But I definitely wouldn't mind getting to know her better," Ian said and turned away so no one could see his face. Was there something he was hiding?

"So, about Hawaii. Are you lazy asses coming along?" I asked, not really caring either way. If it's just Sarah, Ali and Jace, that would be cool. But if the rest of the guys came along, that would work too.

"No way, man. We're going to stay here with Joseph and see what the cops are leaving out. We want to stay around in case dickless tries something. Trust me, we'll take care of him first, then call the cops," Ian said.

"Or maybe we should just call in a favor here and there and have him taken out to the dessert? I know that sounds cold, but after all, he's fucking with our girls now," Alex said and looked ready to kill.

"I don't want you guys to do anything that will get you locked up, again," Jace said.

"Guys, I have to tell you something," I quietly said so the girls wouldn't hear. "I'm going to propose to Sarah while we're in Hawaii."

Ian spit his beer all over the floor. "Dude, seriously? I mean, I love Sarah. She's amazing. But you've known her for like a minute."

"I know you don't understand. But when she wouldn't wake up, when I thought I wouldn't have a chance to talk to her again, or have her arms around me again, I almost snapped. I can't deal with not knowing she's mine. I only hope that she'll say yes. I've been trying to go slowly with her, but I just can't anymore."

"I get it, dude. I asked Ali if she wanted to move up the wedding. At first she said yes, but today she told me she doesn't want to rush things just because Michael hurt her. If I had it my way, I'd take her to one of those little chapels tonight," Jace was smiling.

"You know what my advice is going to be, man. Follow your heart," Alex said with a solemn face.

I fist bumped him and thanked him. I knew this must be hard for him. Now I felt like a shit for not being there for him and Cece. But I felt like it was too late to tell him I was sorry. What good would it do now? How could I go back in time and support him and Cece? I was young and thinking with my dick back then, and I was only worried about myself.

Now all I wanted to do was get a ring, or rather a wedding band, on Sarah's finger and put this complete mess behind us. I had this crazy feeling that if I made Sarah my wife, Michael would stop all his crazy shit and leave her alone, knowing he wouldn't be getting her back. But that was probably too much to ask for, and only wishful thinking.

Ali came into the living room and just had to smile at Jace. "Well, we're going to call it a night. Sleep tight, boys. Don't miss us." Jace put his arm around Ali's shoulder and they walked up the stairs to the bedroom they were using.

"I'm going to get Sarah and call it a night too, boys. Don't stay up too late." I walked into the kitchen where Sarah, Lucas and Ella all had their heads together, deep in devious conversation.

"Baby, want to hit the hay? We have a long day tomorrow. Plus we still haven't packed yet," I said to Sarah, holding my hand out to her.

"Already done, Sir," Lucas said and gave me a stupid salute.

"You're too good to us, Lucas. Thank you for everything. I'm going to go to sleep. Sleep tight all," Sarah said and wrapped her hand around mine as she let me lead her up to our room.

She just climbed right into bed, and as much as I wanted to have her again, I could see the circles under her eyes. She needed some sleep. She was going to need it for all that I had planned for Hawaii.

CHAPTER
SIXTEEN

Sarah

Everything was set. Lucas was coming with us, but Jeff was going to hang back and get everyone ready when the time was right. I knew we couldn't tell the guys until we were ready to get them on the plane to Hawaii. I could not trust their overeager mouths. I was scared they would think this whole thing was crazy and that one of them might even try to talk Matt out of marrying me.

We all woke up on the late side so we were rushing around to get to the airport on time for the first flight. We just made it as they were shutting the doors to the little flight from Vegas to Los Angeles. Then we had to wait three hours in L.A. for our flight over to Honolulu. I was so tired, both mentally and physically after all that had happened over the course of a few weeks.

Ali could tell that I was busy thinking a hole in my brain. She nudged me and asked me to go to the bathroom with her. We were in the VIP holding area, waiting for the flight. The guys were half asleep, and for the first time since I woke up Matt didn't try to escort me to the bathroom.

"What's the matter? Are you having second thoughts?" Ali asked as soon as the door was closed behind us.

"Not at all. I'm just trying to understand everything that's happened and how fast it's all happened. I mean, I was going to marry someone else not that long ago, and now I'm planning on marrying Matt. I'm rethinking my whole career and where I want to live and just about everything else in my life. It's just a lot. But I'm definitely not rethinking anything about Matt. I know where my heart is and what it wants. It wants forever after with him. I just hope he's at the same spot I'm at." I started to chew on my lip with worry.

"Sarah, you're more than just my best friend. We're sisters. I would tell you if I thought this whole plan wouldn't work. I wouldn't want you to get hurt by Matt if I thought he would say no. Plus, even his mom thinks this is a brilliant idea. Just because it happened fast doesn't mean it's not real or lasting," Ali comforted me while brushing my hair away from my face.

"I know. I'm just scared. What if I'm not enough for him? He's a rock star for crying out loud. He'd be giving up so much for me."

"He'll be getting so much you mean. You're it, girl. Now, think happy thoughts and let's get shaking to our plane. I love you, and this is going to be amazing. I promise. Now let's go," Ali said and we headed to the guys.

We waited for security to escort us to the plane, and I was so thankful they were there. There was no press in the airport, but the fans alone were bothersome. I just wanted to board the plane and ignore everyone pushing us and shoving things to sign in Matt and Jace's faces.

When we got onto the plane, I felt like I could breathe. I snuggled closer into Matt's side and we both fell asleep. Ali and Jace slept most of the trip too. I woke up about an hour before we landed and I started to read on my Kindle. It was a romance novel, and I was totally into it. Matt got up to use the rest room, and I was so engrossed in my book that I didn't notice the woman who went after him.

Then I heard a loud yell and looked up to see Ali pulling a pretty woman by the hair. She moved the girl to the seat behind me and pointed in her face fiercely telling her to stay in her seat the rest of the flight, or else.

I looked at Ali with scared eyes. She just smiled at me and told me I could go back to my book. Then Matt sat down next to me and thanked Ali.

"What the hell did I just miss?" I asked in complete shock.

"The chick behind me tried to barge her way into the bathroom, and when I started to leave she tried to attack me. You didn't see, but lucky for me Ali is a light sleeper. She grabbed the chick by her hair and pulled her off me." Matt actually looked like he was blushing over the whole matter.

For the first time since being with Matt, I lost it. Instead of worrying about his fans, I saw red. This was the man who I was going to marry. It was so obvious that we were together. How could someone act that way? I kneeled on my seat and looked at the brooding girl.

"Even look at my man again, and you'll lose that fucking bleached blonde hair for good. Got me?" I yelled at her. She just looked out the window and ignored me.

I turned back to Matt who was all smiles. "Looks like you're getting the hang of this."

"I'm getting there. Slowly but surely. Sorry I couldn't rescue you. I guess Ali has more practice at this than I do."

"You know I love you, Sarah. I'm sorry this crap comes along with me."

"I love you too." I kissed him like I needed to breathe. He was everything I needed.

We kissed the whole way until we landed. When we got off the plane, we were hit with warm and humid air.

The palm trees were rustling in the mellow breeze. The air even smelled sweet and lovely. I was in love, and not just with Matt. I already knew that Hawaii would be my special place.

After we collected our luggage, the car that was waiting for us quickly ushered us to the house. Jace sat up front so that I could sit in the back with Matt, holding his hand the whole ride. Ali and I were like two kids in a candy store, enjoying the scenery that was breezing by.

The house came into view, and I just knew I was going to love it. It was a two story house, with a wrap-around porch with white wicker rocking chairs. There were tons of palm trees and small trees with tons of fragrant white and pink flowers all along the front lawn.

Matt took my hand and pulled a key from his pocket and opened the front door, leading me into the house. Jace had taken Ali's hand and brought her through a side gate to the back of the house. The minute Matt walked me in, I felt calm. There was something about this house. I felt safe, and it was beautiful. It wasn't huge like Matt's place in L.A., but I could see why he always stayed here when he was on the island. The front door opened to the living room which was decorated in light blue colors, with a big light cream colored sofa that wrapped the whole length of the back wall. It faced a huge wall of glass, which gave a view of the ocean.

I walked in silence as I took in the whole first level of the house. The kitchen wasn't huge, but a good size, and there was a breakfast bar. The kitchen was done in beige and blue. It resembled the sand and the ocean. It was gorgeous. I turned to Matt, and he was looking at me with a bit of apprehension on his face.

"What's the matter?" I walked slowly toward him, putting my arms around his neck.

"Do you like it? I really want you to like it." He put his arms around my waist and pulled me even closer into his chest.

"It's perfect, and I haven't even seen the bedroom yet." I wiggled my eyebrows up and down and smiled at him. He was kissing me softly when Ali and Jace walked into the front of the house, running toward the stairs leading to the second floor of the house. Both were laughing and just ran right past us. I could distinctly hear their bedroom door slamming shut.

"They might have a good idea. What do you say?" I asked Matt, pushing into him even harder, feeling his hard on against my belly.

Matt took my hand and led me to the top floor. There was a small hallway with three bedroom doors and a closet on one end that held sheets and towels. Jace and Ali were at the bedroom farthest from us, but we could still hear Ali's moaning through the door. With a little chuckle from both of us, Matt led me to our room. He opened the door for me, but let me walk in first. The room was perfect. There was a huge bed in the middle of the room, made out of a dark wood. There were two nightstands, one on each side of the bed, and a dresser across from the bed. The bed was facing a giant set of glass doors that led out to the lanai, as they call it in Hawaii. On the lanai were two huge overstuffed lounge chairs and a small table. Across from the glass doors was a private bathroom with dual sinks and a huge walk-in shower that could easily accommodate Matt and me, and it would.

I sat down on the bed, looking out the glass doors, and just took a deep breath. I was free. I was free from the incident with Michael, I was free to love Matt, and free to wear my heart on my sleeve and propose to him.

Matt sat down next to me and held my hand. "I know I have no right to say this to you, but you should totally buy this place," I told him. "It suits you so well. It's amazing. Thank you for taking me here."

"I'll let you in on a little secret. I bought it about two years ago. I just didn't tell the guys because I didn't want them bringing ho after ho here. But it's all ours. I'm glad you love it as much as I do." He caressed my cheek.

"I can't figure out what I want to do first. I want to swim in the pool; no, the ocean. No, I want to jump you right here. I don't know. What do you want to do?" I asked, completely letting Matt take control.

"Why don't we go to the beach, and we can always have ocean sex. I've never done that before, and now's as good a time as any. Actually, your even being here with me is a first. I've never brought a girl here, ever. I always thought of this house as my solitude; that's why I wanted to bring you here with me. I want you to feel that way, because you are my solitude too. I feel accepted by you for who I am. You make me feel free and loved. You're so unreal, Sarah. Please, never forget that." Matt dipped his head and lightly kissed my lips. Then he pulled away and started to get our bags from the front entryway.

I looked in the mirror. I hadn't corrected him about this being our place. When we got married, it would be. And I planned on spending a ton of time here with Matt. I could imagine being pregnant here, waddling around with a huge belly, with my feet in the soft sand. This was so right. This all felt right. For once, I was so happy to plunge right into something. I had never known this feeling of pure bliss. But I knew there was one way to make it even better.

Maybe it was the loud moaning that came from the end of the hall, or the beauty around us, but I had to have Matt. NOW! Matt just made it into our room, not even seeming to notice the sounds of Jace and Ali when I looked him dead in the eyes.

"Drop the bags." He did, and didn't ask why or make a move. He just stood rooted to where he was. I slowly lifted the white t-shirt I was wearing from my body and let it drop to the floor. Then I opened the button and pulled down the zipper of my khakis and let them fall to the floor, shrugging out of them. Then my socks were off and I crawled on the bed, looking over my shoulder at him. "Maybe I can't wait for ocean sex. Maybe I need it now, hard and very fast, here, on our bed." I then turned and was still on my knees waiting for him.

Matt tore out of his clothes in record time and joined me on the bed, on his knees, facing me. Then he pushed me over, so I was on my back. He slowly started a trial of kisses that started from my calf muscle to my thigh bone. He put his fingers in the inside of my panties, and I raised my hips to help him get them off me. I was wet already, but the look he was giving me was making my blood scorch.

"Baby, I need you to touch me. Please," I begged. Then I unclasped my bra and let my girls pour out. I fanned my hair over the pillow and bit my lip, trying to look ever the sex kitten for my man.

"I'm just so torn, baby. I want to touch you. I want to touch you with my lips, my tongue, my hands, and my cock, all at the same time. I have to taste you. I'm dying for you." With that, Matt pulled me to the edge of the bed, and he kneeled on the floor. He hooked my legs over his two shoulders and first put a finger to my wet folds. I arched from the bed and picked up my head. That's when our eyes met. "Watch me, Sarah," he breathed to my pussy while keeping eye contact. I gave a slight nod and pulled myself up on my elbows to watch him have at me.

His tongue was making long slow swipes over my seam. I was going to be loud, and fuck Ali and Jace if they didn't like it. My man knew how to get me off, and I wanted him to hear every moan he gave me.

Matt filled me with a finger, while flicking my clit. I

was probably making the worst possible faces, but I didn't care. I was so close to my orgasm. Then Matt pushed another finger in, rubbing at the top of my wall, and that was all she wrote. I was screaming out his name, and shooting lust-filled daggers into his eyes as I came. I was bucking up from the bed, but Matt was holding me down to his mouth, licking at my hot liquid that was gushing out of me. He gave me about a minute and then he started his assault on my clit again. I needed him, more than just between my legs.

"Matt, 69, now." That's all it took. He jumped on the bed, and we were on our sides, his dick in my face, and my pussy in his. I opened my legs for him, and he was fucking my mouth with sharp thrusts of his hips. I had one hand helping me guide him in my mouth and the other one playing with his sack. I loved the feel of his balls in my hands. Our mutual moans were loud and reverberating off the walls. I didn't care. I was so happy I was giving it to him as good as he was giving it to me. I loved the taste of him. The natural smell of his body with the body wash and cologne mixed in. It was getting me so close to the edge.

Matt tried to pull out of my mouth, but I grabbed his ass and forced him to stay inside, sucking and licking as hard as I could. I couldn't get him all the way in, he was too big, but I was close.

"Baby, no, I'm gonna cum. I don't want to cum in your mouth." He tried to pull back, but I was making it too good for him. Then I felt him putting his hands in my hair, moving me with his hips as he continued to fuck my mouth. He let go and roared as he shot into my mouth. I just swallowed all he had to give me.

When I felt that he was empty, I climbed onto his lap and sucked the hell out of his face. The taste of my pussy was hanging on his tongue and I thought it was the hottest thing ever to taste myself on him. I looked at his face, the face of a god. His neck muscles were tight and visibly pulsating. There was sweat on his face and his eyes were almost black with lust and love.

We wrapped ourselves together and then sunk down to lie on the bed. We were a tangle of arms, and legs, and wet sheets and love.

"I love you, babe, so fucking much." Matt kissed my head that was nicely tucked under his arm. I fell asleep with a huge grin on my face and the man of my dreams wrapped around me.

CHAPTER
SEVENTEEN

Matt

We had been in Hawaii for four days now and everything was going great. The girls were having the time of their lives and completely relaxed. The boys at home had nothing to report. Soon I was going to propose to Sarah. Everything was right as rain. Speaking of rain, that's what it was doing at present, so we all hopped into our rental car and headed to a movie.

As far as we knew, news hadn't made its way that we were on the island, and we wanted to keep it that way. Jace took out his face metal and sported a beanie and I wore shades and a baseball cap to try and keep the disguise. The girls got the tickets and food while we sat in the very back row, waiting for them.

"Dude, still gonna pop the question to Sarah this week?" Jace asked in a hushed tone as we tried to be as invisible as possible in the theatre.

"Yeah. I was going to do it tomorrow, but Sarah wants to go snorkeling at Hanauma Bay. Then she set up massages and facials for us at the Four Seasons. So I guess it will be on Monday night. Mind taking Ali out, that way we can have the place to ourselves?"

"No worries, man. I want to take Ali to that awesome fish place we always go to. I'll take her there and leave you two alone."

"What are you two hotties talking about?" Ali asked as she walked past me to sit next to Jace, and then in came Sarah. Both girls were loaded up with popcorn, nachos, and drinks, and a ton of candy was poking out of their purses. That's why I loved them both. No anorexia bullshit going on with either of them.

"We were talking about how amazing the two of you are and how I can't wait for the day you planned tomorrow." I was kissing Sarah's neck, sending goose bumps to her skin.

"Maybe we should do something special tomorrow too? Maybe hit the North Shore and watch some surfing," Jace said to Ali.

"I was thinking of us just hanging around the house and maybe having a little nude sunbathing time. But if you'd rather we go watch some other guys in board shorts, with tan buff bodies surf, I can do that too." Ali was laying it on thick for Jace.

"Right, so we'll be at the house tomorrow if you guys need us."

"As long as I have my girl, that's all I need." I kissed her lips, just as the movie started.

Sarah and Ali were being great sports and had let us pick the movie, which of course had to be a major crazy action movie. Half way through, I think Sarah literally fell asleep. Ali was checking her emails on her phone. But Jace and I were high fiving and loving life.

After the movie, we headed to Aloha Tower to grab dinner at a Mexican restaurant right on the water. Again, Jace and I kept our heads down, and Ali and Sarah did the ordering. We were having a great night, until all hell had to break lose.

"Holy shit! You're Jace Wicks. I love you, man! My name is Cindy." Skank started to pull Jace's chair back and sit on his lap. Jace looked like he might blow chunks, Ali had a dumbfounded look on her face and Sarah was too shocked to close her mouth. "I'm staying at the Royal Hawaiian. What's say you come back to my room and we have a little, or a lot, of fun, depending on whether the rumors of your dick are true." She was trying to kiss Jace's neck, but he was trying to pull away and not dump the girl on her ass. "Who are you, fat ass, and what are you looking at?" she spewed toward Ali.

With that, Ali started to cry and ran from the table to what I assumed was the bathroom. "You fucking cunt! Who do you think you are to do that to my best friend?" Sarah took her drink and threw it at the girl, who turned all shades of red and started to walk away.

"You know, he's never going to stay with a fat ass like her. And he's probably doing you for charity, bitch." Then she tossed her wet margarita hair and stormed out of the restaurant while Sarah ran in Ali's direction.

The waiter came over apologizing and cleaned up the mess.

"I can't believe women keep pulling this shit with Ali. I am going to lose it soon. It's bad enough they know we're engaged, and try to fuck me, but then they always hit her where it hurts, about her weight. I am getting so tired of this, man. I just don't know what to do about it anymore. I wish she would just fucking marry me already. Maybe that would help out." Jace was seriously upset by what happened. He seemed to be taking it harder than Ali was. But I got it. I didn't mind when people wanted to fuck with me, but if they fucked with Sarah, I'd lose it.

"Why don't you guys just get married while we're here? Mom and Dad might kill you, so would Gillian and Sam, but at least you'd be married."

"She won't have it. I already tried. She told me she has her reasons and that I just have to respect them, but she won't tell me what they are. I'm losing it, man." Jace was rubbing his eyes when Sarah and Ali came back.

"I'm so sorry about that, baby," Jace said, standing to help Ali get past him and take her seat.

"Why are you apologizing? You didn't do a damn thing wrong, honey. I'm getting used to this shit by now." Ali said the words, but her eyes told everyone that she had been crying in the bathroom.

Sarah took my hand under the table and gave it a squeeze.

"Truth is, I don't know if I'll ever really get used to women throwing themselves at you, Jace. It all still feels like, at any moment, you'll walk away with them, and where will I be? Left with a broken heart?" Ali's lip started to tremble and she jumped up and pushed her way past Jace and headed toward the ladies' room, with Sarah quickly on her heels.

"Shit, man, this is serious," I said to Jace. "She's really scared you're gonna leave her. What the fuck you gonna do?"

"Matt, she's been like this the last few days. We'll be in the middle of having sex, and she just starts to cry that I'm gonna leave her. I hear her crying in the middle of the night. I don't know how to show her I'm not going anywhere. She won't marry me, she won't set a date, and keeps getting upset." Sarah came back to the table.

"What the hell is going on, Sarah?" I asked.

"I don't know. She's crying and just can't stop herself. I'm afraid that she is going through a deep depression, like when we were younger. Even then, it was horrible to try to get her help. Even after the help with therapy and meds, it took her forever to get better and be back to her old self." Sarah was seriously upset.

"Okay, I know what's going on," Sarah continued. "Jace, go to the ladies room and talk to Ali. I think she's ready to tell you what's what."

Jace all but raced to the ladies' room and Matt was looking at me.

"Do you know what's going on? Are you going to

tell me?" I asked.

"Ali thinks she's pregnant. She's scared that being pregnant is like a trap to Jace. She's scared that Jace will think she did it on purpose. Ali is just so crazy insecure, and being with Jace is not helping her; it seems to be getting worse for her. Then again, what if she is preggers? That could be why she's getting so upset. Do you think I should talk to her about it?" Sarah asked me.

"I think just let her be for tonight. She does have it rough with Jace's fans. That whole thing couldn't have been easy for her. Just let them have some alone time," I said, then changed the topic of the conversation to Sarah. "The way the moonlight is hitting your face, it's breathtaking. I really love you, babe. I hope you never feel like Ali does. I never want you to doubt my feelings, my love, my faithfulness. Please tell me you know that," I said, tightly gripping her hand.

"I know you love me, Matt. I love you too. I don't feel like Ali does. I don't have the past she has. No matter how shitty Michael was, he never tried to change me and have me be someone else. Guys did that to Ali. I believe you, and I hope you understand just how much I love you." Sarah leaned in and kissed me long and hard. Then she took my hand and asked me when we could head home.

When we got back to the house, she let me attack her until the sun started to come up. I felt like I had just fallen asleep when the alarm clock went off waking us up for snorkeling. They only let in a few hundred people to the Bay to snorkel, then they close the entrance, so we had to get moving. We tiredly rushed around grabbing towels and sunscreen, bathing suits and shorts, wallets and phones, and ran for the car, while Ali and Jace stayed at the house. We drove straight to the Bay and were lucky to make the cut. The gates were closed a few cars after us. We slowly made our way down to the beach and laid out our stuff. I went to a shop set up on the Bay and bought new snorkel gear for us, while Sarah bought us donuts and coffee.

We took our time, people watching and enjoying our early morning breakfast. Then after a small rest on the towels, we headed into the water. This was something I always did while I was in Hawaii. I had to feel one with the water, with the ocean and the sand. I was so happy that Sarah had put it on her special day list.

We snorkeled then took a small rest, and then went back out. This pattern followed until around noon. Then we made our way to the car and went to my favorite local spot for lunch. Sarah had done her work and figured out all my favorite things, probably though Lucas. Even though we took Lucas with us, he was at a nearby hotel enjoying a little downtime. We hadn't seen him once.

After lunch of fresh Mahi Mahi sandwiches and fries, we headed to the spa. This was not my idea of the perfect ending to the day, but Sarah was really looking forward to it, and I just wanted to give her anything and everything she wanted.

We walked into the spa and were quickly given a personal tour. Sarah went to the women's side and I was brought to the men's side. I took a quick shower to rinse off the salt water and put on a huge fluffy white robe. It felt good, I must admit. Then I sipped some pineapple water and listened to some music, if you could call it that. It sounded like a running toilet and a drum. But I was relaxing and hoped that Sarah was doing the same.

A very round and older woman named Naila came to get me and walked me to our outdoor cabana. Sarah was already there with another female, Joan according to her name tag. The minute Joan saw me, I thought we would have a problem. She was eye fucking me right in front of Sarah. But then Sarah shocked the hell out of me.

"Joan, this is Matt, my boyfriend. I know he's hot as sin, right? That's why you are massaging me, and lovely

Naila is massaging him. So please excuse us while we disrobe and give us a few minutes to settle in, okay? Joan, Naila?" Sarah took complete control of the situation.

Joan and Naila left us and shut the cabana drapes. Sarah took off her robe and laid it on the table and then got under the covers and made herself comfy. I did the same, looking at her the whole time. I decided I needed to start face down because my wood threatened to give poor old Naila a heart attack.

Sarah

I was honestly shocked that I was able to relax during the whole massage thing. But Joan was doing her job well, and I was momentarily unstressed. I knew that what Ali was going through was hard for her, and maybe after all the cheating and beating Michael did to me, I should have been more cautious with Matt. But I just wasn't. I didn't see why I should be wary of him all because Michael was a prick. Maybe because I knew my dad and Joseph weren't asses, I knew all men weren't the same.

I felt all the stress melt and even heard a few moans coming from Matt's side. Bless Naila.

When we were done with the massages, we proceeded with the facials and body scrubs I had scheduled. The great thing was we were settled into a private bathroom, which was huge with a two-person tub, and were given instructions and then left alone. It was hard to keep my hands from doing naughty things to Matt. But I wanted today to be right on cue, and I had timed out everything perfectly. So there was no time for hanky panky. We both lathered each other with pineapple scented sugar scrub and rubbed away. Then we got into the tub together and rubbed it all off each other. We did have a serious make out session, but we kept it pretty pg-13.

Now came the tricky part. I told Matt to go get his facial and to meet me at the reception area when he was done. He kissed me and walked away to the men's section. That's when I rushed into my clothes and headed to the salon. Lucas and Ali were there waiting for me, with my dress and jewelry, including the ring. They were both practically jumping up and down when I sat in the chair to have my hair and makeup done.

"Everything at home is done, everyone is there and waiting. Your wedding planner is amazing! I might have to fly her to Vegas to do our wedding," Ali said as she handed the hair stylist the small white flowers I wanted throughout my hair. She was already in her dress and Jeff had already done her makeup. She looked stunning. And she seemed to have a beautiful glow about her. I think she was knocked up, but good.

"Oh, honey, as my present, please listen to what I have to say, because I mean if from my heart," I started with Ali. "You're killing poor Jace a slow painful death. He loves you to the moon and back, and you keep pushing him back. Anyone who looks at him sees his love for you. For once, forget what those assholes did to you, see what you have to offer Jace, and just let the poor man love you. That's what I want from you as a wedding gift. That, and for you to take a pregnancy test tomorrow. Please?" I begged with puppy dog eyes and a pout.

"Fine, I'll get a test tomorrow and will try to leave my past in the past. For Jace."

After about an hour, I was set. Makeup, check. Hair, check. Now we needed to haul ass back to the house. I left Lucas behind to bring Matt when it was time. I left with Ali and headed to the house, to get my ring ready and put on my wedding gown.

CHAPTER
EIGHTEEN

Matt

Who knew a facial and shave could take a fucking hour and a half? I did feel baby ass soft though. I went to the reception desk, and lo and behold saw Lucas sitting in a chair, waiting.

"Hey, man, what are you doing here?" I asked, as I bro-hugged him.

"Sarah wasn't feeling well, so she called Ali to take her home, and I'm here to bring you back."

"What's wrong with her? What kind of sick? Is she okay?"

"She's fine. She just felt a little lightheaded and wanted to head home. She was done way before you. Come on. I have a car waiting."

I walked out with Lucas and tried to call Sarah, but her phone went straight to voicemail. She must have turned it off after calling Ali and Lucas. The ride was taking forever, especially when Lucas announced he needed to stop for gas. Then he made a second stop by the pharmacy to pick up something for Ali. I was about to make a run for the house, but knew it would take too long.

When we finally pulled up to the house, I jumped out of the car without Lucas even stopping the car. I heard him honk the horn two times and I was up the stairs racing looking for Sarah. She was standing in our room in the most beautiful white dress, looking purely amazing. I stopped short when I saw her. She looked like a bride. I was dazed by her beauty.

"Come here, Matt." She held out her hand and I slowly walked toward her to take her outstretched hand. She walked me to the lanai and I just followed, still at a loss for words.

That's when she lifted her dress and went down to her knee and looked up at me.

"Matt, you are my knight in shining armor. You are what my heart has always wanted and needed. I feel like I never really knew love until I met you. Even that first night you saw me crying, you were there for me. When I thought you were walking away from me, my heart physically hurt with the pain of losing you. I want to be with you forever. I want to be your wife. I want you to be my life. Look down to the backyard." I did and saw the whole backyard transformed into a white wedding wonderland. Our families were there, and the band. There was a minister waiting. "Matt, in front of the people we care about the most – in every way, they're all family – will you marry me?"

I was stunned. Sarah was proposing, and wanted to get married now. As in, right now.

"Fuck yes!" I screamed and picked her up and kissed her. I heard the cheers from below and knew this was going to be the best day of my life. I was marrying my angel.

"I was hoping you'd say that. Now, I'm going down-stairs to get ready. You get dressed, and I'll meet you at the end of the aisle." Sarah kissed me one more time and left the room, shutting the door behind her. There on the bed was an outfit and a pair of flip flops next to the bed. This woman rocked. I got dressed in record speed and flew down the stairs. When I got to the bottom of the stairs, Jace was waiting for me with Ali. Ali put two leis around my neck, a long green vine one and a white flowered one. Then she kissed me on both cheeks and told me not to fuck it up with Sarah. I laughed and gave her a big hug.

"Give me an early wedding present, Ali. Just let him love you, and believe him. Okay?" I whispered in her ear. With glassy eyes, she nodded yes and walked us out the door to the backyard. I wanted to say hello to everyone, but Jace walked me straight to the little archway that was covered with purple and white flowers. That's when I looked over and saw the guys put their instruments on and Jace left my side to pick up a mic.

Jace started to sing the words to *Come to Me* by the Goo Goo Dolls. I had only heard it once. Right when we landed and were driving the girls around the island. The song came on, and Ali gasped and mumbled something about it being a sign. So I made sure I listened to the words, trying to figure out what she meant. Now I knew. How my baby had managed to do this all, without my knowing, I'll never understand, and I didn't care. I only cared that she did it, and we were getting married. Fuck, rings.

As Jace was singing, I looked to him and he showed me two rings on his fingers. Sarah thought of everything. I turned my attention toward where Jace was singing his heart out, and saw Ali walking down the aisle toward the arch. He had it bad, and I hoped Ali would listen to me.

Then, my eyes clouded as I saw Sarah make her way down the flower and satin runner toward the aisle, with her hand on her dad's arm. I couldn't believe how perfect this moment was.

Sarah was standing beside me and the minister started by welcoming us all to this joyous event. Then I heard nothing more until it was time for the vows. I couldn't listen and look at her and form words all at the same time. I was like a teenage boy who saw his first set of boobs in person. She was taking my breath away and I didn't care what a jackass I looked like.

Sarah recited the form vows after the minister, and when he turned to me, I asked him if I could use my own words. He shook his head yes. I tuned to face Sarah. "Sarah, the first moment I saw you, at Jace's house, I was done. I knew there was no one else for me. You were the light that I had looked for. You are the one woman who could embrace my all-or-nothing ways. When you were hurt, and I thought you wanted me to leave you, my heart shattered. I knew at that moment, when you woke up to me, that I had to make you my wife. In fact, I was going to propose to you tomorrow night. But this is way better. I promise to always love you as you should be loved. I will honor you and treasure you and be faithful to you, not just until we both shall live, but for all eternity. I love you, Sarah."

The minister pronounced us husband and wife and I kissed my bride. Everyone was screaming and applauding for us. It was magic. After that, I finally said a proper hello to everyone and started to make my way around, trying to figure out who knew about this and who didn't. The food started to be passed around, which was incredible, and everyone was having a great time. I saw Sarah grab Ali and Jace by the hands and walk them inside, so I went after her to make sure everything was okay.

I stopped in the hall when I saw Sarah, Ali and Jace, all by the stairs. Then I listened to Sarah's little speech to them.

"Jace, I'm sorry we kept you in the dark about this, but I just couldn't be sure you wouldn't tell Matt. Ali, thank you so much for all you did to help me pull this off. I know I have no right to ask anything more of you, but I want a present for my wedding day. I want you as happy as I am. Why not marry Jace right now, here, while we have the minister? Then tomorrow, when Matt and I go to City Hall for the license, you guys can get yours too."

"No, Sarah. This day is about the two of you. I love Jace, and nothing is going to change that. When we get married doesn't matter to me. I know he's mine and I'm his. Let yourself have this moment with Matt. I love you for your offer. But no. I want our day to come when it's right. Don't you agree, Jace?" Ali was almost near tears. Jace was not going to disagree with her, but I knew deep down he wanted to marry her then and there.

"Ali's right. We'll have our day. Today is for the two of you." Jace hugged me and then Sarah.

We all walked back to the reception. Ali and Jace went to the dance floor. I noticed that Ian and Nell were playing a game of "I Never" with a bottle of tequila in the middle of them. Miles, always the DJ god, took over for the DJ Sarah had paid for and the guy was talking up the wedding planner. Our parents were on the dance floor and Alex, poor Alex, was standing near the water's edge with Joseph. I hoped that Alex would soon get over Cece and at least date someone. It had been about five years since the Cece mess, and he wasn't even looking at other women. He didn't think I knew, but he always left a ticket under her name, no matter where we played, in case she wanted to see him.

I left Sarah on the dance floor and made my way to Alex, just as Joseph walked up the beach back to the reception.

"Alex, man, how you doing?" I asked as I clapped him on the back.

"I'll be fine, Matt. No worries. I'm happy for you. You know, all this time, I blamed just about everyone for Cece and me breaking up. But now, when I look at you and Jace, I see it all differently."

"What do you mean, bro?"

"Sarah and Ali, look at all the shit they put up with. But they're still here. Maybe I've just been kidding myself into thinking we were more than I thought. Cece, if she loved me enough, she would have stuck around. Maybe it's finally time to let it all be buried and move on."

"You do what you have to. No matter what that is, you know we're here for you though." I clapped his back again.

"Thanks, man. Now go back to your bride. I'll be just fine."

I left Alex and went back to dance with my wife. Fuck, I had a wife. I was all grown up now. We were all having an awesome time when a pretty drunk Ian and Nell ran after the minister babbling. It looked like trouble, but I didn't want any part of it. I just wanted my baby.

After dinner and more dancing and cake, Jace and Ali started to gather up the masses and everyone started to leave. Ali told us that we had the house to ourselves as they were going to the hotel with everyone else. We were going to have a big brunch together around noon tomorrow at the hotel. Ali had set the whole thing up. She was amazing.

Once everyone was gone, and the clean-up started, I took hold of Sarah's hand and grabbed two glasses and a bottle of champagne, and we headed to the beach. I didn't want to make love to my wife for the first time with people working outside our house. So we sat in the moonlight and talked about how she managed to get this all together.

"Once I woke up from the coma, I knew we had to get married. I knew you were it. I guess I'm an all-or-nothing kind of gal. I just didn't realize it until I met you."

"Sorry to interrupt. I just wanted to let you know that we're all done. Is there anything else I can get you before I go?" Kailani asked us.

Sarah stood up and hugged Kailani, our wedding

planner, and thanked her. Kailani said congrats to us and left.

"Well, my bride, would you like to join me in the bedroom?" I asked as I grabbed my lovely bride's hand and led her to the house.

"I'm going to go get your surprise ready. You lock up, husband." Sarah kissed me and went up the stairs to our room.

I locked up the front and back doors and grabbed more champagne for my wife. Holy crap, Sarah was my wife. I was the luckiest man alive. That was what I thought, even before I entered the bedroom.

Sarah had candles lit on the dresser. There were rose petals all over the bed and floor of the room. I didn't see Sarah on the bed, or hear anything from the bathroom, so I turned to the lanai and nearly dropped the bottle of champagne.

There in the moonlight was my bride, bare-ass naked and waiting for me, looking at me from the lanai. I slowly undressed out of my wedding clothes and stalked toward Sarah.

"I want you to fuck me outside tonight. I want you to bend me over and slap my ass as you fuck me." Sarah was practically purring to me as she met me halfway.

"Baby, I'm not going to argue with my wife on our wedding day. Do you want it hard and fast? Yeah, that's how I'm going to give it to you tonight, hard and fast, 'til your legs are shaking." I knelt down before Sarah and picked up her right leg, draping it over my shoulder. She had already thrown her head back in anticipation of my mouth on her pussy.

I opened her lips and licked her clit, long and hard. She moaned. I felt how wet she was already, so I pumped a finger into her wet pussy. I licked and swirled my tongue on her clit and finger-fucked her for all I had. I felt her pussy clamp down on my finger as she screamed and came. But I wasn't done with her yet. I hadn't even fucking started. I stood up, and just as she was about to drop to her knees, I held her.

"You won't be on your knees tonight, baby. Let me please you. I want it all about you tonight." I turned her around so she was facing the ocean and bent her over slightly, so her gorgeous ass was shining in the moon. I rubbed my hand over her firm globes and then gave her a little swat to test the waters. I could see goose bumps prick over her back and she was moaning and pressing back into my rock hard dick. But I wasn't ready to take her yet. I wanted something special for tonight.

I wanted her to feel me everywhere. I didn't know if she'd ever done anal, and we never brought it up before. But I wanted to have her screaming and cumming tonight. I put my fingers back into her drenched pussy and lubed them up, causing her to rock into my hand, so she was fucking herself with my fingers.

I pulled my wet fingers out, and ran them over her clit all the way to her ass. She shivered and then reared back into my waiting fingers that were right over her hole.

"Sarah, what do you want? Do you want this?" I pressed against her puckered hole.

"I want you everywhere. I know you're too big for me there. No one has ever touched my ass. But I want to feel you there, I want you everyway tonight, on our wedding night. Please, Matt, fuck me everywhere. I need to feel you everywhere," she was panting and pressing back into my wet waiting fingers.

I gave my fingers one more sweep through her wet folds to make sure I wasn't dry, so I didn't hurt her. I pressed my finger into the tight bud, and it gave way under my touch. Sarah was moaning and begging for more. I was sliding slowly in and almost all the way out of her ass. Her hands were grasping the railing of the lanai so hard, her knuckles were white.

"More, Matt. Now put your cock in my pussy, and give it all to me. Please." Sarah was gasping for breath and panting. There was a sheen of sweat on her skin.

I gave her ass another swat and then positioned my rock hard dick right to her entrance. I waited and held myself there. I wanted to make sure she was ready for all of this. But she let me know she was ready. She backed into my waiting cock, and drank it into her pussy. I moaned. Then I had to keep rhythm, fucking her ass with my finger and her pussy with my cock. I had wanted to do this for her, to her, to fill her completely. It was getting me so close to the edge, hearing her moan and beg for more, all the while she was rocking her hips back into my dick.

"Matt, I'm gonna cum. Feel it." She screamed and I felt her pussy contract and pull my dick. I felt her warm and explosive wetness running down my cock and down both of our legs. It sent me over and I felt my balls tighten and I released into her and slammed into her until I was empty. Then I pulled my finger and my dick from her, kissing her back from her sweet ass all the way up to her long, lean neck.

"Matt, that was the most incredible feeling, being filled everywhere by you. Was it okay for you?" Sarah looked shy, as if she wasn't sure she should have liked what I did to her.

A smile spread across my face as I looked at my wife. "Sarah, that was the single hottest and sexiest thing I've ever done. I had to think of baseball stats to try and hold off cumming too quickly. You feel amazing, everywhere. You look worn out – you okay?"

"I was a bit edgy all day. I was worried I was moving things along too quickly for you. What if you said no?" Sarah asked with a concerned countenance.

"You honestly thought I would say no? Come on,

Sarah. I think you know better than that how I feel." I kissed her lips softly.

"I'd like to think we're on the same page. I guess we are, husband." Sarah kissed me softly.

I lifted her beautifully spent and naked body and walked us to our bed. I gently laid Sarah down on the bed, and covered her with the light sheet and quilt. Even though it wasn't cold, I knew Sarah couldn't sleep unless she was covered.

"I love you, Mrs. Lewis. Thank you so much for today. Thank you for marrying me."

"You're most welcome, Mr. Lewis. Thanks for marrying me. I love you."

I wrapped my arms around my bride and we both quickly fell asleep.

CHAPTER
NINETEEN

Sarah

I rolled over to look at the clock on the nightstand and was surprised that it was after eleven in the morning. Matt and I had to motor to meet everyone for brunch. I looked over at my new husband. He was sleeping so peacefully. I didn't want to wake him up, but I needed to as everyone would be waiting for us.

I was thinking some naughty thoughts about a great way to wake him up when I saw his eyes open.

The dynamite smile that he gave me made my stomach flutter. "Good morning, beautiful. I was almost scared to open my eyes and find out that yesterday was all just an amazing dream."

"No, we're really married. I never thought I could be this happy. But with you, knowing I'm your wife, I am so truly happy." I rolled into his side and snuggled deep into him. I could feel his morning wood, but we didn't have time for that now. So I just giggled at his hard on and swatted him away when he tried to hump me.

"We have to take a shower and get out of here. Everyone is waiting at the Moana Hotel for us for brunch. Wanna shower with your wife?" I asked as I got out of bed and shook my ass to the bathroom.

I think Matt literally jumped from the bed to the bathroom to join me. We washed each other and brushed teeth, and then just as he was about to start nibbling my neck, and make me wet, I backed away and started to get dressed in a light blue gauze strapless dress that Ali and I had bought the other day while shopping at the Flea Market. The guys gladly stayed home that day, but Ali and I had a great time getting some awesome deals.

Matt dressed in a pair of cargo shorts and a tight gray t-shirt and we were headed out.

Almost everyone was there when we arrived. In fact, the only two people missing were Ian and Nell. When I realized it, I looked hard at Matt. I knew Ian had his sights set on Nell, but I knew she wasn't going to be a notch on his bed post either. I had asked Matt to talk him down off the ledge. I tried guessing whether Nell changed her mind and would be arriving here doing the walk of shame, or whether they were both just sleeping late.

I sat down next to my mom and Matt and we all started to order food. I noticed Ali was just moving her food around the plate and not really eating a thing. She had dark rings under her eyes. Jace looked like hell too. But he seemed to be hiding what was wrong, for our sake.

Jace had just stood up, to give a toast I assumed, because he was holding a champagne glass, but his news was interrupted when a fuming Nell came in, followed by a smiling and smug looking Ian.

Nell just sat right down in one of the two open seats, but when Ian made a move to sit next to her, she looked around the table and her eyes landed on Alex who was at the other end. "Alex, could you please change seats with me? If I have to sit next to him, I might carve him with my knife." She huffed out and was already moving to take Alex's seat.

"Sure," Alex said and moved next to Ian.

"Do we even want to know what has you all worked up, Nell, or do our virgin ears need not know?" Matt asked Nell, who looked like she could very well kill Ian.

"Now is not the time. I'm sorry for being late, and for my outburst. Again, sorry we're late." Nell wrapped her arms around herself and looked at the floor.

"I was just about to make a toast," started Jace. "Here's to Sarah and Matt. We all love you, and we're so glad you both have each other. Congrats, guys." There were rounds of applause and cheers from our table and people were clinking glasses. I kissed Matt after we clinked our glasses together.

Everyone erupted in cheers. There were tears of happiness and joy, there were hugs and love, and all was right with the world. All the guys were making their way to us to hug and congratulate us when Ian stood up and started to tap his champagne glass with his spoon, drawing everyone's attention.

"I didn't want to say anything and take away from Matt and Sarah, but I have a major announcement to make as well." Ian looked at Nell, who stood up and gave him a warning look.

"Last night, Nell and I got married too!"

We all looked at each other in shock, and silence enveloped the crowd. I finally hazarded a glance at Nell, who sat back down with her head in her hands, almost in tears.

"I would say congratulations, but Nell does not exactly look happy right now, Ian. What gives?" Matt asked.

"I was drunk. I didn't mean to really marry him. I was drunk and feeling lonely. But then this morning, this jackass refused to get the marriage annulled. I don't want to stay married to you. How could you do this?" With that, she tore away from the table and went running down toward the beach, with Ali and I hot on her heels.

Nell was sitting on the sand, completely crying her eyes out. Ali and I sat down on each side of her. But it seemed as if both of us were at a loss for words. We just kept rubbing her back and trying to soothe her.

"I like him. Don't get me wrong, I wouldn't have slept with him if I didn't like him. But married? I was so fucking stupid. Hammered off my ass, I thought it was just a funny thing to do to marry a rock star. We were both drunk, and I was feeling a bit envious of the two of you. I might have happened to say something about it to Ian, and then he said, let's get married. So we walked after the minister and stopped him, and we got married. Then when we left, Ian said he needed me to sign some papers and I did. I didn't read them. I didn't realize they were the actual marriage license. Now he says that we consummated the marriage, and we can't get it annulled, and he doesn't want to get a divorce because his parents were divorced and it nearly broke him. But how can I stayed married to a man I hardly know? Is he fucking nuts? I mean, he's hot as sin, he's unbelievable in bed, and rich, and famous, and just a huge player. I know he's just going to be sleeping around."

"Honey, I'm sure we can talk to Ian. I'm sure he hasn't really thought this whole thing through and once he realizes that he can't cheat and needs to stay faithful, he'll give you an out," Ali said and looked hopefully at me for more assurance.

"I'm sure Ali's right. Ian is not a one woman kind of man. He'll realize that and let you out of this whole mess."

"You know, that's where I'm so confused. I want out. I do. But when I first woke up this morning, I actually for a moment thought this is pretty cool. But then Ian started in with calling me the little woman, the ball and chain, and I just lost it. I realized that I made a mess of this whole thing. What the hell am I going to do? My brother is going to kill me. That's it! My brother's a lawyer; he can help me out of this whole mess." Nell finally looked a little relieved.

Neither Ali nor I had a chance to answer her because

Ian came and sat down next to me. "Mind if I talk to my wife alone for a minute?"

We looked to Nell who seemed to give us an all-clear, so I helped up Ali, and we headed back to brunch.

Nell

"Look, I know you don't get why I won't end this marriage, but I'm serious when I tell you that I want to really try it. I want us to try and see if we can make this work, Nell. I think you're amazing, and I know I'm amazing."

"And so very modest," I quickly added.

"Just telling it like it is, sweetie."

"Please don't call me honey, or baby, or sweetie. When you call me that, I think you forgot my name and are just using that term to not get in trouble." I meant what I said. I knew I was just one of hundreds that had graced Ian's bed.

"You're my fucking wife. You think I could forget your name? Now look, Nell, I know this isn't a conventional way to get married. But it happened. I like you, and since you crawled into my bed, and enjoyed yourself, and did say yes, I think that you like me too. So why not see if we can make something out of this?" Ian looked sincere, but I was skeptical.

"Ian, have you ever been faithful for more than a week? Have you even ever slept with the same girl more than once?"

"I won't lie to you. No I haven't. But the truth is, it felt amazing waking up to you in my bed. Something you need to understand about me Nell: I tell it like it is, and I don't fucking lie, about anything. I take what we did last night seriously. I'm not going to be fucking around on you, or lying to you."

"Ian, I don't know. I just don't know if I can trust you. I mean, I read all these stories about you in these magazines. How can I believe I would be enough for you?"

"Why can't we just try? How about a deal?"

"What kind of deal?"

"We're set to stay in Las Vegas for the next three months to record. In that time, we stay married and try to make a go at it. If after that time, you really gave it a fair shot and still don't want to stay married to me, I'll let you divorce me. What do you say? It's three months. Can you at least give me that, and a fair chance?" Ian looked serious.

He told me about his family life last night. He told me how his parents divorced when he was young, and each one only gave him attention to piss the other one off. Each one only paid any attention to him to try and seem like the better parent. They constantly paraded other partners in and out of his life. It was a mess for him

My family was the complete opposite. My parents were loving. Everyone ate around the kitchen table, Sunday we went to church together, we always spent time together. At least until my parents died in a car accident. Now it was just my brother and me.

Maybe this was my chance to have that kind of family again. God knows that the guys from Blacking Out weren't going to church, but they were stand-up guys who showed their faithfulness. They cared about each other, and the women in their lives were amazing. Maybe Ian and I could cut out our own little family in this whole mess. He did deserve a chance. I had seen the way he did anything and everything for Ali and Sarah. He hadn't known them that long either. But he told me that they were family now, and he takes care of his family.

"Okay. I think we can give this a try. But I'm telling you, Ian, no other women, or men for that matter, if the rumors about you are true. I won't share my husband. Got it?" I was stern and serious. I wasn't going to share what was now mine, even if only for a little while.

"I promise you ba…, I mean, Nell. I promise you, no one else. Can we go eat now? See, I was busy making love to my wife all night, and I'm kind of hungry now. What about you?" Ian held out his hand to me, as he stood up. I took it, and let him bring me back to the brunch where everyone was busy talking and thankfully not noticing my arrival back.

I noticed that the chairs had been rearranged, and I was sitting in between Ian and Miles now. The waiter arrived to take Ian's and my drink order, and Ian, oddly enough, was a gentleman and let me order first. Then as I tried not to be totally mortified by the scene I caused, I looked up to see Ali and Sarah both raise their glasses to me and wink.

Miles leaned over toward me. I tried to move out of his way, thinking he was trying to grab the salt or something, when he gave a little giggle and moved right next to me. "You know, Nell, he means what he says. You have a lot to learn about the real Ian. But one thing I and everyone else who knows him can tell you is he means exactly what he says and his family is everything to him. Welcome aboard, sweetie." Then Miles went back to his food.

CHAPTER
TWENTY

Sarah

After a very interesting brunch, everyone came back to our house. All the guys were hanging out by the pool and having a blast. Everyone but Jace and Ali. They were nowhere to be found. I walked into the house to see if I could find them, and then I heard crying. I followed the sounds to the second floor of the house.

There, in the hallway, was Jace holding Ali and it seemed like they were both in tears.

"Holy shit, guys! What's going on?"

They pulled apart from each other, and both still had moist eyes with Ali's tears still running down her face.

"Well, it appears that even though I was on birth control, Jace knocked me up. I'm pregnant." Both Ali and Jace were smiling and I was too. I was so glad those were happy tears. Matt found us in the hallway, all holding onto each other, laughing and crying and looking like we were nuts.

"What the hell am I missing?" Matt asked.

"Ali and Jace are gonna have a baby!"

"Holy shit! Congrats, you too! Man, your boys are potent. I'm so psyched for you!"

More hugs and kisses went around. It was a dream come true seeing everyone I loved being so happy. But the fun of our being together was short lived, as the next day everyone had to get set to head back home.

Ali needed to get back to work, and Jace and the boys were going to work on some of the songs while Matt and I stayed in Hawaii. They would start to record once he got back to Vegas. All in all, there was nothing that could ruin my mood and nothing that could dampen my day. It was so sweet to watch Jace fuss over Ali as if she might break at any minute. It was interesting, in an amusing way, to watch Nell and Ian try to discover each other's likes and dislikes. Miles was having a ball with both situations, constantly giving commentary about how all the guys were now pussy whipped. I was happy to see that even Alex seemed to have lost some of his edge and frost. I had seen him talking alone to Matt at one point after the wedding, and since then his mood lightened.

And then there was my husband. My drop dead gorgeous, incredibly talented husband. I was so proud that I was his wife, and that I was part of his big happy band family. The day and night quickly came and went, and it was too soon that we were saying our goodbyes to everyone and wishing them all safe trips back to L.A. and Vegas.

Matt and I stayed on one of the loungers in the back-yard all night. We just stayed wrapped in each other's arms and held each other. It was the first time in my life I had completely opened my heart to someone who didn't hurt me, or use me, or make me feel badly about myself. Matt was incredible. It was so easy to love him.

I woke up, alone, and a little bit startled. Where was Matt? I got off the lounger and made my way into the house. There he was, in the kitchen, making me break-fast. Would he always be this way, so attentive and caring? I hoped so.

"What are you doing up? I wanted to surprise you with breakfast outside." Matt came over to me, wrapped his arms around me and kissed the top of my head.

"I sensed that you weren't there and woke up. I missed you." I snuggled closer into him.

"I love you, honey. Thank you for making me this happy." Matt kissed my cheek and we started our day.

The last few days have been sheer bliss; I should have known that something had to fuck it all up. Not only was a storm brewing to hit straight at Matt and me, but it was the worst shitstorm to rival all.

My phone was ringing. And you would call it either very late at night or extremely early in the morning. I jumped and grabbed it, hoping not to wake Matt. He slept as I looked at my phone. Fuck, it was Joseph. If he was calling at this crazy time, something bad must have happened. Oh no, Mom and Dad.

"Joseph, what's wrong, is it Mom or Dad?" I was shaking already, knowing the news was not going to be good.

"Sarah, where's Matt?" Joseph's tone was even and flat, no emotion at all.

"He's right here, asleep," I answered.

"Wake him up and put the phone on speaker Sarah. Now." I shook Matt and told him that something happened and Joseph was on the phone. Matt woke, but was still out of it.

"He's awake and the phone's on speaker. Joseph, tell me what happened? What's wrong?" I was frantic now and practically in tears.

"Ali and Jace went back to Ali's house when they landed. Michael was waiting for her. He had a gun." I froze, as Joseph continued, "He held them both hostage for a while, and with a gun pointed at him Jace could do nothing but watch as Michael hit Ali repeatedly. Finally, Jace made a move to get to Ali, and Michael tried to shoot him. Ali got in the way. She's going to be okay, but… she lost the baby." I remained frozen, unable to move or speak as tears flowed.

"The bullet grazed her arm, but that's all the damage the gun did. Jace came out unharmed, physically. Fortunately, Raymond called the police to go over there after he had tried to call Jace and hadn't heard back. By the time the police came, Michael was wielding a knife at Ali. When the cops had a shot, they took it. He's dead, Sarah. Michael's dead." I must have looked like a zombie, just standing there, staring blankly and not moving.

Joseph continued, "Ali's in the hospital, and they're keeping her for observation. She's in real bad shape, mentally. She won't speak to anyone, not even Jace. Honestly, that's the only reason I would bother you guys at this time in the morning. They won't release her like this. They've put her on suicide watch and they're holding her until they know she won't hurt herself. I think you guys need to get home as soon as possible. I'm sorry to bother you guys on your honeymoon. But, Sarah, I've never seen Ali like this. She just keeps silently crying and won't eat or talk or anything. Maybe you can get through to her. Matt, I think Jace could really use you. He feels responsible. He keeps saying that if he hadn't made a move toward Ali, she wouldn't have stepped in to save him. He's a fucking mess."

"We're packing now," piped in Matt. "We'll call and get on the first flight there is. If I have to, I'll charter a flight. We'll call you back as soon as we get the flights. Did you call my parents?" Matt was already walking around the room, pulling out our suitcases and throwing clothes in as I was a statue frozen on the bed.

"Jace called them when the police allowed him to make a call. They're here, but they can't seem to get through to him. Everyone keeps trying, but he just keeps saying that it's all his fault, that he should have stopped Michael himself."

"I'm gonna get on my computer now and see when

we can get home. I'll call you right back, Joseph. Bye." Matt hung up my phone, took out the computer and started to look for flights to get us back to Vegas. He still hadn't looked at me or said a word to me. Was he thinking what I was thinking? That this was all my fault?

"Sarah, I got us on a six a.m. flight. Get everything you need and get dressed. We can leave the rental at the airport. The flight goes to L.A., but we can connect and be in Vegas by five in the evening. That is the quickest I can get us there." Matt turned to look at me, and I still hadn't moved.

"Sarah, honey, we need to move. You need to get your stuff ready." Matt worked to keep getting stuff together, and still I had yet to move.

"Sarah, come on. You have to get ready, like now." Matt climbed back on the bed to look into my eyes.

"This is all my fault. All of it. Ali is on fucking suicide watch, her baby's gone, Michael's dead. It's all my fault. How did this all happen?" I was breathing quickly and feeling like the room was spinning.

"Sarah, you need to calm down. You're hyperventilating. You have to slow your breathing down. Look at me, Sarah." I did what he said, but it just helped my breathing, not my guilt. "You didn't do any of this, honey. Michael did it all. He hurt Ali and Jace. He hurt their baby. He made them kill him. He did this, not you. Now I really need you to try and get it together long enough for us to get to this plane. Ali and Jace need us." Matt got off the bed, and raced around getting things ready. Then I heard him calling Joseph while he was in the bathroom. I had gotten up and was trying to move quickly, but I felt like I was sleepwalking and caught in a bad dream. I pulled whatever clothes I could find and threw them in the suitcase.

I did all I could to get ready. We jumped into the rental car and I pulled out my phone to call my mom and let her know we were on our way back.

"Sarah, honey, are you okay?" Mom said in a soft yet strained voice.

"We just talked to Joseph; he told us what happened. We're heading back. I want you to tell me – how bad is Ali, Mom? The truth."

"It's pretty bad, honey. Physically she's fine. She has black and blues and bruises, but no broken bones or internal bleeding. But mentally, emotionally, she's broken. She won't talk to anyone. Poor Jace is terrified. He knows about her past emotional problems. I think it's because of that, that the hospital has put her on suicide watch. Jace won't leave her side. But she won't speak a word to him, or anyone. Maybe she'll talk to you, Sarah."

"I don't know what good I'll be. This is all my fault, Mom. I got her in this trouble to begin with. Michael blamed her and Jace for my leaving."

"Honey, neither Ali nor Jace blames you. This was all on Michael. She needs you, sweetie. Just get home safely. Text the flight info to Joseph and we'll make sure to pick you and Matt up from the airport and take you to Ali. Have a safe flight, honey. I love you."

"Love you too, Mom. Are you going to the hospital today?"

"I haven't left honey. I'm still here. Why?"

"Can you at least tell Ali I'm coming? If she doesn't want to see me, I understand. I don't want to bother her if she doesn't want to see me."

"I'm sure she wants to see you, honey. But I'll let her know. Love you, Sarah."

"Love you too, Mom. See you soon." I hung up the phone. We dropped off the rental car and headed to check-in. By the time we got through the crazy-ass long security line, they were already boarding our flight. We got on the plane and then we endured the excruciatingly long flight back home. Matt and I barely spoke the whole time. Any time he tried to talk to me, I just ended up in tears, so he finally stopped trying.

It took us until almost five o'clock p.m. Vegas time for us to arrive home. Joseph and Raymond were waiting for us at baggage claim. Joseph hugged me, and when I went to let go, he was still holding on. I knew that he really cared for Ali like a sister. Raymond looked like hell. He took my bags from me, gave me a weak smile and welcomed us back, then escorted us to the hospital.

When we got there, the whole crew was sitting in a private waiting room. Apparently none of them would leave, and having a major rock band present was a distraction for the hospital. So we were given a private waiting area.

Everyone stood up and gave us a round of hugs and welcomed us home as we said hello. The only ones missing were Ali and Jace. I asked mom if there was any change and she said no.

"Are you guys sure she wants to see me? I mean, this is all because of me," I said in a low voice, scared of the repercussions that were about to befall me.

"Sarah, this was not your fault. This was that asshat Michael's fault. But at least none of you have to worry about him anymore," Ian said as he came to stand in front of me.

"Sarah, you have to go see Ali. None of us can snap her out of this. You have to help her," Alex said, now standing in front of me too, looking horrible. In fact, they all looked like they hadn't slept in days.

"Are you sure Jace is okay with me seeing her?" I asked Alex and Ian.

"You should know he's not holding you responsible and the thought hasn't even crossed his mind. If anything, he's blaming himself for all of this. Go, see if you can help." Ian gave my shoulders a squeeze and then turned me toward the door.

"I'll walk you to her room," Joseph said and held his hand out to me.

I walked down the hall, holding on to my older brother for strength and support. When we got outside the door, he kissed my cheek and walked back to the waiting room.

I gently knocked on the door and heard Jace say come in. I took a deep breath and pushed the door open. There was a hospital bed sitting in the middle of the room, with Ali lying in it. She was facing away from me. Jace was sitting in a chair facing her, his elbows resting on his knees, face full of grief.

I immediately put my hand to my mouth and tried to stifle my crying. But it was useless. One look at Jace's tormented face sent me flying to him, with tears spilling.

Jace embraced me and tried to calm my crying. This wasn't how it was supposed to be. I was supposed to be comforting them, not the other way around. "Jace, I'm so sorry. Please, please forgive me for this."

"Sarah, there's nothing to forgive. You didn't do this, Michael did. I'm sorry that Joseph called you away from your honeymoon, but no one can get through to Ali. They're talking about admitting her to a mental facility if she doesn't start to talk soon. I don't want that for her. Please, Sarah, get her to talk."

"I'll see what I can do. Why don't you run home with Matt and grab some sleep and a shower, and maybe a real meal. Let me stay with her for a while, see if I can get her talking." I rubbed Jace's back and then moved him toward the door.

I had seen Ali like this twice before: when Jace had lied to her about being a rock star and, years before then, when her ex-boyfriend used her and took her virginity as a bet. When she had come back from visiting Jace in

L.A. and found out that he wasn't just a writer named Ryan Freece, but the rock star Jace Wicks, she was quiet, as in didn't speak.

As I stared at her, I was actually hoping that when she woke up, she would be mad at me. At least if she yelled and screamed at me, I could get her released.

I pulled the chair that Jace had been sitting in closer to Ali's bed. Even while Ali was sleeping, her face showed her sadness and pain. I had caused it. No matter what anyone else said to me, I had hurt my best friend and killed her child, all because I couldn't let people know what Michael had been doing to me. All because I stayed with him and let him keep hitting me and beating me. Then when I did leave, he couldn't take it and snapped.

I was in my thoughts, thinking of all that I would have done differently when I saw Ali's eyes flutter open and meet mine. I moved closer, and thankfully she didn't pull away. But the sight of me brought on a new wave of tears for Ali. She was moaning and grasping her stomach.

"Ali, are you in pain? Should I call for the nurse?" I held the railing on the bed tightly in my grasp.

Ali shook her head no, but kept moaning and crying. Then I was joining her in my own tearful release. I was shocked when Ali moved over in the bed, and patted the spot next to her, indicating that I should join her. I quickly moved to her, and wrapped my arms around her as we cried together, holding on to each other. This was a step, I thought. She had been moving away from Jace's touch since the incident, so holding me had to be a step in the right direction.

"I lost our baby, Sarah. I can't believe I lost our baby." Even though Ali's words were heartbreaking, I was so happy to hear her speak that I actually smiled slightly through my tears.

"I know, sweetie. I'm so sorry, Ali. But I'm so glad you're speaking. You're kind of freaking everyone out, sweetie. What can I do for you, Ali?" I was brushing her hair out of her face.

"I just need time. None of them understands that. I know I wasn't pregnant long, but when I found out I was so happy. So was Jace. I wanted this baby so much. I wanted Jace's baby. But I lost it. I can't do anything right." A fresh wave of crying began.

"I can tell them all that. But you have to understand, they love you, and they're worried about you, sweetie. You have to talk to Jace. He's in really bad shape. He's so worried about you."

"I can't face him right now. I lost his baby. It was all my fault. Michael, he raised his gun right at Jace's head. I just lost it. I jumped on him to stop him, and then he threw me to the floor and kept kicking me. It was my fault, Sarah. And they had to kill Michael because of me." Ali was holding me for dear life. It was like she was going to float away if she let go of me. I just let her claw me and I held her back. I knew this was a big step; she was not only talking, but actually talking about what had happened.

"You did nothing wrong, Ali. I would have done the same thing. You didn't do it to hurt anyone; you were trying to save Jace. They told me you did save his life, Ali. You saved Jace's life. He loves you so much, sweetie. Please talk to him. Do you want to talk about what happened?"

"We landed from Hawaii, and since you were still there, we thought we could just go back to my place. Raymond wanted to stay with us, but we told him to stay with the guys at your place. From the moment we stepped into the house, I felt something off. I just felt like something was different. Everything looked the same, and smelled the same, but I don't know. I just had a feeling.

"Jace went into the kitchen to get us both waters so I could take my pills, and I went to the bedroom. I started to undress and go toward the closet, and Michael jumped out of it. He slapped me across the face, and I remember screaming from the pain. Then Jace ran in, but Michael had a gun, and he had it pointed toward me. Jace tried to reason with him, tried to talk him into letting me go and taking Jace as a hostage. He wanted to hold us so that you would have to come home and see him. He said he would talk you out of being with Matt. He kept telling me that it was all my fault that you were with Matt and that he had to fix the mess I made.

"When we told him that you were in Hawaii with Matt and wouldn't be able to come right back, he lost it. He threw me down to the floor and was hitting my face and my chest, over and over. I was crying and Jace was begging him to stop. But he kept hurting me. Jace was crying, screaming and begging. He offered him money, and that we wouldn't call the police if he just left us alone, but Michael wouldn't stop. He grabbed me back up, looked at me, staring me right in the eyes, and said that I was going to watch Jace die, that I should feel pain for making him feel pain, the pain of losing you. As he was tormenting me, Jace started to make a move toward Michael, and Michael raised the gun toward Jace. I jumped on Michael and the gun went off, hitting my arm. I fell back to the ground, and as I fell I must have knocked the gun out of Michael's hands. He kicked me in the stomach so hard that I threw up, and before he could get the gun Jace grabbed it. Fortunately, the police came storming in and got the gun from Jace, who I'm sure was going to put a bullet right through Michael. And in all the mayhem, before the police could grab Michael, he pulled a knife and said he wouldn't let me go alive. He went to stab me. And they shot him.

"Sarah, it was horrible. He fell on me, and he was bleeding and I could only hold my stomach, and scream and cry, and then everything was like it was on fast forward. They put me in the ambulance and brought me here."

I interrupted, "Please, please calm down and keep talking to me. Tell me, how are you feeling, physically?"

"My stomach hurts, like really bad cramps and pain. I was bleeding a lot, so they had to give me some meds to make the bleeding slow down. The physical pain is nothing. Knowing what I did, that's what's killing me. Sarah, I need time, time away from Jace, time to think. I can't go back to my house. I can't look at the room, or the blood, and remember what happened. I know I made you leave your honeymoon and stuff, and I hate to ask, but can I stay with you and Matt?"

"No, you will stay with me!" Both our heads turned to the door as we saw Jace standing in the doorway.

"Jace, listen. Ali needs some time to get her head straight. I think maybe it would be best if you stayed with Joseph, and Matt and I have Ali stay with us for a while," I said, pleading with my eyes for him to see that this was going to be okay.

"Fuck no! She's my fiancée, and her place is with me. Ali, we should get through this together. We need each other to get through this." Jace was at her side, holding her hand, and all but begging her to speak to him, but Ali just looked the other way and cried. Jace hung his head in defeat. "Ali, you know I have a problem with being shut out. Please don't shut me out this time. It was my baby too. Please, I need you."

"Jace, just give me another minute, then you and Ali can talk." I put my hand on his shoulder. He looked at me like a defeated man, but listened to me and went back out the door. "Ali, he needs you and you need him. Are you sure you don't want to be with Jace to try and get through this?"

"I need time away from him. I need to accept that I

did this, did this to both of us. I should have thought about my baby, but I was only thinking about myself. I should never have jumped Michael. I just couldn't let him hurt Jace. Please, Sarah, I know I'm asking for a lot. But I just need some space."

"You got it. Let me go talk to him." I hugged Ali and went out to the waiting room. Jace must have told everyone that Ali was talking, because someone who looked like a doctor was talking to the group and when he saw me, he asked me if Ali was responsive.

"Yeah, we talked. She just wants some quiet time and space to get through this thing. I'm sorry, Jace, but she wants to come home with Matt and me, and she wants you to bunk down with Joseph until she's ready to talk about it with you."

"I'll see if she's ready to talk to me then," the man with the white lab coat said and walked toward Ali's room. Everyone else was looking pitifully at Jace.

"Come on, Jace. Maybe this is the way she needs to heal. You can stay with me as long as you need to. I know her, man. Just give her time," Joseph said to Jace.

"If I give her time, she might decide she doesn't want to be with me anymore." Jace said it so quietly, it was almost a whisper. Then he slumped down in the closest chair.

"Man, she's just asking for time. She's like you. She's not used to having someone to lean back on. This doesn't mean that she wants things to end. This just means she needs time," Matt said to Jace. "We'll watch out for her, look after her. You have to heal too, you know. You lost your baby too, and you almost lost her. You had to watch Michael beating her. That's a lot of shit to get through, man. Stay with Joseph, and we'll keep tabs on Ali. I promise to keep her safe, bro."

"You have to promise me not to leave her alone. She tried to kill herself once before. She's so upset I'm scared she might try it again. Please, guys, watch her for me." Jace looked devastated and strung out. His emotions were shot. He needed sleep and food and a shower, and time, just as badly as Ali needed those things.

"We promise, man," Alex added.

"I don't have a job for another week. I can watch her during the days while you guys are at the recording studio," Nell added, making Ian smile.

"I'm pretty sure I have no new events after the disaster that was my last event," I said. "So I can watch her too. We're all covered, Jace. I can even stay with her at night to watch her," I continued and leaned into Matt hoping he would understand.

"See, we're all set on this end. Now just get home with Joseph, and we'll let you know when she's sprung and how she's doing," Matt said and walked over to Jace to give him a guy hug.

"Thanks, guys. You're the best. Joseph, I guess I'm all yours. Ready to go?"

"You know you're sleeping on the couch, right, lover boy?" Joseph lightened the mood with his joke and everyone had a good laugh. Joseph physically took Jace and brought him home.

We told everyone else to leave and get rest, since they had been standing vigil for Ali for twenty-four straight hours. Matt and I were going to wait for the doctor to finish up with Ali. They all grudgingly left and headed back to our place. Mom and Dad headed home, and Gloria and Doug headed to the hotel.

Matt and I sat down, and I brought up the subject of Ali staying with us. He didn't mind a bit. If he did, he didn't let me know. He said he was proud of the way I had handled everything and everyone. Then the doctor came to speak to us. He said that they sedated Ali. But she would be free to go home with us tomorrow. She had to see her psychiatrist tomorrow afternoon and set up meetings with her doctor. We agreed with the terms the doctor gave us and then headed home, since we knew Ali would just sleep the whole night.

CHAPTER
TWENTY-ONE

Sarah

Ali had been with us a whole week, and it seemed as if she was getting worse, not better. Jace was a mess too. The guys would go to the recording studio every day, but they would wind up back at our place because Jace was either a drunken mess or didn't show up. Their patience for him was starting to wear thin. But they all seemed to embrace Ali. The guys took turns taking her to her daily therapy sessions. Ian was out with her today, waiting for her. Nell and I took turns sleeping on the couch in her room.

I was getting increasingly worried about Ali. She seemed to be shrinking into a pit of depression out of which none of us could pull her. She would eat, and then cry herself sick and throw up. Her skin looked gray and she was not showering or brushing her hair. She was a complete mess.

Joseph told me that Jace was no better. He wasn't eating, only drinking and then passing out or getting sick. He wasn't showering or shaving, and was stinking up the whole place with self pity. Joseph said that Jace would cry out for Ali at night and was having bad nightmares, where Joseph would have to wake him up from screaming fits.

All of us were at a loss for what to do for our friends. We knew we needed them to get back together, but had no idea how to make that happen. The guys were back from the studio because Jace didn't show up, and we were all sitting around the table. We thought that maybe we should tell Ali what was going on with Jace. If she knew he needed her, maybe it would snap her out of her funk and she'd rescue him too.

"So it's settled. We go get Jace and bring the two of them together. Maybe if they see how badly the other one is doing, one of them will snap out of it and wake the fuck up," Miles said.

"You sure we shouldn't just tell them how badly the other one is doing? I mean, if we get them together in the same room, they might just really lose it altogether," Nell said, thinking that Miles' idea might push Jace and Ali over the edge.

"Jace blames himself about what happened, and so does Ali. If they see that they're both fucked up without each other, maybe they'll at least lean on each other. They need each other," Miles said and went to get a beer from the fridge.

"I think Miles is right. It might backfire, but they obviously need each other. They might get back together only if each one sees how badly the other one is faring," Alex said.

Just then we heard Ian say that they were home. He was holding Ali's hand and Nell actually smiled at him like he hung the moon. Ian walked Ali into the kitchen where she took a seat as we were all waiting for her. Matt, having discussed the issue with Miles earlier in the day and liking Miles' plan, had already gone over to Joseph's house to get Jace. So all we needed to do was keep Ali with us long enough for Matt to arrive.

"I think I'm just going to go back up to my room," Ali said and started to stand.

"Wait, Ali. We want to talk to you for a second," Miles said.

"How was your session? I mean, you don't have to tell us what you talked about, but was it helpful?" Nell asked Ali, trying to keep her in her seat.

"It was okay. My therapist says that she thinks I need to speak with Jace. But I just don't think I can face him yet," Ali said.

We all looked at Miles with a look of dread, thinking that maybe his plan was going to backfire. Miles went to answer Ali, but he was stopped when his phone rang. He looked at it and answered. "Matt, where the hell are you? Ali and Ian are back and we're all in the kitchen." Miles listened to Matt's response, and then he hung his head and started a round of crazy curses. Then he walked into the living room and started to kick over furniture and scream. He threw his phone against the wall and it shattered.

"Miles, what the fuck is going on?" Alex screamed to him.

"Jace is in the hospital. Matt found him in a pile of puke, not breathing. They got him breathing again but he's been admitted," Miles responded while storming around the room. "I can't fucking take this anymore! I'm at that motherfucking hospital every fucking week! I can't take this shit!" Miles turned away from all of us, stormed out and slammed the door.

"We have to go to him now!" Ali was shaking and running toward the door. Alex was practically holding her up, but she was fighting him off and going toward the garage. We all jumped into cars and rushed back to the hospital. Again.

When we got there, Matt was making a hole in the waiting room floor. The emergency waiting room was very crowded and people kept eyeing the guys. But luckily no one was crass enough to try and approach them. Miles was absent, no one knew where he was, and we couldn't call him because he smashed his phone.

"Matt, what happened?" I asked, and when he saw me his eyes softened like he really needed me.

"I went over to Joseph's and the door was unlocked. I found him on the bathroom floor covered in puke and not breathing. I called 911 and started to do CPR on him. The EMTs got him breathing again, but he was throwing up and they think he has alcohol poisoning."

"Is he awake? I need to see him," Ali said.

All eyes turned to her. "Maybe that's not such a great idea just yet, Ali. He's pretty fucked up and out of it. He was screaming and not in his right mind when they got him awake," Matt said. I could tell there was more he wasn't telling us. Apparently, Ali could tell too.

"What aren't you telling me, Matt?" Ali demanded.

"He made me promise not to let you in. He doesn't want to see you," Matt said to her, and then looked down to the floor. Ali looked around, and all the guys were avoiding her. They all loved Ali. But Jace was their brother. They were going to go with what he wanted, not Ali. But Nell called bullshit and gave it to them all.

"Well, that's just too fucking bad for him. She wants to see him, and she's going in!" Nell yelled to them, snapping their heads back up.

"Nell, stay out of this," Ian started to say, but Nell cut him off.

"I know what you're all thinking," Nell said, "but Ali didn't do this to him, he did it to himself. And you all should have known that he was this bad. Now this is what they both need. They both need to physically see how they're killing each other by staying away from each other. Ian, get Ali back there or I'm moving in with Sarah. I'm not fucking around." I was impressed and given a surge of emotion.

"Nell is right. Ali needs to see him like this. Get her back there, Matt, or I'm leaving too."

"You fucking girls always have to stick together, even when you're wrong, huh?" Ian said and glared at

Nell.

"What if it were you? Even if you told Matt to keep me away, wouldn't you really want to see me? Wouldn't you really want me there with you, helping you, you asshole!" Nell yelled at Ian.

"Okay, okay, you have a point. Even if I told Matt to keep you away, I'd need to see you to see that you were okay. Right, Matt?" Ian said to Matt, hoping Matt would back him up.

Miles came through the doors and joined us before Matt could answer. "What's up with Jace?" he asked.

"He's stable," Matt answered.

"Well, why isn't anyone back there with him?" Miles asked, looking at Ali.

"'Cause the idiot doesn't want me back there with him, and the guys won't help me get to him," Ali said, finally sounding like her old self.

"Excuse me, but could you all keep your voices down?" a nurse interrupted. "Mr. Lewis, if you want, you can go back to Mr. Wicks. He's asking for you. The rest of you will have to wait until he's moved into a room and visiting hours start." The bitchy nurse looked Ali up and down as if she were a disease. "I'm assuming you're the fiancée. You might as well go home. Mr. Wicks has given me strict orders not to let you in to see him," she continued then turned to go back to the re- stricted part of the ER.

All eyes turned to Ali. She was literally red and you could almost see smoke coming from her ears. She looked at each of us, and we were all scared as to what was going to happen next. Ali's eyes landed on Miles.

"Miles, get me back there, or so help me God I'll make a scene to end all scenes."

Miles just shook his head and grabbed Ali's hand. They moved toward the back of the ER. Whatever Miles said to the charge nurse got her attention, because she opened the restricted locked area and gave them entrance.

Ali

I knew that Miles was on the same page with me. Jace was getting me whether he liked it or not. I was holding Miles' hand and we made it to the back of the ER. We stealthily went about trying to find Jace's curtained-off room. When we found it, I was bullshit. The same bitch nurse was practically throwing herself at a half-tanked Jace. I saw red. Luckily Miles knew I was going to lose it.

I made a mad scramble toward her and grabbed her hair, and pulled her off Jace, with her loud screaming filling the curtained room. Jace sat straight up and looked at me like I was crazy. Bitch kept screaming for me to get off her, and Miles was pulling me away but not hard enough to really make me lose my grip.

Security quickly came in and took me from Miles. They tried to pull me out of the curtain, but before they could, bitch nurse jumped me and started to hit me in the back of the head. Then she yanked my hair, and Miles grabbed her and pulled her off me, as another security guard burst in to take hold of her.

"This is a hospital, not a wrestling match!" the security guard who had me held back said. "Now both of you calm down and tell us what the hell is going on here. Or do you both need to be removed from this hospital?"

"I came in here to see my fiancée and this bitch was trying to kiss him," I spat to the guard, looking daggers at the nurse.

"I was listening to what he was whispering. What he was saying was that he didn't want her in his room.

Right, Jace?" bitch said, looking lovingly at Jace, who was sitting up on his elbows.

"Don't fucking call him Jace. He's your patient, not your boyfriend. Bitch!" I yelled back.

"He doesn't want you here, isn't that right?" nurse again directed at me.

"Well, Jace, is that true? Do you want me to leave? 'Cause so help me, if you fucking throw me out of this room, I will kick your fucking ass to tomorrow. Do you hear me? Fucking tomorrow!" I screamed at him.

"Ma'am, calm down and stop yelling at the patient. Sir, is this woman really your fiancée?" the guard asked Jace.

"Yes, but she...." That was all Jace got out, before he slumped back on the bed and started to cry.

"Sir, I'm sorry but we need to know if you want her removed or not," one of the guards said to Jace.

He found my eyes. "You left me," he whispered.

"But I got my head out of my ass, and I'm here now. Let me stay, let me fix this, Jace," I begged.

"I don't know what to say to you anymore, Ali," Jace again whispered.

"Jace Ryan Freece Wicks, look at me, and look good, in my eyes. I'm sorry I fucked up. I'm sorry I've been totally useless and not there for you. But I am here now. I'm trying to be here for you. Are you saying you don't want us anymore? 'Cause if you tell them to make me leave, that's what you're saying. And let me tell you, I did not go through all this pain and grief just for us to break up. Now man up and deal with me and tell them to let me stay. Because even if you tell them to take me out, I'm not leaving. I'm not leaving you. I finally see that we might not have our baby, but we have us. And I'll fight for us. But you need to fight too. Do you hear me? I'm not leaving. You can't get rid of me. I love you, asshole. I fucking love you and I want you to help me and I want to help you. Please, Jace, just forgive me and tell me I can stay. Please, Jace, tell them." I was shaking and crying freely.

At last Jace was looking at me. Maybe he would see how sorry I was, how much I needed him. He had to. But if the worst happened and he still wanted me gone, I wasn't going without a fight. When I thought I had lost Jace, something in me snapped. The darkness about the baby was wiped away. I would always love and miss the baby. But Jace was here and I couldn't lose him too. I loved him. I loved him too much to just walk away and wallow in self-destructive behavior. I needed to be the strong one now, and Jace needed me.

Jace opened his mouth, "I want my fiancée to stay with me, please." Then he gave me the faintest of smiles. The security guard released me and I flew to Jace. He was so weak, but he managed to hold me.

"I'll go tell the guys that all is well in lovebird land. Glad you made it back to us, Jace. No more shit, brother." Miles made his exit and so did the security guards and bitch nurse.

"I love you so much. What were you thinking, Jace. Alcohol poisoning? Did you seriously not realize how much you were drinking?" I asked as calmly as I could, but I was pissed all the same.

"I didn't care anymore. I honestly thought I had lost you. Losing the baby, our baby, and then reliving that night over and over in my head, reliving you getting beaten and shot. I could have lost you too. Then know-ing that we lost our baby because of me. I know that's why you had to have space from me; it was my fault that we lost the baby, and you didn't want to be near me."

"Jace, you are so very, very wrong. I wanted to be away from you because it was all my fault we lost the baby and I thought you shouldn't have to look at me, or be around me. I thought I was giving you a way out from having to be with me. I don't blame you at all, Jace. I was the one who jumped Michael, and didn't think about the baby. I was the one who should have known better. When Michael said he wanted to kill you, I realized that was all my fault too. I almost got you killed because Michael wanted me to suffer. I love you so much that I could only think about losing you, and that killed me. And I lost it. I'm so sorry. Please forgive me," I begged.

"Baby, no, there's nothing for you to apologize for. It was my fault."

"Jace, we can go back and forth this way all day and all night. Maybe we both just say we forgive each other and we try to move on. What do you say?" I asked Jace, hoping that he wanted to get past this with me by his side.

"Ali, I love you so much. I just can't make it without you. Marry me."

"I will, idiot. You know that," I laughed at him.

"No, I mean like now. Marry me now. As soon as I'm outta here, just marry me. You don't know the hell I've been through this week, not knowing if I had really lost you. I can't feel that way again." Jace's eyes started to tear up.

"Okay. As soon as you're out of here, we'll get married. But if you want to wait, you have to realize a little space never meant that I didn't want you. It just meant that I had shit to work out in my messed up head. But if moving the wedding into hyper drive will help you and make you feel better, I'll get everything set. Okay? You just get dressed and show up. But first, you have to get out of here. I have to tell you, I'm scared. I'm scared that your drinking got this bad, this fast."

"I know. I think I need to see someone to get through what happened. Maybe the psychiatrist you see would be a good idea. I obviously need some help and I think I need to hear from him how to help you when these dark days come around for you, in case there are any more. I promise to try to do whatever I can to keep them away, but when I can't I don't want to be shut out again, baby."

"That sounds like a good start. I love you, honey. Please don't scare me like that again."

"Mr. Wicks. Hello, I'm Dr. Woodmin. I was the doctor who brought you back here. Glad to see that it was worth it. You have to be admitted for a few days. I'd say you should be out by Thursday or Friday at the latest, if all goes well. You're going to have to get cleared by a psychiatrist since you basically overdosed with alcohol. Do you have any questions for me Mr. Wicks, or any from you, Miss…?"

"Ali, I'm Jace's fiancée. I have a question. Did the alcohol poisoning have any permanent damage?"

"He seems to be doing well. The poisoning wasn't the main problem. You asphyxiated on your vomit and stopped breathing. But it seems like it had just happened when you were found, and your friend was knowledge-able enough to start CPR, so it appears as if there was no permanent damage. You're very lucky, Mr. Wicks."

"I know I am, and I will not be a repeat customer for you, doctor." Jace was again smiling.

"Glad to hear it. Now, we need to move you up to your room. I'm afraid it's after visiting hours, so you might as well go home, Miss. You can visit with Mr. Wicks at ten o'clock tomorrow morning."

"I guess I have to go. I don't like leaving you here, Jace." I was holding his hand for dear life and looking into his eyes.

"I'll be fine. You'll be in good hands with Sarah, Nell and the guys. I'm sure they're all out there waiting for you. Go home, get some sleep, and come back to me tomorrow. I'll be waiting for you. I love you, with my whole heart. Now go home and get some sleep. We have a wedding to start planning tomorrow." Jace kissed my hand, but that wasn't enough for me.

I kissed his lips. He smiled at me and winked. I let go of his hand and walked out to the waiting room. Everyone was in fact still waiting for me.

"How is he, Ali?" Sarah asked first.

"The doctor came in and said that he's going to be fine. You saved his life, Matt. If you hadn't gone to see him, and started CPR, he wouldn't have made it. Or he would have had brain damage. How can I ever thank you enough?" I hugged Matt and, again, I was a crying mess. But this time they were happy tears. Happy that Matt found Jace in time. Happy tears that I was given another chance with Jace.

"I think we need to get you home, little one," Matt said and put an arm around me. He put his other arm around Sarah and we all started to file out of the ER waiting room.

"Seriously, we have been at this hospital several times over the past three weeks, and never for happy reasons. Can we cut all this drama shit and just have dull lives for a while?" Miles piped up.

"I don't know about the rest of you, but I think that's a wonderful idea," Sarah said.

"One more thing. Jace wants us married, right away. They say he'll be out by Friday, so if you guys have nothing to do, I think we'll get married, say, Saturday night? I'm not sure where yet. I'll get working on that tomorrow. But I hope you can all make it," I said, knowing full well they had nothing else to do.

"I'll check our calendar, but I think Nell and I are free. Need a photographer? My wife happens to be a fabulous one," Ian said.

"How would you know whether I'm good or not?"

Nell answered back at him.

"I've been looking up your work online. You're amazing," Ian added and made Nell smile.

"I'd love Nell to do it, only if she can still have a good time too. I don't want you to just work. I think that we all need to let loose and have a good time," I said.

"You think?" Miles asked.

We all let out a loud round of laughter.

CHAPTER
TWENTY-TWO

Sarah

I walked Ali to her room and was about to enter the room with her and stay the night with her, but she stopped me at the doorway. "I think I'll be fine by myself tonight, Sarah. I'm really better. I promise. I have only happy things to look forward to." Ali hugged me and I could see no tears in her eyes for the first time in weeks. I gave her an extra tight squeeze and walked down the hall to Matt. He was in our bedroom, taking his clothes off, and stepping into the shower. I just watched him from afar.

He didn't hear or see me, and I was glad. He might be my husband now, but I was being a bit pervy watching him undress and step into the shower. I had been so worried about Ali that I hadn't thought about how Matt was feeling about what was happening to Jace. I knew it must have been a heavy weight to save your brother's life. I'm sure there were a bunch of "what ifs" running through his head right now. So I gave him a few minutes to himself. I hadn't unpacked, and truthfully, it could wait.

I shrugged out of my clothes and was searching for something comfy to wear to bed. But I was stopped by two warm and wet hands on my ass. Matt was rubbing my globes and making me pant.

"I didn't think that after the day you've had you would be in the mood. I was just giving you time to process everything. You want to talk about it?" I asked.

"We'll talk after. Right now I need you. I need inside of you." Matt nipped my shoulder and just bent my naked form over the bed. I went from watching him naked, to having him play with my pussy for a minute or two, to getting ready for a good fuck. Then he thrust into me with all he was. The slamming of his hips against my raised ones was the only sound that echoed through the room. I was moaning into the mattress so no one would hear us. Matt's hands were grabbing me hard; there would be hand prints on me for a while, but I didn't care. He needed me hard and fast and I needed him the exact same way.

Watching the pain the guys and Ali were going through tonight, thinking they would lose Jace, had sickened me. I wanted to know we were all fine. I wanted to feel and not be numb anymore. Matt was ramming into me, making me feel amazing. It wasn't long and my orgasm was there, and Matt was right with me, flowing over the edge. He lay on top of me, panting in my ear and kissing my neck.

"I couldn't have gotten through this without you," Matt said to me as he lifted me up and laid me down on the bed.

"This is all because of me, Matt. Seriously, I'm the one who brought Michael into our lives. I should have ended things with him long, long ago and then none of this would have happened."

"You didn't make him go crazy, Sarah. You could have broken up with him months ago and he still could have freaked that we were together. He still could have blamed Ali and Jace. You know, you were with Michael a long time. You were even going to marry him there for a while. How does it feel knowing he's gone?"

A tear slipped down my face. No one had asked me about that until now. The truth was I had pushed my own feelings and thoughts about Michael to the back of my mind while trying to take care of Ali. Honestly, I was so confused in my feelings.

"I would be lying if I said I was unhappy he's dead. After what he did to me, to you, Ali and Jace. I feel a small sense of peace that we'll be free of him. But there's also a piece of me that feels responsible that he's dead and that it's my fault. I just wished it all worked out differently. That when I ended things, he took it well and just moved on, and we were just going on with our lives separately."

"I spoke to Raymond about the night he died. The police ran a toxicology panel. He was really high on meth, Sarah. They said there were signs everywhere at his place, and by the way he was acting that he had been on it for a while. That and coke. Did you know?" Matt gently asked me.

"I didn't know for sure. But I figured he was on something because of the way he was hot and cold."

"The drugs messed him up, honey. It wasn't you."

"But there's still so much that is messed up for all of us because of him. I lost my job, and Ali will probably lose hers for all the time off she's had to take. You guys are behind in recording the album. Jace is in the hospital. Everything is turned to shit."

"Hey, look at me. Nothing is shit. Okay, you lost your job, but I told you a while ago, we need a manager and you would be perfect for the job. So as soon as you want to jump in and help, you have a job. Ali can find a job in L.A. if she wants one. She said she doesn't want to go back to her house and that, other than you and your parents, nothing is keeping her here anymore. We'll get recording as soon as Jace is out of the hospital. We have plenty of time and stuff is all ready to go. Look at all the good you have brought us. Ian has Nell. Miles is finally being an active part of us, not just an observer. Alex seems to have gotten over Cece. Look at how you saved us all. I know you saved me."

Still teary eyed, I thought about the end results of what I had brought to the band. Maybe things were going to be okay after all. I snuggled close to Matt and let sleep come. It was the first time I had a good sleep with him in weeks and I was enjoying every moment of being held tightly to his side.

The next morning I was awoken to loud voices from the kitchen. I got dressed, noticing Matt was gone, and made my way downstairs. Everyone minus Jace was crowded around the table waiting for Matt to finish up breakfast. Ali was helping him, and for once she didn't look like she had circles under her eyes.

"Morning, everyone," I said and went to kiss Matt.

"Jeezus. Can you not do that while I have yet to find a girl?" Miles said and started to fake puke on the floor.

"Shut up, Miles. It's either you or Alex next. Every-one is arked up into pairs," Ali added.

"Arked?" Alex asked.

"Yeah, like paired up for Noah's ark. Arked up," Ali answered.

"I like that," Matt said, and went back to flipping pancakes.

We all ate together as a big family. The guys were sitting near each other talking about the recording time they were going to have to fill today. The girls were talking about helping Ali with the wedding. Luckily when you live in Vegas, things can get thrown together on the fly.

Nell and I were taking Ali to the Bellagio to make all the arrangements. Ali had been up early and had already called some places. The Bellagio was available, and she wanted to get married as the grand fountains were going off behind her. So that was set. After the

Bellagio, we were stopping by a bridal shop for dresses.

"The dress code for you guys is black jeans, a white long sleeve button down shirt, sleeves rolled to the elbow and black chucks. Ian, get the hawk redone; it's growing in and I like it short. Girls, you are wearing black dresses with a pink sash and I'm wearing the opposite. Any questions?" Ali demanded, glaring as if daring anyone to answer back.

New no-nonsense Ali was pretty fun to watch around the guys. It was like they were scared of her. It was fun to see. No one had a problem and we all quickly ate to get on with our day.

On the way to the Bellagio, I told the girls Matt's idea about managing the band.

"I think it's a great idea. That way we can have some control over where they are, and how long they're away. This way the record label can't just plow them to be always on the go. You will rock it, Sarah," Ali said.

"I agree with Ali. I think it's a great idea. And if you need photos of the guys, Ian's wife would be perfect," Nell laughed at her own self-promo.

"That goes without saying, Nell."

"I think I should finish up the year, but then I'm giving notice. I think I want to go back to L.A. with Jace. I love his house and he feels so much freer there. We don't get bothered by paparazzi. Everyone's used to him being there. What do you think?" Ali asked Nell and me.

"You have to do what's best for you guys. I understand your not wanting to go back to your house," Nell said.

"I'm with Nell. You have to do what's best for you. But you're not going back before the album's done, right?"

"I have another month and a half to finish the year.

We'll rent a place until the album is done and then we'll see. Maybe by then I'll feel safe here again. But I want to put the house up for sale. I can't go back in there. I don't even want to go back to pack it up. I'm going to hire someone and Jeff said he'd go oversee the packing. There's a house up the block from your place, Sarah. I'll call the realtor and see if they want to rent it to us for a while."

"That would be awesome! It would be great to have you and Jace so close. But you know you can stay with us for as long as you want. All you guys can stay as long as you want. I kind of like having the house full." I meant what I was saying. I liked having everyone close to Matt and me.

"I know, but I think Jace and I will need some private time to get things back on track."

"Maybe Ian and I could move into Ali's room. We've been staying at my place, but it has to be fumigated, and Ian hates it. Would that be okay with you, Sarah? Besides, I think Ian misses Miles a bit when we're at my place. I swear those two are like a married couple."

"I don't mind at all. I like having people around. You can move now; I can bunk Miles with Alex to free up a room for you guys."

"I'll wait until Ali goes. I don't want to piss off Miles and Alex. Miles is kind of having a hard time with Ian and me together."

"Why do you say that?" Ali asked.

"Ian was Miles' wingman. They used to troll for hoes together. Ian's days of hoes are done, at least for now," Nell looked momentarily sad.

"You needed to stop that sentence awhile back. Forget the 'for now' part, Nell. Give Ian and this marriage a chance. Was it conventional? No. But does Ian do anything conventional? No," Ali said to Nell.

"Ali has a point. Just give this all a chance, Nell," I said.

Nell shrugged her shoulders and we were quiet the rest of the way.

When we got to the hotel, they were smart enough to treat Ali the right way. We were given champagne and little nibbles of food to taste. It was only three hours later and we had a time, food, music and a cake all ready to go for Saturday. Soon, Ali would marry Jace and start their happily ever after.

Next we headed to the same bridal salon where Ali had gone to get a dress for me for my wedding. True to her vision, Ali picked out a petal pink strapless gown that was tight until the waist and then flared out in layers of ruffles. There was a big black sash that tied in the back and rode all the way down the train. We had mini strapless versions but in black with a petal pink sash.

Ali then took us to the mall and treated us all to crazy-ass expensive shoes to match our dresses. Then we headed to the hospital to drop Ali off to stay with Jace. Matt had just left and headed to the recording studio. I took Nell to her apartment so she could start to pack up her stuff, and Ian's, and move over to our place.

I was in the house, all alone, and no one was going to be home for hours. I didn't know what to do with myself. I figured this was as good a time as any to try and prove to the band that I could be their manager. I took out my laptop and, before anything else, realized that I hadn't checked my emails in almost two weeks.

Four hundred emails awaited me. Great. I started deleting a bunch, as most of them were junk and ads. Then I saw an alert about my name on the Yahoo page. I opened it, and there were all kinds of buzz about Matt and me getting married. Then there was talk about how I was knocked up – I wish – and that's why we got married so quickly. There were alerts about Ian and Nell, and the news hit about Jace having alcohol poisoning and being in rehab and that he and Ali were done. I knew what I had to do. But I needed the guys to tell me it was okay first.

I grabbed my car keys and headed to the studio. I called Nell and picked her up on the way. After I finished with the guys, I would go to Jace and Ali and see what they wanted me to do for them.

The guys were all sitting around, and Matt was in a booth. Recording was underway for his part of the song. When he saw me, he stopped and came running out of the booth.

"Sarah, what's wrong?" he asked as he stopped short in front of me.

"Not too much. But I think you guys and I need to have a little meeting, like now," I said. Matt led me over to the couch where the rest of the band, minus Jace, was sitting. Nell was sitting on Ian's lap.

"I have these message alerts linked to my email when my name gets press, since I always want to see how my events go. Well, I was fishing through my emails today and a ton hit me. There's some pretty shitty stuff bouncing around about Jace, you and Ian. They're saying you married me because I'm knocked up, same thing about Ian and Nell, and that Jace overdosed and is in rehab, and that he and Ali are over. Now, I know this is a lot to throw at you guys, but Matt had asked me to step in as manager until you can find someone else, since you have no one right now. If it's okay with you guys, I want to release some press statements about all these rumors. But I need to know what you want me to say."

"I didn't ask you to take over until we find someone else, Sarah. I just want you to take over, period. I already talked to the guys about it, and they're all on board," Matt answered me, as he ran his fingers up and down my arm.

"Jace needs to tell you what to say about his shit, but as far as I'm concerned, what do you say, Nell? They know we're married anyway. Mind making an announcement about how you swept me off my feet and I just couldn't help myself and put a ring on your finger? How does that sound to you?" Ian asked Nell.

"Better than the truth, that we got fucked up and said, 'why the hell not get married?'" Nell answered back, throwing her arms up in defeat.

"As far as we're concerned, you can handle our statements. Just be honest and say what you think is the right thing. I trust you, baby," Matt said and kissed me.

I looked at the rest of the guys and they all agreed. Then they said that they wanted to do a small show in a few weeks, to try and set something up. I left Nell there with Ian and the guys, and then made my way to Ali and Jace.

Jace must already have heard the news that he had overdosed, because when I got near his room, there was screaming from Jace behind his door. Oh boy, here it goes.

I pushed the door open and walked into Jace, barely dressed, heatedly arguing with a nurse. "Jace, what the hell is going on?" I asked in as calm a voice as I could manage. Right behind, Ali opened the door and came in with the doctor from the other night.

"Doctor, I know you wanted to keep him another two days, but since your hospital doesn't see fit to keep medical matters private, you can understand why Jace would like to be released as soon as possible," Ali explained to the doctor.

I guess Jace saw the Yahoo report. "Doctor, I am Mr. Wicks' manager, Mrs. Lewis. I think it would be best for Mr. Wicks and the hospital's reputation to release Mr. Wicks today as long as he is in good health. If you release him today, I can personally guarantee that there will not be any legal action from Mr. Wicks," I said and looked the part of the threatening manager.

"Mr. Wicks has indeed shown complete recovery from the other night. I think as long as he sees someone for a possible drinking problem, he can be released tonight. How does that sound, Mr. Wicks, Mrs. Lewis?" the doctor smiled at me.

"Thank you, doctor. We'll just slip outside so that you can get dressed, Jace." I walked out the door with the doctor.

"Thank you for calming him down, and for there not being repercussions toward the hospital. I assure you, I will get to the bottom of who divulged Mr. Wicks' stay here."

"Doctor, I have to tell you, I don't plan on telling the whole truth of what happened to Mr. Wicks. He was in a bad place, having just lost his child, and almost losing his fiancée to a crazed stalker. I think it would be better for everyone involved if Mr. Wicks had an allergic reaction to his medication for migraines and mixing them with an alcoholic beverage. I don't think the whole world has earned the right to know about Mr. Wicks' loss, do you?"

"I am bound by patient confidentiality so no one will know anything. Whatever you say, I cannot go against you. But I do appreciate the heads up. I'll make sure that anyone who still wants to have a job here understands that a patient's privacy is imperative." The doctor shook my hand and bid me a nice day and left me to wait for Ali and Jace.

The door opened and Jace and Ali walked out, holding hands and looking shaken up. The hospital even let Jace walk out on his own, against the whole wheelchair rule, since he promised not to sue them.

I went ahead and got the car and met them at the

back exit. There wasn't anyone around that way. They piled in the car and I took them back to our place.

When we got home, we went to the kitchen where it seemed all major decisions got made.

"You guys have to tell me how much you want the press to know. I already talked to the doc and he's going to keep quiet about the alcohol poisoning. I think it would be best if we twisted the truth a tad. I think you had an allergic reaction from your migraine meds because you took a drink shortly after having them. What do you say?"

"No, I don't care if the truth gets out, but I don't want people to think I'm in rehab. I'll own up to the stupid mistake I made. But I want the truth out. A stalker tried to kill me, Ali jumped in, we lost our baby, and the stress made me act out of character. I'm not going to lie to my fans. If I lose some, so be it. I'm only human. If you ladies will excuse me, I want to take a shower and get the hospital stink off of me." Jace kissed Ali's head. "I'll be back in a little bit, baby." With that, Jace walked up to the second floor of the house to take a shower.

"I know it may hurt him in the long run, but he wants the truth out, Sarah. Can you spin it to make it not as bad as it looks?" Ali asked me concerned.

"Leave it to me, sweetie. This is my job, to take care of all the guys now. You just worry about Jace and getting married." I hugged Ali and got out my cell phone and laptop.

I started to put together a press release for the guys. Ali went about making lunch for Jace and us as I worked in the kitchen. "Ali, how is Jace? I mean, how is he really doing?"

"Seriously, he's fine. I think I just pushed him over the edge when I shut him out. But just like you, when I thought that I might lose him, for good, all my old bullshit went away. I'll always be insecure about my looks and the fact that I'm not waif thin. But I've seen how much he loves me, and how much I hurt him. I never want to do that to either one of us again. I have to keep reminding myself what those thoughts felt like. I just don't want to be here without him with me."

"I'm glad to hear he's okay and that you're going to try and curb your idiotic ideas that he should be with someone who's a stick. He loves you so much, Ali. I just want you two to be happy."

"We are now. And we will be. We're even talking about how I should stay off my birth control. Because of the D&C we can't do anything for a while anyway. But he really wants me pregnant badly. I think he wants to make sure he has a reason for me to stick around. He's scared I'm gonna run again. No matter how much I keep promising him I won't."

"You won't run will you, baby?" Jace walked into the kitchen, freshly shaved and showered in sweats and a t-shirt.

Ali walked over to him and wrapped her arms around his waist. "No, I'm never going to run away from you, from us, again. But you still don't quite believe me. Maybe after we're married you'll believe me."

"I believe that you love me, babe. But this life I chose is not easy. That's what worries me the most. I want you in this crazy life, not running from it." Jace kissed Ali until I started to blush and clear my throat.

"So. Jace, do you want to read what I wrote to release to the press?" I turned my computer so that Jace could read what I wrote.

"Looks amazing. You're good at this, Sarah. Welcome to crazy land." Jace hugged my shoulder and sat down next to me. We all had sandwiches for lunch and salad that Ali made us. Then Ali and Jace went out with the realtor to look at the house up the block from us, while I put out the press release.

I spent the rest of the afternoon talking to the boys' record label and making arrangements for the guys to play a show here in town in a few weeks. I was still on my computer when the boys came back from the recording studio. They all came in. Matt came straight to me, and kissed my cheek.

"Gather around, boys, and look at this." I pointed to the screen at their published press release. They all stood around reading it, except for Miles. "Miles, don't you want to read the press release I just put out?" I asked him as he was busy grabbing a beer from the fridge.

"I trust you, Sarah." That's all he said and then asked us all what was for dinner.

"I think this is great, Sarah. You really are good at this manager shit," Ian said and kissed me head.

"I agree with Ian. I like the way you worded everything and how it all looks like a positive foot forward for the band," Alex said and then grabbed beers for himself and Matt.

"I knew you were smart, honey, but the way this reads, you're a fucking genius. Jace was cool with all the shit about him and Ali?" Matt asked me.

"Yeah. Jace wanted me to tell the truth and be honest. He said he owed it to your fans not to lie or even sugarcoat the matter."

"I'm proud of you, baby. This is great. I bet we're already getting positive feedback on Twitter. Too bad I hate social media and could care less about checking my accounts." Matt kissed my cheek again and then lifted me from my chair and hugged me.

"Well, I'm looking at my Twitter account, and it's lighting up like crazy," said Alex. "So far a few negative comments, but tons of positive feedback and best wishes coming in to you, Matt. And you, Ian. And tons of best wishes for Jace."

"Best wishes from whom?" Jace asked as he and Ali walked into the kitchen hand-in-hand together.

"Sarah released the press release and social media is lighting up. Let's check our website." Alex got to work logging on to the band's webpage.

"Same thing here. Tons of positive feedback. Seems like our fans are loyal as hell and still love us, even with the women on board now," Ian said.

"I love how you put that, Ian. God I wish Nell were here to hear that," Ali answered with a smirk.

"Speaking of my wife. Since she's not here right now, I want to thank you all for accepting her and being so nice to her. I really want to give this marriage a shot, and she's finally softening up on the idea about staying together and making this work. I think it's in part that you guys are so nice to her. So thanks." Ian looked at each of us and gave us each a chin lift.

"She's easy to be nice to. I'm happy for you, Ian. Shocked as hell, but happy. After all, I think you were the last holdout when it came to Jace and me. But I'm willing to overlook it all since you let me cut your hair into a Mohawk." Ali went to Ian and gave him a hug.

"Okay, get off him. I know you love me, but I hate seeing you even hug another guy. Now, all the mushy shit done with for one night? What's for dinner?" Jace asked.

"I vote for pizza. Because that's what I thought to bring," Nell called as she carried five boxes of pizza into the kitchen.

"See how well she takes care of me? I knew you'd make a great little wife." Ian grabbed Nell and started to assault her mouth in the kitchen.

"Okay, let's get these into the living room to eat, since these two need to fuck each other in the kitchen," Jace said and took the boxes from Nell. We all walked into the living room and gave Ian and Nell a little private time.

"Well, sorry to end the whole communal living thing we have going on, but Jace and I rented our own place. It's right up the block, so we'll basically be here all the time anyway, but with our moving out, Nell and Ian can take over our room. We'll be out of your hair after the wedding," Ali said before starting to eat her pizza.

"You guys know you don't have to do that, right?" Matt asked Jace and Ali.

"We know. But I think right now we need some space to get shit back on track," Jace answered.

"When do you think you'll be ready to get recording, man?" Miles asked Jace.

"I want to get to work soon. I was thinking of coming in with you guys while Ali and the girls handle the house shit. It's all furnished, so other than moving our bags in, there's nothing much to do. I hired someone to pack up Ali's house and we're moving that stuff into storage for a while, until we figure out our next move."

"I like how you assumed the girls had nothing better to do than help me. I was going to ask them for help you know," Ali said while hitting Jace on the chest.

"I'm bringing Jeff and Lucas in for you too. Sarah, do you mind helping Ali get stuff set up at our place?" Jace asked me.

"Not at all. I do have to ask my boss. Oh, that's you guys. Can I have time off to help your future wife?" I sassily asked Jace.

"Smartass," Jace said and continued to eat.

Nell and Ian walked into the living room to join us. "I can help," Nell added. "I only have a boudoir shoot Sunday afternoon. So I'm good Sunday until three o'clock and also am available early next week."

"What's a boudoir shoot?" Ian asked.

"Where ladies, or even gentlemen, dress in lingerie for their partners and I take sexy yet tasteful photos of them. I have a real knockout coming. I can't wait to shoot her," Nell said as all the guys' mouths hung open as they were staring at her.

"People pay you to take their photo while they're in lingerie? Nice, baby. Can I see the proofs?" Ian wiggled his eyebrows toward Nell.

"No, asshole. You only get to see me in lingerie from now on. Remember the whole getting married thing we did?" Nell countered.

The rest of the night went really well. I was so happy about the way the guys took to my taking charge. Matt was proud of me too, I could tell. I thought I handled the whole situation well, and their fans were happy for them and supportive. We all joked and drank and laughed the rest of the night.

I was exhausted when Matt and I got to our room, so we just snuggled close and I fell asleep before I knew it.

CHAPTER
TWENTY-THREE

Sarah

I awoke realizing that Ali and Jace's wedding day was here. I had never seen two people calmer and cooler about getting married. Ali woke up at our place, so she couldn't see Jace until the wedding. Most of the guys were at her and Jace's place. Jeff, Lucas, Nell and I all stayed at my house with Ali. She woke up like it was any other day. And it wasn't an act. She was perfectly calm and happy about marrying Jace.

Jace had the house set up for all of us to have massages before getting ready. It was divine. We had our massages, then a light breakfast, and then we all started to get ready. Jeff and Lucas did all our hair and makeup and we all felt like we were princesses for the day. The car arrived and we were whisked to the hotel.

"I can't believe how calm you seem, Ali. I mean, don't get me wrong, I'm happy you're calm and all, but this is like a 180 from just last week," Nell said to Ali who was sipping some pink champagne from a flute.

"What can I say? Like I told Jace the night he was in the hospital, I finally got my head out of my ass and realized what I really wanted. Don't get me wrong, it's still going to be a while 'til I can understand why Jace wants me, but I'll take him as long as he'll have me."

I was proud of Ali. She was making great strides in therapy and working really hard to accept that Jace loved her because she was a wonderful woman.

We arrived at the hotel and there waiting for us was Ali's wedding planner, Shea. She was ready with our bouquets and led us to the private room where we would wait until the ceremony was ready to start.

"You're sure the guys are already in their room, Shea?" Ali asked, for once sounding nervous.

"I already escorted them there a half hour ago, and right before I left to meet you I popped my head in and told them to stay put, or else." Ali and Shea hugged. It seemed that Shea used to teach with Ali before Shea decided she'd rather plan weddings than change soiled pants on pre-k kids.

Now Ali was relaxed again, as we all followed Shea to the private waiting room. Jeff and Lucas gave us all kisses and left us to join the boys.

Mom and Gloria came into the room a few minutes later.

"Ali, I'm so happy for you, honey. I have something I want you to have today," Gloria, Matt's mom and Jace's adoptive mom, was gushing to Ali. "I know you wanted a bit of tradition, including not seeing Jace before the wedding, so I thought you needed some wedding items. Your dress is something new, and here is something blue." Gloria handed Ali a blue garter belt.

Why hadn't I even thought of this stuff? I was the matron of honor, although I asked to be called the lady of honor, because matron sounded old and lonely.

"Now here's is something old. They were my mother's pearl earrings, and I would be honored if you had them and wore them today. I always wanted to give them to Jace's bride, and that's you, baby girl." Gloria handed Ali a beautiful pair of huge white pearl earrings. Ali was welling with tears. She had been close to Gloria since the first moment they met. I wasn't jealous because I knew the bond between Ali and Gloria was a special one.

"And I have something borrowed for you. I forgot to bring this to Sarah on her wedding day, but at least one of my daughters can wear it. I know you aren't the old-fashioned type, but I'm lending you my mother's pearls to wear with Gloria's pearls. They match, look." My mom put the necklace around Ali's neck and Ali was overwhelmed with emotion. Not bad for having two sets of parents now, when her own sucked.

"You look beautiful, Ali," I told her, and I meant it. She was practically glowing with happiness and acceptance.

"Sarah, can I talk to you a minute alone please?" Gloria asked, and I shook my head and followed her to the hallway.

"Sweetie, I don't want to leave you out of the gift giving. This is a little something for you too. I am so mad at myself for forgetting to bring it to Hawaii. But please take this, sweetheart. It was my mother's bracelet, and I want you to have it. I would love it if, when you're comfortable, you could call me mom." Gloria had tears in her eyes and I hugged her with all my might. I was so happy that Matt's mother liked me and accepted me too. When I pulled back, she fastened a gold and diamond bracelet onto my left wrist. It looked beautiful and seri-ously crazy expensive, and I loved it. I couldn't see myself taking it off, ever.

"Gloria, this is just my taste and I love it. And I love you, too. I guess now is the right time to start calling you mom, if you don't mind. And thank you."

"The bracelet is nothing, sweetheart. What you've given my Matt, I've never seen him happier."

"I love the bracelet, but that wasn't what I was thanking you for. I was thanking you for Matt. Thank you for raising him so well, and for never changing him. I know he told me he has always been impulsive, and that you and Doug always embraced it rather than trying to change him. I love that about him. Thank you for trusting me with him. I promise I'll be the best wife to him that I can be."

Gloria and I hugged some more and had to wipe our eyes so as not to ruin our makeup jobs. When we walked back into the room, Ali was laughing and talking with mom, Nell and Shea.

"What did we miss?" I asked.

"Nothing. I was telling Ali that when Jace was told he was to leave his boots on, and he didn't need to wear the crazy tux shoes, he dropped to his knees and was saying that Ali was the best woman in the whole world." We all laughed, totally seeing Jace doing that.

"Let me see if it's go-time yet. Do you need anything else, Ali, before I go?" Shea asked.

"I'm good to go as soon as you say it's time. Oh wait, where's Joseph? Is he ready?" Ali asked, again a little nervous.

"He's on his way here; we're just waiting for you," Shea answered and waited to see if Ali needed anything else.

"Could you do me one favor, Shea? Tell Jace I'm ready." Ali smiled brightly and the nervousness faded away.

Ali talked to my dad and asked him if he minded that she wanted Joseph to walk her down the aisle. I think dad might have been hurt, but he had just walked me down the aisle to Matt, so he was still in father bliss. It was right for Ali to have Joseph do the honors. He had taken great care of her over the years. Ali stood up from the makeup table after applying a fresh coat of lip gloss, and stood in front of the floor-to-ceiling mirror and did a little twirl, watching her dress spin around her waist.

"I'm ready. What do you say we start this?" Ali asked just as there was a knock on the door.

"Everyone decent in there?" Joseph yelled through

the door.

I opened it to see my brother looking absolutely gorgeous in a tux and his black chuck sneakers. That's what all the guys were wearing. But Jace loved his boots, and Ali wanted him to be himself on this special day.

"Wow, you girls look divine. Mom, Gloria, time for you two to take your seats. Shea sent me here to get you girls going." Joseph walked to Ali and gave her a kiss on the cheek and then wrapped his hand around her looped arm.

Mom and Gloria went first, taking their seats in the little chapel. Nell was to walk first, with Ian, and I was going to be flanked with Miles and Alex. Matt was already standing by Jace's side.

The wedding march started, and the doors opened. Nell and Ian started the procession, then Shea signaled the guys and me to start.

The chapel was beautiful. It was small and filled with family and friends all there for Ali and Jace. The chairs had champagne colored gauze seat covers, and there were sheets of white and champagne colored gauze hanging over the walls and meeting in the middle to make there appear to be a tent in the room. The altar sat in front of floor-to-ceiling glass, and just as we started our walk toward Jace and Matt, the fountains went off, exploding water hundreds of feet into the air. All the guests were clapping, and Ali hadn't even made her entrance yet.

Just as the fountains settled down to a smaller show, Ali and Joseph entered. She was breathtaking and smiling from ear to ear. Her eyes were set to Jace, and I snuck a look at him. His eyes watered as he watched her step slowly closer to him.

Any fool could see the love radiating off the two of them. As Ali got closer, I saw Jace mouth, "I love you, baby. You're beautiful," to her. She smiled more brightly, and mouthed, "I love you too."

I looked over to Matt and he had his eyes on me. We both smiled. It felt good to see our best friends so happy and with each other.

"Ladies and Gentlemen, we are gathered here today to unite Jace and Ali. Although I usually don't say the next part, the bride and groom have insisted I do so. If anyone here does not fully embrace this joining, please get the heck out now. Sorry, son, I don't say the f word." The minister turned to Jace who gave him a thumbs up while the crowd laughed.

Ali and Jace had written their own vows, and it was a little scary that they mimicked the exact same sentiments with a lot of the wording being almost identical. Boy, these two really were meant to be together. There wasn't a dry eye in the room by the time the vows were over. After the vows, they exchanged rings, and they were married. Now the party started.

We were all brought to a small room for the reception. There was a DJ spinning music and we were all dancing like crazy. We hated when the food arrived and we all needed to sit down. But it was also time for the toasts. I went first.

"I would like to propose a toast. To Ali and Jace. I can't see two people more well-suited for each other and more in love. I wish you always happy days, but when those happy days are far away, I wish you both get through those days, together, as one. We are all here for you tonight because we love you, and we hope our love for you both always stays with you. Congrats." The guests lifted their champagne flutes and drank.

Matt next stood up with his glass. "You may not know this, but Jace didn't tell us about Ali at first. We found out about her on his Twitter account. And I'm ashamed to say that we, the band, we weren't very open about Jace being tied down. For that, Jace, Ali, we're all very sorry. We should have seen how happy he was with you, Ali. But we were all selfish and stupid and, well, jealous of what he had. Ali, we owe you the biggest apology. From the first moment you met us, you were kind to us and sweet and understanding and accepting. You didn't judge us. You just loved us because Jace loved us. We love you too, Ali, and not just because Jace loves you. We love you for the amazing woman you are, and the woman who has Jace's back day in and day out. You're a lucky man, Jace, and we're all very happy for you. To Ali and Jace."

Jace stood up and hugged Matt in that hug, back slap kind of thing they do. Then Jace put his glass down and addressed the room. "I just want to thank everyone for coming tonight. It was short notice, but I had to marry Ali before she changed her mind about me. In the past seven or eight months, a lot of changes have taken place for me. Two of my brothers are married, new sisters have been added into my crazy mix, and I fell in love for the first time. Lord knows I've given Ali plenty of reasons and chances to run away screaming from my crazy life. But she never has. She's always there when I need her. I love you, Ali. I love the life I have now, all because of you being in it. And to my new sisters, Sarah and Nell, thank you for adding in the love too. Matt, Ian, Alex, Miles and I are very lucky to have you, all of you. Thanks for taking a chance on us. Thanks, girls. We love you all."

Again tears were moistening my eyes. That Jace would acknowledge us all at his wedding, which was his and Ali's special day, was too much. I felt love, nothing but love.

We ate lobster and filet mignon. We drank champagne and had caviar. It was a magical night. It was a magical life. I couldn't have asked for more.

THE END,

for now.

REVIEWS

Reviews and word of mouth are among the best ways for authors like me to succeed. If you enjoyed reading this book, I would love if you left a review, even if it's only a sentence or two, on Amazon or Goodreads (see my author links below). Your reviews make all the difference and are appreciated in ways I could never express. Here is a review of one of my books that made my day:

> "I loved this book! This is the first book I read by this author and I'm glad I discovered her. I love finding new good authors! I really enjoyed the story, the characters and the emotional twists. Matt is so easy to love, as is the entire band. Sarah has had a rough past and it's wonderful seeing her get through it all. I really enjoyed the close bonds among the characters, which made the rock stars seem like people who could just as easily be friends of mine. A great story, a happy ending, and characters you can relate to - what more could you ask for? I'd recommend this books to anyone who loves a good romance novel. Five stars!"

Also, check out Diemme Black's other published books:
Rocking Me at https://amzn.com/B00V6IVIZQ
Inked My Life at https://amzn.com/B00JAG7AQW

Please visit and follow Diemme Black at:
https://twitter.com/diemmeblack
https://www.facebook.com/diemme.black
https://www.facebook.com/diemmeblackauthor
https://www.instagram.com/diemmeblack
http://amzn.to/2bxJyoz
http://bit.ly/goodreadsDB
http://www.diemmeblack.com

www.ingramcontent.com/pod-product-compliance
Lightning Source LLC
Chambersburg PA
CBHW051418170626
46809CB00006B/2224